FINAL
JUSTICE

FERN MICHAELS

FINAL JUSTICE

**Doubleday Large Print
Home Library Edition**

KENSINGTON BOOKS

or phone the office of the Kensington Special Sales Manager: Kensington Publishing Corp., 850 Third Avenue, New York, NY 10022. Attn. Special Sales Department.

Kensington and the K logo Reg. U.S. Pat. & TM Off.

ISBN-13: 978-1-60751-483-1

Printed in the United States of America

...from the office of the Kensington Special Sales Manager, Washington Publishing Corp., 850 Third Avenue, New York, NY 10022, Attn: Special Sales Department.

Kensington and the K logo Reg. U.S. Pat. & TM Off.

ISBN-13: 978-1-60751-483-1

FINAL
JUSTICE

Chapter 1

Maggie Spritzer leaned back in her chair and stretched her neck muscles. She wished she could prop her feet up on the desk the way she'd done for years at her old desk. But those days were gone, and she missed them. No point in lying to herself. Right now, tired as she was, she knew if a hot tip came in on a story she was following, all her tiredness would be gone, and she'd be in hot pursuit of whatever lead she was chasing down.

She liked her new job but it was so *routine.* She couldn't remember the last time she'd had an adrenaline rush, the rush all reporters lived for.

Maggie looked out through the plate glass windows of her office, which she'd decorated to suit herself. It wasn't exactly homey, but it was comfortable, with soft leather chairs, green plants, and colorful prints on the walls. She'd had the office painted a misty green, hoping to get the cigar smoke from her predecessor off the walls and out of the fiber shades on the windows. It didn't work. Every so often she thought she caught a whiff of one of Liam's cigars. She sighed as she continued to stare out at the newsroom, which was quiet at the moment. All the rushing around and the sound of computers clacking away had died down two hours ago when all the other newspaper employees had packed up and gone home for the day—which was exactly what she should have done.

Maggie rolled her head back and forth on her neck, hoping to work the kinks out. Maybe she should get a massage tomorrow or go to Harry Wong's *dojo* for a good workout. She leaned forward and scribbled a note to herself, a note she would probably end up ignoring when she arrived back in the office the next morning.

She knew she was delaying her departure because she hated going home to an empty house and an empty refrigerator. There was a note someplace on her desk reminding her to stop at the grocery store. That note was at least two weeks old, which meant she'd have to stop for some takeout if she wanted to eat tonight.

The empty house was three doors away from Jack Emery's house in Georgetown. A find, really. Jack had clued her in when one of his neighbors had told him he was going to rent out his house because he was being transferred to England, and had asked if Jack knew anyone interested in leasing it for two years, fully furnished. She'd snapped it up before Jack was finished with his spiel, and the *Post* had picked up the lease. She paid half the rent, and the *Post* paid the other half.

The house was a bit on the masculine side, but with a few of her treasures set about, some plants, and colorful rugs on the shiny oak floors, the Tudor became hers in short order. The funny thing, though, was that she'd been in the house almost a year and had yet to bump into Jack. Maggie grimaced. She'd rather thought they would pop in on each other, shoot the breeze, and maybe have a beer once in a while. It never happened. Yet it was comforting in a way to know he was just three houses away in case she needed him in the middle of the night for something or other.

Maggie sighed again as her stocking feet sought her heels under the desk—though she hated high heels, she wore them at the office every day because she had an image to present to her staff. The designer jacket was another thing she wasn't fond of. The truth was, she hated getting dressed up. Reporters never got dressed up, and they wore running shoes all the time.

The only thing that hadn't changed was her old backpack. She still carried it every single day, and there was no way she was going to stuff her life into some crocodile briefcase that cost more than most people earned in six months. Her L.L.Bean backpack suited her just fine, thank you very much.

Maggie was reaching for her coat when

she heard a knock on the door of her office. She whirled around, her breath catching in her throat. Ted Robinson. She tried to take a deep breath and almost succeeded by the time she motioned for him to come in.

This was a new Ted standing in front of her. She wasn't sure if she liked this new Ted or not, but she'd transformed him into who he was these days, so she was stuck with the new, improved version of her old lover. Somehow she managed to ask, "What's up? I thought you left hours ago."

"I did leave, but I came back. I wanted to see and talk to you alone because I . . . I wasn't sure you would want anyone to see me talking with you one-on-one. It's important. At least I think it's important. Yes, it really is, Maggie. Look, it's not about us, so don't go there if that's what you're thinking. Look, I haven't had any dinner, so what do you say to grabbing a quick bite? We could pop into The Nest for a burger and a beer. Even a salad if you want. My treat and, no, I'm not going to put it on my expense account."

Maggie surprised herself by saying, "Okay, let's do it."

Ted beamed with pleasure.

Maggie surprised herself even more on the ride down in the elevator when she asked how Mickey and Minnie, Ted's cats, were.

"Minnie was sick a few weeks ago. I had to leave her at the vet's for two days. Mickey was so lost he just lay by the front door and waited for her to come home. When I brought her back I put her on the couch, and he curled up next to her and stayed right by her side. Tell me that isn't true love."

"Sounds like it to me," Maggie said. That's how it had been when she and Ted were together. She hated the anxious tone in her voice when she asked, "She's okay now, isn't she?"

"Yeah, she's fine. I wouldn't have brought it up, but you asked."

Maggie knew she was supposed to say something that referred to the time in their lives when they'd talked of marriage and retirement. It seemed like a lifetime ago. "I . . . I was very fond of Mickey and Minnie. Actually, Ted, I think I loved them as much as I . . . loved you at the time. You can't . . . you just can't turn . . . what I'm trying to say here is . . ."

"That you loved me and I screwed it up for us and you still can't forgive me but you still love my cats. It's okay, Maggie. Just so you know, I still love you. We aren't supposed to be talking about *us.*"

"I know." Stupid answer. It's all she wanted to talk about, but she wasn't going to let Ted know that. She blinked away a tear. Suddenly, a vision of herself twenty years down the road floated in front of her. She was alone and crying.

Out on the street she stopped in midstride, turned to the right, reached for Ted's windbreaker, and pulled him forward. She planted a lip-lock on him that made her toes curl up inside her pointy-toed high heels. When she released him, she gasped for breath.

Ted's eyes rolled back in his head. "Jesus!" was all Ted could say.

"We will not talk about this . . . ever."

"Yeah, yeah, right. We won't talk about this . . . ever. You want to go home and have sex?"

"Sex? What? You think I'm easy? Just

because I kissed you doesn't mean I want . . ."

Ted was still rooted to the sidewalk. "It was a yes-or-no question, Maggie. You didn't answer the question."

"Yeah. Yeah, I do."

Ted almost fainted. He felt like scooping her up, slinging her over his shoulder, and running down the street. Why the hell not? He grabbed her, threw her over his shoulder, and started running as Maggie squealed and laughed and pedestrians clapped their approval.

"Put me down, Ted! Let me take off my shoes, and we'll *run!*"

Run they did.

Two hours later, the new editor in chief of the *Post* and the *Post*'s star reporter snuggled in Ted's big bed with the two cats, who were purring so loud it was hard for the humans to hear their own words.

"That was the best sex I ever had," Ted said sleepily.

"Yeah, it was pretty good," Maggie agreed. "You got anything to eat in this place?"

"Everything under the sun. Help your-self."

"I don't mean leftover takeout. I mean food."

"Check it out, Miss EIC."

Maggie padded naked out to the kitchen and opened the refrigerator. She blinked at the array of food inside. Fresh fruit and vegetables. Half a ham covered in Saran Wrap. A plate of leftover fried chicken. Milk, juice, beer, eggs, bacon. She didn't know what to reach for first. She turned around when she felt Ted's hand on her shoulder. He was just as naked as she was. She smiled. This was familiar ground, some-thing she'd missed the past year. Sex, pil-low talk, raiding the fridge. Companion talk. Easy, comfortable. "Want a sandwich? What's up with this loaded fridge? I was expecting to see a ton of take-out cartons."

"I've been staying home a lot. Cheaper to cook than eat out. I've been running and exercising a lot lately. I didn't know what to do with myself. I actually like cook-ing. I meant it when I said I missed you, Maggie. I've been trying to be the kind of person you want me to be. I paid attention to everything you said. I need to know something, though. Was . . . is this just a hit-and-run? Or are we . . . Whatever it is, I'm okay with it if it's what you want. I might not like it, but I'll do whatever works for you."

Maggie pretended to think as she sliced the succulent ham. "I think it's whatever we make it. Look at us, we're standing here naked. I'm slicing ham, and you're spreading mayo on bread. Neither one of us is bothered by our nakedness. I guess that has to mean something. It can't be the way it was."

"I know. We could start over. No secrets this time around. That was our problem, you realize that, right?"

Maggie stiffened. She did realize it. She also realized it was make-or-break time as far as Ted was concerned.

Seeing her discomfort, Ted stopped what he was doing. He reached over and pulled her close until they were eyeball to eyeball. "Look at me, Maggie, and listen to me. I know you're one of the Sisterhood. I think I've known it for the past year. You changed when you joined them. That was your choice, but in my own defense, I reacted to that change in you. For God's sake, Maggie, we talked for hours, days, for weeks and months about how we were going to spend the rest of our lives together. You shut me out, babe."

Maggie nodded. She didn't trust herself to say anything.

"Listen to me, Maggie. I actually like the new me. I felt like a ton of bricks dropped off my shoulders when you ordered me to cease and desist where the vigilantes were concerned. I admit I was obsessed. Beyond obsessed. It actually felt good when I finally let it go. And the reason I was able to do that was I didn't want to hurt you in any way. I *know,* Maggie. Do you want to hear something really weird?" Maggie nodded. "Knowing you the way I know you, I knew you wouldn't have joined that pack unless you believed in them with your whole heart and soul. I still believe that.

"I also know who the owner of the *Post* is. Don't worry, I can't prove it, and that's okay. It's the de Silva woman. I'm not asking you to confirm or deny. I know because they made you the EIC. I'm not going to interfere, Maggie. I swear to you on Mickey and Minnie."

Maggie licked at her dry lips. Suddenly, she wasn't hungry. It didn't look like Ted was hungry, either. She sat down. Ted sat down across from her. "What did you want to talk to me about when you came to my office?"

"Want a beer?"

Maggie nodded. Ted uncapped both bottles and held up his hand for her to wait a minute. He ran to the bedroom and returned with two ratty old robes. He handed one to Maggie.

Maggie slipped her arms into the robe she'd worn many times. It smelled like Ted. She tied the belt and sat back down. She held up her bottle of beer, and they clinked bottles before Ted spoke.

Ted cleared his throat before he spoke, but he never took his eyes off Maggie. "I wanted to give you a heads-up on something. I have a source at the FBI, and I met him for lunch. He's a good friend as well as a source. Don't worry, you don't know him. He's golden, never steered me wrong.

"As you know, the buzz in this town for the past month has been the president's appointment of Bert Navarro as director of the FBI. With the advice and consent of the Senate. I lost track of the number of articles we published on the topic during the past month. Navarro has been vetted up one side and down the other. The Judiciary Committee has been holding hearings, as we reported. Right now we're waiting for the committee to vote and pass it on to the Senate. We don't know which way they're going to vote, but either way, with or without a recommendation, once the nomination is out of committee it can come up for a vote in the Senate. If they approve, Navarro is in as director of the FBI.

"My source has a source who told him there's one hang-up for Navarro. It looks like it might be a go for him except for one thing."

Maggie felt a ripple of alarm at Ted's words. "What?" she asked. "Are you going to make me drag it out of you?"

"Maggie, I'm a damn good reporter. I dig and dig, and my instincts are every bit as good as yours are. We both know that. I know that Navarro and Jack Emery and that guy Wong have been helping the vigilantes. Nothing else makes sense. I'm not the only one who thinks like that, either. We both know that, too. Anyway, my source's source told him the hang-up on Navarro is his friendship with Jack Emery and Harry Wong. It seems when the FBI did the vetting background check, that all came out. Jack's previous engagement to Nikki Quinn and knowing Myra Rutledge. I guess all kinds of stuff came up, like Bert's being front and center when the vigilantes were running fast and loose, and those guys ran with it. My source told me there are those within the FBI who are jealous of Navarro and never liked his close relationship with Elias Cummings. Cummings is the one who had the president's ear, and he recommended Bert replace him. Elias's vote carried a lot of weight. It's politics like you've never seen.

"My source's source told him the Senate should be ready to take a vote on Friday. Friday of this week, Maggie. Today is Monday. My source told me if Navarro loses, he's going to resign from the FBI."

Maggie's hand snaked out to reach for a slice of ham. Her mind was racing. Was there any way for Charles and the girls to know the way this was playing out? Probably not, she decided. Her eyes narrowed as she stared across the table at Ted. He met her gaze without flinching.

"You and the others need Navarro, so you better get in touch with someone and do something in the next few days," Ted said quietly.

Maggie nibbled on her bottom lip. Ted was right. But . . . was he setting a trap for her? Evidently the question she wasn't asking verbally showed on her face.

"Maggie, get dressed and go home. Do what you have to do. I'm not going to do a thing. Personally, I think Navarro will make a hell of a director. When my source told me Navarro is prepared to walk away rather than give up his friendship with Emery and Wong because that's what it will take to get him appointed, I had all I needed to know about the guy. You're the go-between. Take care of it, Maggie."

Maggie shoved the ham to the side of the table. She leaned across and was mere inches from Ted. "All of this," she said, waving her arms around, "was and is wonderful. I enjoyed every single minute of it. If you're setting me up, Ted, there will be no place for you to hide. I will come after you with all my new friends. Just so you know. For both our sakes, I hope the new you is here to stay. If you are setting me up, I will fire your ass, and you will be grist for the mill. I'll make sure you never work again for a newspaper. That's assuming you're still alive at that point. Thanks for the heads-up."

Ted dipped his knife in the mayo jar. "Hey, what are friends for?"

Ted was munching contentedly while slipping tidbits of ham to the cats when he heard the door to his apartment close with a loud bang. No kiss good night. He winced. Then he shrugged. This new Ted wasn't one bit worried about anyone coming after him. He was walking the straight and narrow these days. His conscience clear, Ted decided to make a second sandwich. Sex always made him hungry. Really, really good sex made him ravenous.

Outside, her stomach churning, Maggie hailed a cab and gave the driver Jack Emery's address. How weird that just a few hours ago she'd been sitting at her desk at the *Post* thinking about her neighbor Jack

Emery and how they never ran into one another. She looked down at her watch and saw that it was almost eleven o'clock. She knew for a fact that Jack never went to bed before midnight. She, on the other hand, was usually in bed by ten and soon sound asleep.

How was she going to explain all this to Jack? If she gave up Ted, Jack wouldn't believe her, and she couldn't blame him. She wondered if she was making a mistake going to see Jack instead of calling Nikki or Charles. Maybe she should have called Lizzie Fox or Judge Easter. *Well, it's too late now. Let Jack make the decision.*

The traffic was light at that hour, and the cab sailed along, missing just about every red light on the way. Maggie leaned back and closed her eyes. She felt physically wonderful. She even felt good mentally. Her world was suddenly right side up. She absolutely refused to wonder if it would last. It was what it was for now. She smiled when she remembered how Mickey and Minnie had run to her when she entered the apartment with Ted. Oh, to be so loved by two precocious cats even though they'd hissed their disapproval when she left the apartment.

Ten minutes later, the cab pulled alongside a parked car in front of Jack's house. She paid the driver, asked for a receipt, and pocketed it before she climbed out of the cab.

The house was lit up from top to bottom, and that could only mean Jack was home. Maybe he didn't like the dark. She didn't, either. She wondered if he was as lonely as she was.

Maggie rang the bell and waited. When it opened, she said, "Hi, neighbor! Can I come in? I need to talk to you right now. It can't wait, Jack."

"What? No cake? Aren't new neighbors supposed to bring a cake or a pot roast or something?"

"Well, yeah, but you have it backward. You were supposed to bring me the cake or the pot roast. I'm the one who is new and just moved in."

"Yeah, like a year ago. What's up? You want a beer, coffee?"

Maggie realized she hadn't eaten. She thought about the ham and the fried chicken in Ted's refrigerator. She should have taken some to go. "You have anything to eat?"

"Crackers and cheese. Some fruit. I didn't have time to shop on Saturday. How hungry are you?"

"Starved." Sex always left her starving for some reason.

"How about a Hungry Man TV dinner?"

"I'll take it. And the beer."

As Jack bustled about the kitchen, Maggie started to babble. When she was finished she said, "My source is impeccable, Jack, and don't ask because you know I can't tell you who it is. You only have till Friday to turn this around, or Bert is not going to be confirmed."

"Are you sure, Maggie?"

"I'm positive. Bert doesn't even know your friendship is why he won't be confirmed. He might suspect but probably won't believe it. At some point during the vetting process your name and Harry's came up. My source told me Bert was ordered to sever his relationship with you both, and he refused. That's what I call a good friend, Jack."

"Aw, shit!"

"Yeah."

The microwave pinged. Jack removed the TV dinner and slid it across the table to where Maggie was sitting.

"I hate these things," Maggie said, digging into the Salisbury steak dinner. "Maybe you should heat up another one and call Harry to join us."

"Harry only eats weeds and tofu. It's late. Harry gets real pissy if you wake him up."

"Ask me if I care. I'm up. You're up. I rest my case. This thing tastes like cardboard," Maggie said as she shoveled mashed potatoes into her mouth.

Jack got out his cell phone and pressed the number three on his speed dial. "Yeah, I know. Wash it down with the beer, that kills the taste. I don't have to walk you home, do I?"

"I live three houses away, Jack. You can stand on the steps and watch me till I get inside. I'll take another beer."

Jack stated his business, waited, then without saying anything, put away the phone and got Maggie her second beer.

"Well, is he coming or not?"

"Yeah, but he was jabbering in Chinese or whatever the hell language he speaks. He likes to mix them up to confuse me.

That's another way of saying he's pissed. Big-time."

"Too sad, too bad, oh, boo-hoo," Maggie said, upending her longneck.

Years of friendship that were sometimes up and sometimes down allowed Jack to talk to Maggie like the old friend she was. "You're awful chipper this evening. You get laid or something?"

Maggie started to laugh and couldn't stop. Finally, she managed to gurgle, "Or something?"

On the way out the door she called over her shoulder, "Call Judge Easter right away, Jack. Timing is everything."

"Yeah, yeah, yeah," Jack said, picking up his cell phone. He grinned when he thought about how Judge Nellie Easter was going to react to this new set of orders. With extreme gusto. He started to laugh out loud and, like Maggie, couldn't stop.

Chapter 2

The high from the previous night's encounter with Ted and the late dinner with Jack was still in effect as Maggie Spritzer dressed for the day. She risked a quick glance at the digital numerals on her bedside clock. As she hopped from the shoe rack back to the bathroom and out again to the closet, where she donned a freshly cleaned designer jacket, she tried to keep the red numbers in her line of vision. She didn't want to be late for her breakfast meeting with Lizzie Fox.

One of the perks of her new job was that she had transportation to and from work, so she knew that the car and her driver would be waiting for her. If she was lucky, she'd make the breakfast meeting right on schedule. And then the day would take off like a rocket. Well, she was ready to fly.

As she rode down in the elevator, Maggie found herself thinking about Ted and how they'd stepped back into their old ways with hardly a misstep. Until Ted confessed to knowing she was one of the vigilantes. Was her secret safe with him? She wanted desperately to believe it was. But if it wasn't . . .

The elevator door swished open. Maggie marched across the tiled lobby and sailed through the revolving doors. Her car was double-parked. The driver had the door open within seconds, and she was inside in a heartbeat.

Daniel West had the car in gear the moment he said, "Good morning, Miss Spritzer. Where to?"

"Good morning to you, too, Daniel. Take me to Finnegan's Café. I have an early breakfast meeting."

"Lots of traffic this morning. Might take us an extra ten minutes. You might want to

consider calling your breakfast companion, and it wouldn't surprise me if he or she
is going to be late, too. The town is busy
this morning with the presidential debates.
Do you still think Martine Connor is going
to land the highest office in the land?"

"You know it. She's running way ahead
in the polls. No one can touch her, and the
country is really ready for the first female
president. She's a shoo-in."

The driver laughed. "Thanks to the
Post's support. That was a really good
article in this morning's paper about Connor and her dog. Great human interest. My
wife reads every word about Connor. She
says she's for the people. Robinson writes
a great article."

Maggie felt like preening. "He's a ter-
rific reporter. You know what else, Daniel,
Robinson is a great guy in person." Oh,
God, did she really say that?

"I guess he is to write a piece like that
with so much heart."

Fifteen minutes later he said, "I hate to
say this, but there's a bottleneck up ahead.
If you get out here, you'll get to the café
before I will. It's just a block. Are you okay
with that, Miss Spritzer?"

Maggie looked down at the hated high heels. "Sure, Daniel, no problem. Pick me up in front of the café in forty-five minutes. Then I'll see you tonight unless I call you."

"Okay, Miss Spritzer."

Maggie started off at a brisk walk. God, how she hated these damn heels, with the pointy toes. By the time she walked all the way to the restaurant, she'd either have blisters or corns. A second later the heels were in her hands and she was sprinting toward the café.

Two minutes later she saw Lizzie standing next to the hostess as she waited to be seated. Lizzie turned around to look at Maggie and burst out laughing when she saw the shoes in her hand.

Maggie followed Lizzie through the cheerful café, which smelled of fresh-roasted coffee and cinnamon, to a secluded table in the back. Lizzie's table. Lizzie, as Maggie had found out, had a table at just about every restaurant in town.

Both women ordered hash browns, scrambled eggs, bacon, wheat toast, and a large glass of freshly squeezed orange juice with crushed ice. Coffee was poured, and the two women settled down to discuss business, confident they were out of earshot of anyone who might have an interest in the two of them.

Lizzie took the lead. "Myra called yesterday and asked me to meet with you. She wants me to go to Las Vegas to check on something for her. She said I was to fill you in because you might want to send one of your reporters, possibly Ted Robinson, along with me. She said to fire up the Gulfstream if you're okay with it. If not, I fly commercial—it's your call. Having said that, she has an old friend who lives in Vegas. Annie and Judge Easter know this person also. From way back, childhood. They haven't seen or heard from each other in over fifty years. The friend's name is Beatrice. Myra calls her Beats. She, Beats, has seven last names, meaning, of course, that she has buried seven husbands. Her current last name is Preston, as in Alonzo Preston—also known for the shipping empire that he bequeathed to Beats. Beats inherited the whole ball of wax, not just the shipping fleet. She did the requisite ten-day mourning thing and now she's running in high gear because people are after her daughter.

"Before you ask how Miz Beats got in touch with Myra, I will tell you she contacted Nikki's old law firm, who then contacted me. At that point, I turned it over to Charles."

Maggie frowned. "And the story is . . . ?"

"The daughter is in trouble. I'm sketchy on details at the moment. I guess I'll find out everything when I get there. All I know for certain is the daughter is in jail, and she's estranged from her mother.

"I want you to get in touch with Martine Connor and explain that I'm out of town. But I don't want her to know why, at least not right now. I can't risk having anything I do rub off on her. A week from now I might feel different. Everything seems to be going well for her at the moment, so why look for trouble. Martine is so far up in the polls I can't imagine anything that could bring her down, but you never know. It's only five weeks to the election, so we all have to be on our toes."

Maggie nodded, wondering where all this was going. While Lizzie was here physically, she was in another place mentally—Maggie could tell. "Are you okay, Lizzie?"

Lizzie pondered the question. "Yes, I'm

okay, Maggie. But my gut is telling me something's wrong somewhere. I hate being across the country when all the action is here at home." She shrugged her elegant shoulders. "Let's just chalk it up to paranoia on my part."

"Something did happen last night. I should have called you when I got home, but I . . . well, I didn't, that's the bottom line."

Lizzie looked around at the bustling café with its young waitresses, who looked fresh and dewy-eyed even so early in the morning. Since waitressing was such hard work, she wondered how they did it. *By being eighteen years old,* she told herself. She knew for a fact most of the waitresses in town were college students. Young, young, young. She brought her attention back to Maggie. "So, tell me now."

Maggie told her everything Ted had shared. She spared nothing, even elaborating on her romp in the sack with Ted, right down to her visit with Jack. "Lizzie, girl to girl, do you believe it's only possible to love once? Real, true love, that kind of thing?"

Lizzie chose her words carefully. "I do believe that. But . . . and it's a big 'but,' I

believe you can love again. It's just different, but love all the same. As a very wise
man told me not too long ago, you have to
be open to it." She was, of course, referring to Jack Emery, but she wasn't about
to tell Maggie that. "You're wondering if
you can trust Ted, is that it?"

Maggie nodded. "He's different these
days. On the straight and narrow. I think
what convinced me was that his refrigerator was full of food he cooked himself. He's
been staying home a lot. He's one of the
best reporters I know. Even my old boss
said the same thing. He's from the old
school, journalistically speaking, and that
counts in my book. I think he really loves
me. I do love him, Lizzie, but I will never do
anything to bring attention to . . . to the vigilantes, to you, either. You know that.
Maybe I should resign and go off to some
cabin and write my memoirs."

Lizzie laughed. "No way. There's too
much juice left in you, Maggie. My advice
would be to go with your heart, but don't be
blind. Now, what did Jack have to say?"

A perky waitress with a little too much
makeup set down their food in front of

them while another young girl poured orange juice from a crystal carafe.

When they moved out of earshot, Maggie said, "Jack called Harry, and he was on his way over to Jack's, but I was tired and left. I don't know what if anything they decided. I would imagine whatever they came up with they would have to run by Charles. That's all I know."

Both women, who had earlier professed to be starving, picked at their food. Lizzie nibbled on the crisp bacon, while Maggie chomped on dry toast and stirred the eggs around on her plate.

Lizzie looked at her diamond-studded watch. "I should be going. So, what do you think, the Gulfstream and Ted or not? It will get him out of your hair for a while or until you get your head on straight. I don't know why, but my gut is telling me there's more to this than a young girl in jail. This could be a rip-roaring series for your paper if my gut is right. No matter how you look at it, Las Vegas is a gambling mecca, and that's fodder for the media."

"Sure, no problem. What time do you want to leave?"

"Wheels up by noon if you can manage it."

"You gonna look up Rena Gold while you're there? She has some powerful friends in the underbelly of Vegas."

Rena Gold had been the paramour of the president of the World Bank when the Sisterhood brought him down. The Sisters had cut Rena enough slack to turn her, and sent her on her way with the promise to help them if they ever needed someone in Vegas to, as she put it, shill for them.

"I have thought about it. We'll see how it goes. So, should I just be at Dulles at noon?"

"That'll work." Maggie motioned for their waitress and handed her a credit card. "Go ahead, Lizzie, I'll take care of this. I'll send Ted and will make sure he's at the airport on time. I'll call when I know more about Bert and the guys."

Lizzie stood up, all six feet of her, and straightened her short leather skirt. The Silver Fox, as she was known, had the sudden attention of every male in the café. Maggie frowned. On her best day she had never looked half as good as the Silver Fox. Oh, well, Ted loved her as she was. So did Mickey and Minnie. Which brought up another problem. Who would watch the cats while Ted was in Vegas?

While she waited for the waitress to bring back her credit card, she yanked her cell phone out of her backpack and called the pilot in charge of the Gulfstream to tell him to be ready to fly to Vegas at noon. Her second call was to Ted. She issued orders like a general. She half-expected him to squawk and complain, but he simply said okay if she would watch his cats. She agreed.

"Tell me the truth, Maggie, are you trying to get rid of me because of last night?"

"No, Ted, I am not trying to get rid of you. Lizzie said there's a story there. You'll get the scoop. You should know by now that when Lizzie is involved in *anything,* it's news. Big news."

"What about Martine Connor? You said you wanted daily articles. I can't do that if I'm chasing Lizzie around Vegas. Which brings up another point, I'm going to need some cash."

Maggie's tired brain clicked into gear. "Espinosa can do the articles. He's got a feel for Martine just the way you do. By the way, my driver told me this morning his wife loves your articles on Connor. He said that she said you're humanizing her, which is what the public wants. Don't go getting a swelled head, now. Stop by Accounting and tell them I okayed two thousand dollars cash. Sign for it, Ted, and have them send the chit to my office for my signature. Make sure you keep all the receipts. Use your credit card for anything else."

"Yes, Mom. I love you, Maggie."

She knew she was supposed to say, *I love you, too, Ted.* Somehow the words wouldn't roll off her tongue. She nodded until she realized Ted couldn't see her. She said, "I know," before she broke the connection.

Maggie scrawled her name on the credit card slip, stuck the receipt and the card back in her wallet and into her backpack. Her watch told her she had ten minutes until Daniel was due to pick her up out front. She finished her coffee and juice as she people-watched until it was time to give up her table. She wondered why she wasn't hungry. She was almost out of her chair when she remembered to put on her shoes.

On the ride back to the office, she let her mind race. *Tomorrow I'm supposed to fly commercial to North Carolina to attend a party on the mountain. But Jack said something about driving.*

She wasn't sure what it was all about, but Charles had said it was an invitation she shouldn't even think about turning down. In other words, a command performance. Something was going on, she was sure of it. And it wasn't the business with Bert and the guys. Something else entirely. Like Lizzie, she suddenly had a bad feeling and wasn't sure why.

She was going to have to put in a long day to make sure things would run smoothly if she had to go to the mountain. Charles had called it a party. A party was usually a festive affair, not something to dread. Charles had said *everyone* was going to be there. She wondered who "everyone" was. Would Bert be there? Highly unlikely, if he was under such intense scrutiny. Lizzie wouldn't be there, so *everyone* wouldn't be there.

Five minutes later Maggie stepped out of the elevator. She removed her shoes and carried them down the hall, across the newsroom, and into her office, where she dumped them in a corner. She slid her feet into a pair of scuffed loafers and settled down to put her office to rights in preparation for her trip. She looked up once, an hour later, to see Ted staring at her from across the newsroom. He blew her a kiss. She smiled and waved.

She felt so giddy she didn't know what to do, so she blew a kiss in return, which brought a smile to Ted's face.

"He's not setting me up. He's not. He wouldn't do that to me again. I trust him. I really do. Well, mostly I trust him," she muttered under her breath.

The big question was, should she stay at Ted's apartment or take the cats to her house? If she stayed at Ted's, she could spy on him, check out his computer and whatever else he had lying around. Like she would really do that. She'd end up doing his laundry, cleaning the apartment, feeding the cats, and changing the sheets. It would be okay to leave the cats for an overnight trip as long as she fixed the litter boxes and put down plenty of water and food.

She blinked when she heard the strange buzz from the cell phone Charles had given her. She dug it out of her backpack and opened it. Her heart picked up an extra beat when she realized that the caller was Jack Emery.

Chapter 3

Dawn was just moments away when Jack Emery slammed his way into Harry Wong's *dojo.* He was shivering and sweating at the same time as he jumped around from one foot to the other. "It's cold out there," he said to a startled Harry.

"What the hell are you doing here at this hour of the morning, Jack? I thought we said we'd meet at ten. It's not even six yet."

"I wanted to make sure you didn't weasel out on me, Harry. You were pretty pissed when you left last night. We can't screw this up. Everything hangs on our pulling it off and making it legit. You got any hot tea?"

"What's with that *we* shit, Jack? Tea isn't ready yet. The reason it isn't ready is because I just got here myself. And the reason I just got here was I was at your place till two this morning. Then I had to go across town on my cycle and almost froze my balls off. It took me two hours to thaw out, and that means I only got an hour's sleep."

"You're missing an hour. I thought you could count."

"I tossed and turned after I thawed out. I hate you, Jack."

Jack waved his arms in the air. "Enough of this male bonding. You need to stop saying that or you're going to start believing it. I'm your best friend. Actually, I'm your *only* friend aside from Yoko. I still don't know what she sees in you."

"Shut up, Jack. It's way too early to be having this stupid conversation. Class starts in forty minutes. I still think you should tell Bert and not blindside him."

"If we do that, he won't react the way we want him to. It has to look real. Look, Harry, we beat this to death last night, we're not changing course now. It's too late."

"I'd feel a hell of a lot better if Charles

knew about this cockamamie plan of yours. I was really looking forward to going to the mountain today. Think about this scenario, *Jack*. We step out of that cable car, and there's Charles and *Kathryn* waiting for us. I'd sooner face a firing squad. You can't mess with her, man. Then you know damn well the rest of those women are going to side with Kathryn, and before either one of us can blink, we'll both be rolling down the mountain, and I didn't even get to what Charles is going to do." Harry took great pleasure at the look of terror on his friend's face.

"It will be okay when we explain," Jack mumbled.

"You really are a dumb shit, Jack. I can't believe I hang out with you. Didn't you hear what I said? Kathryn is going to kill us. Then you better think about what Nikki is going to do. Those women are glued to one another. You and me, Jack, we're just window dressing. Those women have it going on, and they scare the living shit out of me. If they don't scare you, then you have a few screws loose up there," Harry said, clipping Jack on the side of the head.

Jack snorted, but he had the grace to

look uneasy. "Isn't that damn tea ready yet?"

"Fix it yourself," Harry sniped.

"'Fix it yourself,'" Jack said, mimicking his friend. "You are the crankiest son of a bitch I've ever met." Before Jack could take a second breath, he was on the mat, flat on his back, the wind knocked out of him. He'd never seen the lightning swing of Harry's foot.

Jack rolled over on the mat, his hands clutching his stomach. "You feel better now that you vented?" he managed to gasp.

Harry sniffed. "You make my brain ache, and my hair hurts when I'm around you. No, I don't feel one bit better." He reached down to grasp Jack's hand and pull him to his feet. It was Harry's way of apologizing. Jack accepted the apology.

Still clutching his stomach, Jack's voice was tortured at best when he said, "Look, if you have a better way, let's hear it. Last night you drew a blank. I'm not saying this is a perfect caper, but I can't think of anything else. If you think for one minute this isn't killing me, you're wrong. I love Bert like a brother, the same way I love you, Harry."

This was Jack's apology and, just as Jack had done, Harry accepted it.

Wincing, Jack slapped his buddy on his back before he headed for the door. "So, I can go off knowing you're going to take care of matters?"

"Yeah, Jack, I got it covered. Don't be late for our trip up to the mountain. You want the tea to go?"

Jack sucked in a deep breath. "No, but thanks for the offer. I'll be on time. See ya, Superman."

Outside, Jack looked to the left, then to the right. After debating a whole minute about whether he should jog to the courthouse or hail a taxi, he limped to the curb and hailed a cab. The moment he buckled up, his cell phone rang. He hissed a greeting. Maggie Spritzer. He listened.

"I just left Harry. He's got it under control. How are things on your end?" He listened again.

"Yeah, okay, we're good to go. I'll see you this afternoon for our ride to the mountain. Charles said he didn't want a paper trail, and there will be one if you fly. Jesus, Maggie, if this doesn't work, Bert is screwed." He listened again. He rolled his eyes. Maggie counseling him. What was wrong with this picture?

Jack leaned back and closed his eyes. He hated what he was being forced to do and at best it probably wasn't going to work, but he had to do *something.* Only three days to ensure that the Senate backed Bert.

The cab pulled to the curb. "Ten bucks, buddy."

Jack pulled some bills out of his pocket and sprinted across the pavilion to the massive front doors that would take him to his office. Everything had to be routine. Now he had to head for the coffee shop to get a bagel and coffee that he would carry outside to the back of the building, where he could smoke as he drank his coffee. He always ate the bagel on the elevator. The same people he rode up with every day would say he was right on schedule. If anyone had even asked, that is. The smokers would be gathered outside, alongside a tub filled with sand. Ordinary. Nothing different. Business as usual.

Jack's thoughts were all over the map as he stood in line for his bagel and coffee, kibitzing and making small talk with colleagues. *I'm pulling this off, I really am.* An MRI of his stomach would have said otherwise.

Outside, he fired up one of the few cigarettes of the day. He shivered in the brisk October air. His gaze followed a puff of smoke as it sailed upward to meet the gray clouds of the day. It was going to rain before long, making for a messy trip to North Carolina. But gray clouds and rain were the least of his worries.

Jack jerked his attention to the left when he heard someone call his name. Brad Devane, a colleague from his softball team. A guy he had a beer with occasionally. "What's up, Brad?"

"Same old, same old, overworked and underpaid. I heard you're going to let that guy Josephson plead out. True or false?"

Josephson? Jack drew a momentary blank before it came to him who Josephson was. He forced a grin he didn't feel. "Decided to save the taxpayers some money. He'll be back in ten months, then we can throw away the key."

"Call me next week, and we'll have a

beer," Devane said as he crushed out his cigarette in the sand.

"You got it. Next week is wide open." He wondered if that was true. He followed suit and stuck his cigarette in the sand, then followed Devane, who was holding the door for him.

As the two attorneys walked to the elevator, Devane asked, "You think your buddy Navarro is going to be confirmed on Friday? Pays to have friends in high places."

Jack stiffened. He'd heard the envy in Devane's voice. "Navarro is no friend of mine. You need to update your information, Brad. I personally don't give a good rat's ass if he's confirmed or not."

Devane pressed the elevator button, stepped back, and said, "Whoa! Hey, I thought you guys were friends. The scuttlebutt . . ."

"Look, Devane, I don't care about scuttlebutt, and I don't like discussing my private life in public. Just drop it, okay?"

"Sure, sure. No problem. Sorry I brought it up."

The two men were silent as they entered

the half-filled elevator and rode upward without further comment. When the elevator stopped at the fifteenth floor, Devane got out, waved airily, and turned right. Jack waved his index finger and turned left.

"For whatever that was worth," Jack muttered as he entered his office and hung his jacket on the hook hanging over the door. He sat down and turned on his computer. Checking his e-mail was the first order of the day. He grinned from ear to ear when he clicked and clicked again to bring up his home e-mail to read the note from Nikki.

The message was short and simple. "Love you, am counting the hours till I see you." As always she signed the e-mail with a question mark.

Still grinning, he clicked back to the government e-mail and read those that had come in during the night. He decided there was nothing that required his immediate attention, so he unwrapped his bagel, refilled his Styrofoam cup of coffee from the urn out in the kitchen, and settled down with the morning paper. He knew if someone quizzed him in an hour he wouldn't be able to tell them what he'd read.

Every two minutes, Jack looked up at the huge white clock on the wall. The hands were moving like snails.

While Jack was eating his bagel and watching the clock, Maggie Spritzer was chewing on her bottom lip, wondering if anyone involved in the day's activities would take the time to figure out where the tips were coming from in regard to Bert Navarro.

It wasn't exactly news when Elias Cummings, the current director of the Federal Bureau of Investigation, visited the White House. Maybe a mention on page eight in a two-line paragraph. Even when Cummings journeyed to the White House with his right-hand man, assistant director Bert Navarro, it was still a page-eight, two-line item. All the news was about the upcoming election in November, just weeks away. Boring political news. Hard to believe there was no scandal going on in Alphabet City, and the populace had to do with page after page of hashed and rehashed political garbage.

Well, that will change in a few hours. Childishly, Maggie crossed her fingers. A shadow crossed her doorway and she motioned for Joe Espinosa to come into her office.

"Talk to me, Joe."

Espinosa licked at his dry lips as he looked at Maggie. Once she'd been one of them, his partner's lover. They'd had some good times and some bad times as well, but she'd been one of them, not the establishment. He suddenly felt inferior, and he didn't much like the feeling.

It was the first time he'd been in this office since Maggie took over. He wasn't sure how he was supposed to address his new boss.

Maggie changed all that when she asked, "Joe, you waiting for a bus? What? This is me, Maggie. Talk to me."

Espinosa heaved a sigh of relief. "I thought this was Ted's gig. I just got my orders an hour ago, but I hustled. I called some friends at the *Daily News* and the *Sentinel*. Just another day covering the White House, with one slight difference. I was just getting ready to leave and wondered if you had any last-minute instructions."

"Get me good pictures. I'm going to run

with it above the fold. Do it right, and you can count the bylines on both hands. The television stations will be covering it all day and night."

"Why the hell is this guy so important all of a sudden?"

"Where have you been, Espinosa? Nobody has the right to tell another person who his friends should be and hold a promotion over his head for a relationship that goes back years. Jack Emery has an impeccable reputation, so it doesn't make sense. Washington politics suck. I want an in-depth interview with both Cummings and Navarro. Both will run under the fold. You following me, Joe?"

"Got it. If that's it, I'm on my way. But before I go on my way, do you want to step outside this office so we can *talk?*"

Maggie laughed. She let him off the hook when she said, "Yeah, I guess this office is intimidating." She could have said *she* was intimidating, but that would have frazzled Espinosa's delicate psyche.

Outside the "intimidating" office, Maggie was once again one of the guys.

"You want to tell me what the hell is

going on? Is there any way any of this can backfire on me, you, the paper? I'd just feel better if Ted were here. He's got instincts I'll never have. I do better when I know what's going on."

"All you have to do is show up, cover the scene, and get me some good pictures. The interviews have all been arranged for four o'clock this afternoon. Just show up at Cummings's office. Get me the interviews on time. He's expecting you. You're right about Ted, but today is one day he doesn't need to be at 1600 Pennsylvania Avenue for reasons I won't go into right now."

Espinosa offered up a sloppy salute of sorts and loped off toward the elevator.

Maggie returned to her office and clicked on her television. She sat glued to her chair, her eyes fixed on the screen.

An hour later, a Channel 5 news commentator suddenly appeared on the screen, the reporter rattling off a pre-arranged opening. A running banner under the full screen said, BREAKING NEWS. "We don't know why this emergency meeting is being held here at the White House, since it wasn't on the president's schedule today.

We assume it has something to do with the upcoming Senate vote this Friday on Bert Navarro's nomination to succeed Director Cummings."

The reporter's cameraman let his pictures do the work as he panned the parked car that belonged to Director Cummings. The reporter started speaking again, saying, "These meetings never last more than twenty minutes. We're told that Cummings and Navarro have been in with the president for over forty minutes, which is an indicator to those of us in the media who know about these things that something serious is going down or will shortly. Back to you, Stu," the reporter said.

The morning anchor on Channel 5 resumed his report on a firebomb going off in Pakistan. Maggie rubbed her eyes when suddenly all hell broke loose on the screen in front of her. The anchor turned the screen over to the reporter at the White House, who was shouting about ninja forces invading the grounds of the White House.

Maggie's eyes popped wide when she saw black-clad masked figures leaping and pirouetting as smoke clouds sprang up everywhere. Bedlam ensued as Secret

Service agents appeared out of nowhere, guns drawn. The ninjas covered from head to toe in black garb, continued their high-flying antics as more smoke enveloped the area. Maggie heard curses and shouts the network wasn't able to drown out. More agents appeared as more smoke clouds erupted.

Maggie flinched when she saw Bert and the director flat on the ground, gray smoke circling overhead. She knew she wasn't imagining things as she saw the look of stunned surprise on Navarro's face when one of the black-clad ninjas leaned down to say something to him. When a giant cloud of smoke sailed upward, guards, agents, and pedestrians, as well as all traffic, came to a screeching halt. Car horns blasted the morning as shrieks and shouts permeated the air.

When the smoke cleared, the ninjas were gone, and the Secret Service agents were obviously chasing their tails all over the place. Even to Maggie's eyes they looked foolish. Her nerves twanging, she continued to stare at the screen until she saw Joe Espinosa talking to one of the agents.

Sightseers hoping to see themselves on the noon news could be heard shouting about which way the ninjas had traveled. They seemed to be saying, *"Straight up in the air, then they disintegrated into a fine mist."* She almost fell off her chair when she heard one of the agents ask Espinosa if that was all true and did he see it the same way.

With a straight face, Espinosa said, "That's how it looked to me. They went up in a cloud of smoke and disintegrated."

Nine blocks away, Jack Emery stared at the screen and muttered, "You can't make up this shit. No way, no how."

Chapter 4

By the noon hour Maggie had her headline for the *Post,* complete with pictures. She giggled as she approved the bold black letters. NINJAS ATTACK FBI! The pictures made her laugh out loud. Espinosa came through.

She looked up at the reporter, who was standing in the doorway, and paid him the supreme compliment: "I couldn't have done it better myself, Joe. If you hurry, you can catch Emery. He should be leaving the courthouse in"—she looked up at the wall clock—"precisely ten minutes."

Espinosa was gone before she could blink.

The entire front page of the *Post* was dedicated to the ninja attack. *Damn, I'm good.* She hoped Charles, Annie, and the others were proud of her. She took a few seconds to wonder what Ted would think when he watched the news or went online to check out the latest happenings in the District. Not that it mattered what Ted thought. *That's a lie, and it does matter,* she told herself. She shrugged because there was nothing she could do about Ted. At least for now.

Maggie continued to giggle and smile as she read the brief interviews Espinosa had done with the director of the FBI and Bert when they left the hospital after being checked out, at the insistence of the president. Navarro had suffered the most, with two black eyes, a dislocated shoulder, and other assorted bumps, bruises, and scrapes. The ninjas had apparently taken into consideration the director's age and potbelly by going easy on him. A sprained wrist, a twisted ankle, and a few jabs to the stomach were minor compared to the humiliation and embarrassment, he said.

A picture of Bert wearing sunglasses, his suit jacket hanging in tatters as he was being helped to a government car, made her wince.

The best line in both interviews was, "We do not discuss ongoing cases, whether it concerns ninjas who evaporate into thin air or aliens who are invading our planet." The last thing to be uttered, and not part of the interview, was something this intrepid reporter overheard as Navarro was helped into his government-issued vehicle. "You'll pay for this, Emery, and your vigilante friends won't be able to help you." When pressed for an explanation, Navarro offered up a single-digit salute as the ambulance sped off into traffic, siren wailing.

Maggie's fist shot into the air. "That should do it." Her gaze moved to the television on the wall and the nonstop coverage Channel 5 was running.

Her ears perked up, and she bolted upright when she heard the anchor say, "We're outside Harry Wong's martial-arts establishment, where he trains local law enforcement as well as the FBI. We can't prove this, but it has been said CIA agents have been known to come here for refresher courses. We also cannot confirm, but it has been said over the years that Wong is on the CIA's payroll and goes out to McLean on a regular basis to train the men and women who work for the CIA. Right now we're hoping to get a comment from Wong about what happened at the White House today."

"Oh, shit!" Maggie muttered. Major screwup on her part. She should have anticipated what was currently going down and sent Espinosa to Harry's *dojo* first instead of to the courthouse to speak with Jack Emery. Maybe, just maybe, Espinosa would take some initiative, tune in to his iPod, and show up. That was what Ted would have done. But Joe Espinosa was *not* Ted Robinson. She whipped out her cell phone and punched in Espinosa's number.

Before she could say a word, the reporter said, "I'm on it. I should be at Wong's *dojo* in three minutes. Call Emery and set up a meet someplace else, and call me back with the details."

"Okay. If Harry sees you, he'll give you an exclusive. Play that up, Joe."

"I'm not some cub reporter, Maggie. I know what to do."

"I know, I know. I'm just a little jittery today. I'm holding four inches of space for this interview." Maggie closed her cell phone when she realized she was talking to dead air. She returned to the television, her eyes fixed on the screen and the scene playing out in front of her.

A good-sized crowd was gathering outside Harry's *dojo.* For some reason people just seemed to gravitate to any place where they saw more than one police officer and a reporter. She squinted to better see the faces, but to no avail. Her eyes still on the screen, her hand snaked out to grapple with the pile of junk on her desk until she found her glasses and put them on. Ah, now she could see some of the *Post*'s rivals, friends of Ted and Espinosa. Police were pacing near the entrance. The lookie-loos were starting to multiply near the entrance, and the cops were trying to push them back to the curb. It looked like it was going to get unruly any second. She spotted Espinosa as he did his best to inch his way to where the Channel 5 reporter was standing. *Good spot,* she thought. Harry would be sure to see him.

All the jabbering and babbling suddenly stopped when the door to Harry's *dojo* opened, and he stood in the doorway. The aggressive reporter from Channel 5 pushed forward and jammed the microphone in Harry's face. Maggie groaned. No one invaded Harry's space. *No one.* She watched as with one finger, Harry jabbed out at the reporter's nose. His free hand knocked the microphone out of the offender's hand. One of the gleeful lookie-loos picked it up and started to whistle into it.

Harry eyeballed the Channel 5 camera, and the man lowered it. "Turn it off," Harry ordered.

The cameraman backed away, but a Fox reporter used his own camera to catch the Channel 5 cameraman turning his camera to the OFF position. It was a clear signal that you didn't mess with one Harry Wong. The reporter himself moved off to a respectable distance, his camera steady. Maggie wondered if Harry knew the cameraman was still filming.

Harry's eyes spewed sparks when, hands on hips, he asked, "What? You're here because some *actors* stirred up things at the White House? You came here because I'm the number two martial-arts expert in the world and you think I'm somehow involved because of my friendship with District Attorney Emery? I have no comment. Now, get the hell out of here before you make me angry."

Espinosa raised his hand the way a schoolchild would. "Not me, Mr. Wong. I don't think that's all, and neither does the *Post.* I came here to get your spin on it because you *are* the number two expert. Personally, I think you should be the number one expert. I've seen you in action. I know you wouldn't have anything to do with that fiasco. Joe Espinosa from the *Post,* sir."

"Oooh, I love the way you suck up, Joe. Good going," Maggie mumbled to herself.

Harry stared at Espinosa as though he was contemplating his next move. "Okay, okay, the *Post* always gets it right—unlike these other guys, who make it up as they go along. Come on in, I'll talk to you."

Maggie burst out laughing when Espinosa turned to the Channel 5 reporter and flipped him the bird. "Well, damn," she muttered. Yoko was going to be so proud of Harry. She wasn't sure if Ted would be proud of Espinosa, not that it mattered. She was proud of him, and that was all that counted.

She watched a few moments longer and saw Harry motion one of the cops to come closer. She couldn't hear what was being said, but the cop backed away and, with his fellow officers, started to move the crowd farther back. The television media, sensing favoritism, started to squawk. The cops ignored them and moved the crowd back fifty feet from Harry's *dojo.*

"Show's over folks, let's move it along now," one of the cops could be heard saying.

Maggie sighed as she leaned back in her chair. "Guess that takes care of that," she muttered to the empty space surrounding her.

Maggie looked at the clock. Two hours to go until it was time to meet Jack, Harry, Judge Easter, and Pearl Barnes, retired justice of the Supreme Court, for the trip to the mountain. She crossed her fingers, hoping Espinosa could get the interviews with Jack and Harry in to her before it was time to leave.

Maggie blinked when her e-mail chirped. She looked up at the name of the sender and saw that it was Espinosa, who was winging his interview by the seat of his pants and sending it on to her at the same time, knowing it would be blue-penciled within seconds. Modern technology. She was convinced now that Espinosa had learned more from Ted than she had thought. *No matter, Espinosa is coming through,* she thought as she gleefully read what was coming to her, one e-mail after another.

Her e-mail pinged again. Ted. She grinned when she read the short message: "What the #%&#%^$ is going on?"

Maggie took a few seconds to respond to Ted. "Read tomorrow's paper, and you'll see." She sent off the reply and went back to Espinosa's interview, one eye on the clock, the other on her computer screen. She chewed on her lower lip, wondering how Espinosa was going to meet with Jack and get his interview in on time. If it came down to crunch time, she could write the interview herself. If she gave Espinosa the byline, no one would know but the two of them. Three, if you counted Jack, who wouldn't care one way or the other.

When Espinosa's last e-mail on his interview with Harry came through, Maggie printed it out and scanned it thoroughly before buzzing Tillie, her secretary, to take it down to editorial. She quickly scribbled a note on a sticky pad that read, "This is bare bones, add enough filler to fill the four inches I allocated for this interview." She added a scrawled *MS* at the bottom of the Post-it. *One down and one to go.*

Maggie leaned back and closed her eyes. She hated stress, all forms of stress, and at that moment she was stressed to the max. She sat upright and took deep, gulping breaths, then exhaled slowly. She did it ten times and didn't feel one bit better. *What I should do is change my clothes and go for a long run.* For some reason, running always worked out the kinks and calmed her. Sometimes a banana split with gobs and gobs of warm marshmallows on top had the same effect. *Like that's going to happen today of all days.*

Thirty minutes later her e-mail pinged, and Jack Emery's interview flooded the screen. For some reason, Espinosa was sending the full interview in one e-mail. Maggie calculated the words—two inches. Jack was being testy in the interview, and that was a good thing. She burst out laughing when she read the last sentences in the interview. "Yes, I'm considering a lawsuit. I'm an officer of the court and do not take kindly to having my character impugned. My lawyer? Lizzie Fox."

Maggie ripped the e-mail from the printer and slapped a sticky note on it, yelled for her secretary, and said, "Tillie, get that to editorial and don't bother waiting for the elevator. *Run!*"

Maggie headed for her private bathroom, where she quickly changed into a warm running outfit and sneakers. She hung her designer suit up neatly, then saluted it. She looked at herself in the mirror and decided to stay with her makeup because she knew she looked better with a little war paint. She brushed her teeth, all the while listening to the television. The three twenty-four-hour networks were still running with ninjas invading the nation's capital. Talking heads out of their depth had little to contribute as far as ninjas' disintegrating or evaporating into thin air.

One intrepid soul finally found his voice, and said, "I think it's all a trick to cover up something else."

Maggie gurgled with laughter as she bent down to tie her sneakers.

Back in her office, Maggie changed the channel and heard that calls were flooding the station's switchboard, from worried people wanting to know if they should take their children out of school.

A squeaky-voiced caller had the audacity to say, "If ninjas can go after the director of the FBI and the man being considered to replace him, who is going to take care of the citizens?"

Someone else called in to ask if, after the disintegrating, there was any residue found on the ground. Maggie almost choked as she waited to see what the anchor, who was wearing enough makeup to cover a battleship, would tell the caller. He said that it was a very good question, and he would see what he could find out.

"Asshole," Maggie mumbled as she gathered up her backpack. She looked around, checked her bulletin board and all the sticky reminder notes, which now had red *X*'s through them. She nodded in satisfaction. Her first rule when she'd moved into that office was: I'm in authority here, and that gives me the right to delegate. So far the rule was working just fine. She could leave knowing the paper was in good hands. Besides, she asked herself, what could possibly go wrong in just a few hours? She'd be back in control in a relatively short time if she followed through on her plan to leave the mountain at sunrise or a little before. But before she did any of that, she had to settle Ted's cats and make sure they would be okay until her return.

The cable car swayed in the strong wind, whipping across the mountaintop. When it slid into its nest, the party of five ran across the compound toward the main building. They were soaked within minutes.

"You lucked out, Jack. Kathryn won't dare do anything to you in front of everyone," Harry cackled gleefully.

Jack gave him a mighty shove that sent him into a prickly holly bush. Harry continued to laugh, the others joining in as he picked himself out of the wet, thorny mess.

"Are they always like this?" Pearl Barnes asked Nellie Easter.

"Most of the time," the judge shouted in return.

"*All* of the time," Maggie said.

The huge oak door of the main house opened wide, and the little group barreled through. Myra and Annie held out fluffy yellow towels as Nikki led the little parade to the back end of the house, where dry clothes waited for all of them.

Twenty minutes later they were assembled in the huge family room, a roaring fire crackling in the fieldstone fireplace. Everyone started talking at once.

"Why the command performance?"

"What was going on?"

"Did anyone see the news?"

"What is the press saying?"

"What's the big secret about this 'command performance'?"

Charles, Myra, and Annie simply smiled as they handed out yellow slickers for a walk across the compound to the huge dining room, where a celebratory dinner awaited them.

Maggie's eyes were full of questions for the others, who simply shrugged, which meant that they knew as much as the guests.

Jack and Nikki were holding hands, as were Harry and Yoko. Kathryn simply looked lost, her brashness and sharp tongue buried somewhere.

Jack let go of Nikki's hand and walked over to where the former truck driver stood next to Isabelle. "He's okay, Kathryn. Trust me. It was all a plan. Bert knows that. It had to go down the way it did, so Bert would react just the way he did. He's fine, and he'll be calling you in short order. I guarantee it."

Thinking he had allayed Kathryn's fears and wanting to prove to Harry he really had it under control, he offered up a smirk in Harry's direction. Jack turned when he heard Kathryn call his name. He pivoted on one foot, and in the time it took his heart to beat twice, he had sailed through the air and landed hard on his butt. He saw stars, heard bells, and felt like he was going to toss his cookies. "What the hell . . . ?"

"That's for not telling me first . . . you . . . you . . . *scoundrel!*"

Scoundrel? Jack's mind raced as he grappled with the pain in his rear end. "I wanted to tell you, but Harry said not to." He knew he could die on the spot for such blasphemy, but Yoko stepped forward before Kathryn could lay hands on her beloved.

"Enough of this boyish tomfoolery," she said, using one of Myra's pet phrases.

"She's right," Charles said. "We'll discuss all of this after dinner. Right now I want everyone to put on their festive faces, don your slickers for this momentous moment in time. Follow me," he said, buttoning up his slicker.

Jack was the first one through the door because he didn't want either Kathryn, Yoko, or Harry anywhere near him. Nikki made soothing sounds as she ran after him.

Jack stumbled when he heard Yoko say, "No, darling Harry, you will not kill Jack. I will do it for you."

"Aw, shit!" Jack groaned.

Chapter 5

The excited group removed their slickers, hung them up, and looked around. Someone, probably Annie and Myra, had spent a lot of time decorating the dining room for the special dinner that was about to take place. The long table held a bowl of deep orange and bronze chrysanthemums at each end. The autumn flowers matched the gold tablecloth perfectly. Even the dishes matched the cloth and flowers, and were a rich rust color, with a colorful autumn leaf in the middle of each plate. Directly in the center of the table, between the saltshakers and pepper mills, sat nine gifts wrapped

in shiny gold paper with bronze satin ribbons. The women stared at the gift-wrapped
packages as they whispered among themselves and speculated about what could
possibly be inside the elegant wrappings.

But it was the huge bouquets of colored
balloons that drew the most attention. They
were everywhere, huge clusters of balloons tied to the backs of the chairs, and
anywhere else they could be tied down.

"There must be hundreds of them,"
Alexis said, awe ringing in her voice. "When
I was a little girl, I had a balloon once. I
cried for days when the air leaked out. I
only ever had one."

The next ten minutes were filled with
reminiscences of childhood and how balloons were always associated with happy
times.

Charles waited patiently until all the
stories were told before he said, "And now
it's time to have a champagne toast. And
for this particular occasion, nothing but
the best: Krug Clos du Mesnil 1995."

The women watched, their eyes full of
unasked questions, as Charles poured the
bubbly into exquisite Baccarat flutes. Jack

and Harry longed for a heavy stein of beer but graciously accepted the long-stemmed crystal.

"Who or what are we toasting?" Isabelle asked.

"Our first toast is to the happy times of our past, our lives as they are now, and to a safe, secure future," Charles said. "A bit wordy, but it needs to be said. I'll let you all pick your own toasts when dinner and dessert are over. Tonight we are drinking and dining, and only conducting business later. Having said that, I hope you all enjoy my dinner."

"And what is on the menu?" Kathryn asked. This was the same Kathryn who had a cast-iron stomach and would eat anything that wasn't moving. In an anxious voice, she said, "Please tell us it isn't everything pumpkin, like last year."

"No pumpkin, dear," Myra said. Her face glowed with happiness in the candlelight.

"I made up the menu," Annie said shyly. "I asked Charles to make all of . . . of my family's favorites. I know I don't have a family anymore, but sometimes I long for all the things I used to make specially for my husband and children. It's nothing fancy, and I hope you like the food and aren't disappointed."

"Just so it isn't pumpkin soup, pumpkin bread, pumpkin salad, pumpkin meat loaf, and pumpkin pie," Kathryn grumbled.

"There isn't a pumpkin on the mountain," Myra said. "Charles learned his lesson last year when we ate pumpkin *everything* for a week."

"So what are we having?" Nikki asked.

"A bit of a smorgasbord," Charles said. "Weenies, hamburgers, grilled cheese, tomato soup, spaghetti, gingerbread cookies, and my attempt at homemade Twinkies and homemade pizza. Soda pop, hot chocolate, and coffee."

"That works for me," Kathryn said when she got over the shock at hearing the menu. She'd been expecting some colossal gourmet delight, as were the others. She risked a glance at Annie, whose eyes were moist and sparkling.

Jack clapped his hands together in an attempt to cover his disappointment. "Bring it on, Charles."

And Charles brought it on. Huge platters found their way from the kitchen, the aroma of garlic and onion filling the dining room.

Sensing this particular menu was extremely important for some reason, the others chimed in about how the menu contained all their favorites, too. The moment the food was on the table they all dug in as they again reminisced about when they were kids and lived on such delectable fare.

Within seconds, a party atmosphere took over, right down to the food fight that ensued when the last of the dessert was finished. Nikki started it by throwing a gingerbread cookie at Isabelle, who then threw her Twinkie at Jack, who reached over and stuck a piece of pizza crust in Harry's ear as Yoko raced around the dining room untying all the balloons. They all got up and tried to catch as many as they could before the balloons raced for the ceiling. As one they presented all the captured treasures to Alexis, who started to cry.

"I'm crying because I'm so happy," she blubbered. "Only all of you would understand how important that one balloon was to me."

There wasn't a dry eye in the dining room when they all took their seats and waited while Charles cleared the table. "No, no, you are all guests. I'll clean up even though I cooked, then we'll get to the presents. However, it's a one-time deal. As you know my rule is, I cook, you all clean up. Today is special, hence the exception."

Annie poured more coffee as Myra walked out to the kitchen and returned with a tray of clean wine goblets. She set it on the sideboard along with a single bottle of champagne—this time the precious Louis Roederer Cristal 1990.

Then they waited, their hands clasped in their laps for what was to come.

Finally, Charles took his place at the table and settled himself. He looked around at the excited faces and said, "Unfortunately, we're shy two of our members, but I hooked up a webcam so Lizzie will be with us electronically. For reasons you will all understand shortly, Bert will not be a part of this private party, but he has been apprised of what we're doing. Myra has Lizzie's permission to open her package, and Bert graciously gave me permission to open his. So, without further ado, Annie will hand them out, since this is her party and the honor belongs to her."

After setting out the packages Annie sat on her hands. She hoped her nervousness wasn't telegraphing itself to the others. She was worried. What if her little brood had changed their minds? Myra had assured her that would not be the case. Charles had echoed Myra's assurances. Still, one could never predict another's emotions. She sucked in her breath and waited for the first reaction to the packages. She risked a quick glance at Nikki, who looked devastated at not receiving a gift. Myra had said she would understand. Charles agreed. Still, Annie wished she could wipe away the strange look on the young woman's face.

The ribbons undone, they were picking at the paper, trying not to rip it. Then they were all looking at a simple cream-colored file folder with a gold seal. Annie watched as they picked at the seal and the folders were opened and nine sets of eyes were staring at the crisp papers Lizzie had drawn up.

Adoption papers.

"I know it's taken longer than expected,

but we finally managed to dot the last *i* and cross the last *t*. I just want to say it's iron-clad. I . . . hope . . . none of you changed your minds. I think this is one of the happiest days of my life. I know I said this before, but I want to say it again, I will never try to take the place of your own mothers because that simply can't be done, ever. I don't want to be a stepmother, either. I just want to be a pretend mom. I . . . uh . . . I know how to do that because I was a mom once a long time ago. It was the most rewarding time of my life. I . . . miss being a mom. I really do. If any of you want to change your mind, I'll understand. Lizzie said we can undo this in the next few days." Annie looked around, hoping she wouldn't see anything negative in the faces of what she now considered her family. She was relieved to see a smile on Nikki's face. She understood, she had already gained a stand-in mother in Myra, who had adopted her when she was a young child.

It was Yoko who got up first, tears streaming down her cheeks. She rushed around the table to drop to her knees. Her head fell into Annie's lap. "I never knew my mother. I know you promised to adopt me when we were in Japan but I . . . I thought perhaps you were just being kind to me because you felt sorry for me. I don't know what to say, Annie. I am honored to have you as my mother. I know Harry feels the same way."

Then it was bedlam, with Lizzie screaming into the webcam.

This was Annie's moment, so Pearl Barnes, Judge Easter, Charles, Nikki, and Myra moved closer to the sideboard.

"This is so wonderful. Thank you for inviting me, Myra. I wouldn't have missed this for the world," Pearl said.

Nellie echoed her sentiments. Charles simply beamed.

Nikki hugged Myra. Her words were simple, and from the heart. "Everyone needs a mother, and every mother needs a child. Annie will love all of them with all her heart. I am so proud of her."

The lawyer in Nellie came through. "Her estate . . . that vast wealth of hers? Has that been taken care of?"

"Absolutely. Lizzie handled all the details, and while it was a bit tricky, it's all in order. All ten of her new children inherit equally," Charles said.

"Nine children," Nellie corrected.

"No, ten, Nellie. Annie included Nikki in her will."

Nellie nodded. The lawyer in her kept speaking. "And the name change?"

"Simple. Jack de Silva Emery. Harry de Silva Wong. Yoko de Silva Akio, Alexis de Silva Thorne, Isabelle de Silva Flanders, Kathryn de Silva Lucas, Elizabeth de Silva Fox, Margaret de Silva Spritzer, and Bertram de Silva Navarro.

The lawyer in Nellie continued to speak. "That will do it, then. What are the chances of these particular adoptions ever becoming public?"

"Zero chance. That's why everything took so long," Charles responded. "The adoptions took place in different court-rooms across the country. Lizzie knows her business. I hope she isn't feeling left out, being out in Las Vegas."

"Look!" Nikki said, pointing to the web-cam where Lizzie was talking to the others. She was laughing and holding up a glass of champagne of her own. "I think that should address your worry. Lizzie always makes things work. By the way, what was the rush to get her to Vegas, Charles?"

Charles wagged his finger. "All in good time, my dear."

The cork flying out of the champagne bottle sailed upward, the signal that the last toast of the evening was ready to take place. Myra carried the tray to the table, and Charles carried the champagne bottle.

Suddenly the atmosphere turned solemn. The women all seemed to be teary-eyed, while Jack and Harry were trying hard to keep it together. Annie simply beamed, her face alight with joy.

Charles poured the champagne carefully. He looked around the table. His mood was serious and solemn. "We need to make a toast." He took a step backward to allow the others to decide.

In a heartbeat, Yoko stood up. She held her glass aloft, her eyes shining with tears. "To our mother."

Harry bounded to his feet, his arm snaking around Yoko's shaking shoulders. The others were on their feet in an instant.

And then they all got silly, laughing and crying at the same time. Annie simply basked in the love of her new family.

"I've never seen Annie so happy," Nikki whispered to Myra.

"There's a reason for that, dear. Annie has never been this happy. I've known her all my life, and I've never seen such love as she has for all of you. I'm so happy for everybody."

Nikki squeezed Myra's hand to show she understood and, at the same time, telling Myra how much she loved her.

An hour later, Charles declared the party over, telling his little flock it was time to adjourn to the main house to discuss their next mission. "Unless, of course, you feel impaired with all the bubbly you've consumed, in which case we can adjourn till tomorrow."

Nikki threw a wadded-up napkin at Charles and ran to put on her slicker. The others followed suit.

Annie lagged behind and was speaking to Lizzie on the webcam. "Darling girl, I am so sorry you aren't here. I wanted to hug you and thank you for all you've done for all of us. I love you, dear girl."

Lizzie laughed. "It was my pleasure, *Mom.* I'll be back before you know it. Or, maybe you'll be here before you know it.

I'll talk to you tomorrow. Sweet dreams, Mom."

"And the same to you, darling girl." Annie swiped at her eyes. How wonderful it all was. She looked at Myra, and said, "Imagine having nine children!"

"Just be glad they aren't in diapers or toddling around. You have the grown-up version. I'm so happy for you, old friend. So very happy. Now, come along, we have a mission to plan. You have the rest of your life to be happy. Right now we have a childhood friend who needs our help."

Once inside the main building on the mountain, Pearl tactfully excused herself and walked down the hall to her assigned bedroom. The others marched into the huge conference room, which they laughingly called Charles's lair.

This room was different from the climate-controlled underground war room back in McLean. It was also different from the war room on top of Annie's mountain in Spain. While this room still had a bank of computers and wall-to-wall television monitors, all tuned to the twenty-four-hour cable news channels, it also had windows.

The furniture was cushioned, soft, and easy on the eye. There was even a thick Berber carpet on the floor, on which sat a large round table and matching chairs.

Charles pressed a button on one of the remote controls. A blow-dried, waxy-looking reporter was instantly replaced with Lady Justice and her scales. It was Charles's way of calling the meeting to order.

Tonight there were no colored folders on the table, which meant the mission was going to be open for discussion.

"Before we get down to business, I know all of you want to hear from Jack, Harry, Maggie, and Nellie. Maggie, I think since it began with you, you should start off."

Maggie nodded as she looked around. "I don't know if I should start off by apologizing to all of you or not for acting independently. I knew I could help, but my window of opportunity was short, so I took matters into my own hands. I did what I could, then turned it over to Jack and Harry, who in turn enlisted Nellie's help.

"One of my guys came to my office the day before yesterday and told me a story he got from a reliable source. The story was that Bert Navarro was not going to be confirmed by the Senate on Friday because he refused to give up his friendship with Jack and Harry. That didn't sit well with me. I knew . . . know how important it is to all of us to have Bert appointed to the top position in the FBI. Knowing how stubborn and loyal he is, I went to Jack that night and told him what was going on."

Maggie looked across the table at Kathryn, who was picking at her cuticles as she pursed her lips, and addressed her next comment to Kathryn alone. "We opted to keep Bert in the dark, Kathryn. We wanted him to react to the event, and he did. It was all so bizarre, I don't think anyone was any the wiser. The same goes for Director Cummings. Both men were taken to the hospital, where they were checked out, treated, and released, and they're okay. Angry but okay. Now it's Jack's turn."

Jack took the floor. "I called Harry, and together we came up with the invasion of the ninjas. Harry's people, of course. Harry needed to have an airtight alibi, which his class gave him. It was a diversion, nothing more. The media ran with it like we knew they would, right down to a fistful of human ashes from one of Harry's guy's ancestors—which are currently being analyzed. Director Cummings allowed himself to be pummeled a little more than necessary, but it just appeared that way. Bert put up a fight to defend his boss, which played out well.

"Cummings gave all the credit to Bert, who was heard to say that Harry and I were not friends—which I, of course, confirmed, as did Harry when we did our interviews with Joe Espinosa. Harry gave a very good interview to the *Post.* Maggie devoted the entire front page of the paper to the incident. She played up the human-ash part big-time. The story's all in living color, I might add. Harry, you want to say anything?"

Harry nodded. "Just that I think we pulled it off. Every member of the Senate gets a copy of the *Post,* so they'll read that front page in the morning with their morning coffee. What they don't know but will learn when they flip open the paper is Cummings's story. I think Judge Easter can pick up here."

Nellie looked around and smiled. "Jack asked me to call the airlines and book two tickets to Las Vegas for Thursday, which I did. We're to leave before the president makes his announcement. One ticket in my name and one ticket in the name of Elias Cummings. Both tickets were booked, confirmed, and paid for a little after nine o'clock that same night. It seems that Elias and I are getting married in Las Vegas. It was the only way we could think of to get Elias out of town to push the president to install Bert as director as soon as the Senate confirms him on Friday. No one is going to want the FBI to be without a director even if there is an acting director, what with the brown stuff splattering all over the place."

"You're getting married!" Annie exclaimed. "Nellie, how wonderful! I so love weddings. Goodness, what a day this has turned out to be."

Nellie groaned. "No, Annie, I'm going to pick a fight with Elias when we get there. No marriage. Well, maybe we'll get married if we don't have anything else to do." She twinkled. "Then again . . . if things work out and time permits, Lizzie and the *Post* reporter are to be our witnesses if the marriage comes off."

The room erupted in sound as the women clapped and hooted, congratulating Nellie.

"And Elias Cummings is going to go along with all this?" Nikki asked, a frown building on her beautiful face.

"He doesn't know yet, Nik," Jack said, doubling over with laughter. "He's going to read it in tomorrow's paper like the rest of Washington. He's no fool, he'll get the drift right away. It was the only way to get him out of town. Even the president isn't going to foul up a man's wedding plans."

"Well, since that seems to be taken care of," Charles said, "I suggest we get down to business. Girls, how does a trip to Las Vegas sound?"

Chapter 6

Jack was the first to speak. "We have no backup in Vegas. Law enforcement out there doesn't mess around. Everyone knows the casino boys run that town. One little infraction, and you get locked up. Those guys kick ass and take names later. Dicey from Harry's and my perspective. That's assuming we're invited to go along."

"It should be exciting. *Ka-ching!* I do love the sound of slot machines," Annie said. "The shows, the twenty-four-hour frenzy, and I understand there are no clocks in any of the casinos. Will we be high rollers?

Everything is free if you're a high roller. Hotel suites, drinks, food, limousine service, the whole nine yards. I have a book on gambling I bought online. There's no way you can cheat—they have ceiling surveillance, and every casino has at least a thousand security guards," she said breathlessly. Then, as an afterthought, she added, "Count me in."

Kathryn snorted. "Annie, Annie, get real, it's only free on the surface. Even though they give all those perks to you, and if you add it up for, say, a two-day, even a three-day weekend, the tab might be three grand, tops. The chances of your only losing three grand is about nil. If you're a high roller, you're guaranteed to gamble a hundred times that amount. There are no free lunches, Annie."

To Annie's chagrin, Kathryn directed her next comment to Charles. "What's in Vegas, and why are our services needed? It seems like an odd place for the vigilantes to go. All that sharp-eyed security is going to make me *very* nervous."

The others nodded but waited patiently for Charles to spell it all out for them.

"A message came through to Nikki's law

firm. It was pretty straightforward, a request for our help, but contact was needed for the details. Then a second request came through a few days later. It was the same party. There was a note of desperation in both pleas. Nikki had her old office manager call the sender for details, which I'm about to share with you. Before I do that, though, this person is someone Annie and Myra used to know when they were little girls, although the sender did not trade on that relationship. I came across it when I ran a check on the sender of both requests just to make certain it was the same person. Myra and Annie confirmed the childhood friendship. Neither Annie nor Myra has seen the woman in over fifty years. Nor have they had any contact.

"Then two other messages came in through the message boards. I can't be one hundred percent certain, but I think they came from Las Vegas and were not from Myra and Annie's old friend. I have people working on that end of it."

"What does she want?" Isabelle asked.

"Nothing for herself. It's her daughter who needs the help. That's why Lizzie is in Las Vegas. First, let me tell you about the woman who is seeking your help. The name she signed on her request was Beatrice Basson. Basson was her maiden name and is the name Myra and Annie knew her by. She's been married nine times. Her latest husband's name was Alonzo Preston. The Preston shipping lines," he added for clarification.

Annie poked Myra's arm. "Nine times! Mercy! I never thought she could snare even *one* man. How'd that happen, Myra? Beats, as we called her, didn't have much going for her." Myra just rolled her eyes. "Remember how she said she was from 'Loo-zee-anna'?" To the others she said, "That's how she talked. She was from Louisiana. Beats came to McLean to her granddaddy's plantation for the summer. Four summers, is what I remember. I think we were eleven the first time she came. I remember that the summer I turned fifteen, she wasn't there for my birthday party, but she came for a visit a few weeks later. We never saw her again after that or even heard anything about her that I can recall."

"That's pretty much how I remember it," Myra said. "Her grandparents died when we were sixteen, and the farm sat empty for years and years. I remember my father talking about titles that weren't clear and land grants, that kind of thing. As a young-ster it simply didn't interest me."

"What happened to the nine husbands?" Nikki asked.

"They all died. Natural deaths, before you can ask. All were extremely rich. There were a few lawsuits with some of the hus-bands' families because Beatrice, as the wife, inherited the bulk of all their fortunes. Everything was eventually settled, and everyone walked away happy, especially Beatrice. She only had one child, with her second husband, a girl named Marble Rose Barnes.

"Marble Rose had a series of nannies from birth. She attended an exclusive pre-school, followed by a boarding school, then on to Harvard, where she won a Rhodes Scholarship. Brilliant young woman. My investigation has not turned up anything positive in the way of a mother-daughter relationship between the two of them. Mar-ble Rose visited during holidays for a day here and there, but summers she was sent to a special camp for gifted children. By the age of fifteen the young lady stopped visiting her mother altogether. One can only speculate as to the reason. It might be because every other year or so there was another new husband, or perhaps the young lady had a very busy life.

"Her father left her a robust trust fund, so money was never an issue in her life. The trust fund is substantial enough that she never has to work a day for the rest of her life. However, she does work. She teaches sixth-graders in a public school, and she's finishing her dissertation on the gambling industry—at which point she'll be known as Dr. Barnes."

"She sounds like a fine young woman. What's the problem? Is the mother or the daughter the prospective client?" Alexis asked.

"The way I see it, the mother is asking for help for her daughter. The daughter at the moment is languishing in a Nevada jail. That's why I sent Lizzie to Vegas."

Chairs moved, deep breaths were taken, eyebrows raised. The interest level heightened with a chorus of whys.

"I can only tell you what I know, which is not all that much. My research is ongoing.

Because mother and daughter are not close, Miz Preston's information is sketchy at best, so it's up to Lizzie and me to make sense out of it. She probably left out more than she told me or will tell Lizzie. Clients do that for some reason, and the lawyer gets blindsided. This is what I know so far. Sixteen months ago, Marble Rose was mugged when she left a local gym around nine thirty at night. She was robbed and severely beaten and was in intensive care for five days before her mother even heard about it. By the way, I forgot to tell you the mother lives in California but is currently in Las Vegas.

"Marble Rose had a severe head trauma. Her recovery was long and, no, mother and daughter did not bond during her rehabilitation. The mother was sent packing with a lot of bitter recriminations. Miz Preston returned to California and only returned to Las Vegas last month when Marble Rose was arrested for the fourth time. This time she refused to leave, but Marble Rose will not allow Miz Preston to visit her in jail."

"Why? What did she do?" Jack asked.

Charles cleared his throat. "I don't know

how to answer that. In a way she did nothing, and in a way she turned Las Vegas on its ear. It would appear, and I stress the word *appear,* that Marble Rose's head trauma left her with . . . an extraordinary sense of some kind. At least that's what the mother *thinks.*"

Isabelle leaned forward. "Are you talking about something like what happened to me when I had my car accident? When I could, at times, *see things?* I was tested, retested, then tested again, like a guinea pig. The only thing the doctors could ever come up with was my sixth sense had something to do with my head injury. They wrote me up in some medical journals. We could go back and check that out. The worst part was that the things I saw came true. But I saw them after the fact. That awful sense, or whatever you want to call it, stayed with me for two years. And then it just faded away. It's a good thing, too, or I would have lost my mind. Is it possible the same kind of thing happened to Marble Rose?"

"It might be something like that, Isabelle. I just don't know. It's hard for me to believe the mother knows any of this, considering the relationship she has with her daughter. I assume she's speculating. The alternative is that she's trying to arouse our curiosity for reasons we have yet to discover."

"What's Marble Rose charged with?" Jack asked.

"She isn't charged with anything. The police are saying she isn't even in their jail or the system. The mother insists that she was carted off to jail and booked, according to the private detectives on her payroll. I couldn't find a record of any arrest. Lizzie is looking into it and will be meeting with the mother shortly.

"So, ladies, are you interested in this case? If you are, you'll be taking on some of the smartest individuals in the security business and some of the smartest lawyers Nevada has to offer. Because, believe it or not, this has something to do with Marble Rose's gambling and winning *big.* I can almost guarantee it, and while Miz Preston didn't say so, I think she believes it, too. She also said it's not wise to make an enemy of the people who conduct security for the casinos."

"Are they any match for Lizzie Fox?" Annie asked.

"I can't answer that, Annie, because at the moment I simply don't know. I'm just telling you what you're going up against. Like I said, are you interested?"

As one, the women gave off a resounding *yes.*

"Where does that leave Harry and me? Are we to stay behind?" Jack asked.

Charles frowned. "If you were to go, you would have no authority of any kind in Las Vegas. Now, if you can secure a week or so of vacation time, I see no reason why you can't make a trip to Nevada. I think, though, Jack, you should remain behind this time around unless I can come up with a foolproof reason for you to be taking a vacation at this particular time."

Jack grinned. "I might not have any legal authority, but I should receive some courtesy acknowledgment. Harry, now, he has authority just by being who he is, no matter where he goes. And those in the know will remember him because he won the martial-arts competition three years in a row, and all three of those competitions were held in Vegas at, where was it, Harry?"

"The MGM Grand," Harry said. "Sellout crowds all three times."

"I rest my case," Jack said. To Charles he said, "Work it out, Charles, I want to go. I can't be of any use here."

Kathryn squirmed in her chair. "What about Bert?"

Charles looked at Kathryn and chose his words carefully. "Bert will be apprised of what's going on. Right now we have to let matters where he's concerned go through the proper channels. We need to see him confirmed, and we're still not sure if that will happen. In other words, it will be Bert's decision on what and how to proceed. It's the best information I can give you at the moment, Kathryn."

Kathryn nodded as she kneaded her hands, which were folded in her lap. Murphy, her huge German shepherd, sensing her unease, nosed her leg for attention. Kathryn unlocked her hands and reached over to stroke the dog's great head.

Maggie pushed back her chair. "Is there anything else you want me to do? If not, I have to be up at four, so I think I'll say good night now."

"Just saturate the front page with whatever you can make work for all of us," Charles said. He looked at the monster clock on the wall and smiled. "I think the *Post* is now online. Shall we all view it in living color?"

Suddenly the room was a beehive of activity. Everyone was talking at once as Charles used a pointer to jab at the different pictures and articles on the front page. The girls rushed to Maggie and swooped her up as they congratulated her on a job well done. She glowed with pride.

Jack clapped Harry on the back as Charles used his pointer to pinpoint a small mound of what looked like ashes. "Where'd you say you got those ashes?"

"One of my guy's long-dead ancestors. He didn't have a bit of trouble giving them up because he's going to reclaim them and put them back in their little nest as soon as the lab confirms the ashes are human. Labs take very good care of stuff like that," Harry said with a straight face.

"Just like that, he's going to go to the FBI's forensic lab and take back his ancestor's ashes?" Jack asked, disbelief ringing in his voice.

"Well, yeah, Jack," Harry drawled. "He's a ninja. If he can disintegrate into thin air, I think he can pull it off. You want to make a little wager?"

"Hell, no. I was just asking, Harry. I'm sorry I brought it up. No, I'm not. Just hold on here a minute. When those eagle-eyed forensic people test those ashes, aren't they going to be able to tell how old they are?"

"Well, yeah, Jack," Harry drawled a second time. "It will just perpetuate the ninja myth that they come back to life, then return to their . . . uh, other form."

The others listened to Harry's explanation with wide eyes and dropped jaws. None of them were going to touch that explanation with a mile-long pole. Jack shrugged as he stared at the picture still on the screen. He just knew the son of a bitch was going to pull it off. He should have known better than to even think about questioning Harry.

Maggie's cell phone took that particular moment to ring. She looked down at the caller ID and mouthed the words "Joe

Espinosa." "Yeah, Joe, what's up?" She listened a moment, and with her index finger indicated that Charles should turn to the Fox News Channel. "What do you mean, where am I? First of all, it's none of your business where I am. I ask the questions, remember? Everything's ready to go. I'll be in by nine. I'm sleeping late because I'm treating myself to a job well done by you. Stay on it, Joe. I know what time it is. You have the rest of your life to sleep. Screw this up, and you won't like what I do."

She powered down and then made the decision to leave immediately instead of in the early hours of the morning, regardless of what she'd just told Joe. Nellie elected to go with her.

Harry poked Jack on the arm. "See, they're all chasing their tails. Now they don't know what to do since the ashes were human remains. Not to worry. By morning those ashes will be nothing but a memory." He cackled gleefully as he walked out of the room with his arm around Yoko's shoulders.

Jack doubled over laughing as he gasped to Maggie, "Make sure Espinosa is on top of this and the paper runs with the theft. Play it up, Maggie, the ninjas came back for their . . . whatever term ninjas use for their remains."

Maggie offered up an airy salute. At the door, she turned around and asked Charles if she was going to Vegas.

"I'm not sure, Maggie. You might do us more good here. I'll let you know by noon tomorrow."

"Okay, works for me. You ready, Judge?"

"I'm ready, dear."

Maggie ran over to Annie and whispered in her ear. Annie hugged her and, like every other mother in the world, said, "Drive carefully, dear. Call us when you get home safe and sound."

"Will do, *Mom*."

Chapter 7

Lizzie Fox sauntered into the Babylon casino, Ted Robinson at her side. In appearance, they looked like all the other couples who were milling about or gambling. And just like any other visitors to Las Vegas, they were awed at the flashing lights, the bells, the whistles, the scantily clad waitresses just waiting to serve their free drinks.

Lizzie decided they were dressed appropriately, nothing to distinguish them from the other guests. She was wearing dark slacks, a yellow sweater, and loafers. She carried a matching gold suede jacket on one arm, a large Chanel carry bag on her shoulder. Ted wore pressed khakis, a white button-down shirt, and a tweed jacket. His pack was nestled securely on his back.

"Let's walk around. I want to get a feel for this place. We have forty minutes till we meet Ms. Preston. Remember, Ted, you're my assistant. That means you keep quiet, you listen, and you make sure your tape recorder is on. I hope you put fresh batteries in it." No need to tell the reporter her own recorder would be on inside the pocket of her slacks. Lizzie was big on doubles of everything. And she fervently believed in the old adage of Murphy's Law, that what can go wrong, will go wrong. Each tape would record for a full sixty minutes. If the interview went past the hour mark, she'd have to excuse herself and head outside to flip the tape. She really needed to get a digital recorder.

Lizzie chatted amiably with Ted as they strolled along like neither had a care in the world. "Do you know if they have monitors in these places that pick up sound?"

Ted grinned as he watched a white-haired grandmother feed twenty-dollar bills into a slot machine at the speed of light. She looked grim, like she was going to kick out at the machine or explode with frustration. "Not for a fact. This particular casino has over two thousand security cameras. I don't think I'm comfortable talking about this right now. Later, when we leave here, we can take a stroll, and I'll tell you what I've managed to come up with. Maggie has been text messaging me all day, so I have to combine all that she's told me with what I already have. It's awesome, Lizzie. All this crap they have here—Homeland Security wishes they had it themselves." He stopped, fished around in his pocket for a dollar bill, and slid it into one of the slot machines. "This is just a guess on my part, but I think you have met your match here, Miz Fox."

"You think?" Lizzie watched the wheel spin and laughed out loud when Ted won five dollars. "Take your four-dollar profit and move along."

Ted cashed out his winnings, and mumbled, "Yeah, I do think that. You're good, and I give you that, but these guys are better. No offense."

Lizzie laughed again. "And none taken."

She winked at him, and Ted almost wet his pants. "See that machine over there? The jackpot is $187,444. Imagine that." Five minutes later, when she turned around, the numbers read $187,993. "I hope some construction worker from New Jersey and his wife win it."

"Just out of curiosity, can you practice law here, Lizzie?"

"Yep, I can practice law in every state except South Dakota. Don't even ask why I don't want to practice law in South Dakota. I thought you knew I'm billed as the female Clarence Darrow and a legal whiz who has no equal. You need to get with it, Teddie," Lizzie said airily, as her gaze raked the rows and rows of slot machines. Since Marble Rose wasn't into blackjack or roulette, Lizzie gave the tables barely a glance.

Ted frowned as he tugged at one of his earlobes. "All of that aside, there's a first time to fumble. Happens to the best of us." He hated it, absolutely hated it when Lizzie one-upped him.

"I'm not you, Teddie, and it isn't going to happen. I have secrets that have secrets. I know people who know other people. A long time ago I decided I didn't need just a plan but a *master* plan, so I formulated one. It's all up here," Lizzie said, tapping her head. "You look . . . scared, Ted. Why is that?"

"Because you scare the shit out of me, that's why. Listen, I forgot to mention I'm going to amble over to wherever the *Review-Journal* is and talk to a few of the local reporters. I want to get the *real* skinny on this place. I might hit up the *Sun* and the *Northern View,* too. The single guys are the ones I want to talk to. But that's for later, after our walk outside and after your meeting with Ms. Preston."

"That sounds like a plan. I think we should head back to that cocktail lounge and order a drink. I've seen enough. I cannot imagine working a full eight- to twelve-hour shift in a place like this. A person's nerves must be twanging all over the place when they leave at the end of the day."

"This ain't nothin'. You should see these casinos come eleven o'clock at night. That's when everything goes through the roof, and the high rollers come out to play." At Lizzie's quizzical look, he said, "I read a lot and go to the movies even more. Vegas is a gold mine in the entertainment business. People can't get enough of it."

Lizzie's gaze swept the rows of slot machines until she found the one that had read $187,993 at last look. It now read $188,311. Absolutely amazing. She made a mental note to check the machine one last time before calling it a night. She might even do what Ted did, put a dollar in to see what kind of return she'd get for her investment.

In what looked like a tiki bar, Lizzie settled herself in a comfortable rattan chair. Battery-operated candles sat in the middle of all the tables. Tiki torches with the same kind of battery lights were placed strategically around the huge bar area. Dried palm fronds and other assorted dried foliage were everywhere. Lizzie decided she would rather sit in a well-lit chrome-and-glass bar where she could *really* see what was going on.

"I assume we're being watched here, too, right?"

"You assume right. Bartenders are known for giving friends free drinks, adding an extra jigger to the glass. Everything here is suspect. This is just a guess on my part, but I'd wager there are at least two cameras in here, probably glued to all that fake palm crap. It's hard to be honest in a place like this. It's called temptation."

A waitress who was pretty and shapely enough to be a Hollywood starlet bounced over to their table to take their order. She smiled, and the room lit up. "What can I get for you wonderful people? Welcome to Las Vegas."

Lizzie smiled in return. "Scotch on the rocks," she said. Ted ordered a Corona.

"Bet you can't guess how much these girls make in a night," Ted said.

"Probably a couple of hundred if they smile at the guests. Waitressing is hard work, you're on your feet for your entire shift, and those girls wear high heels, so no matter what they make in tips, they earn it. Okay, how much?"

"Eight, nine hundred a night. Most are girls working their way through college. Like I said, I read a lot. So, is she late, or are we early?"

"We're five minutes early. You look nervous, Ted. Relax."

Their drinks arrived, and the waitress

made a production out of setting up the napkins and the small bowl of trail mix, then offering to pour Ted's beer. He declined the offer and immediately took a swig out of the bottle. Lizzie dug around in her purse and pulled out her American Express Black Card and handed it over. Ted noticed.

"The Centurion Card, eh? Guess they do pay you the big bucks. I heard that card is titanium and makes a different sound when you drop it on the table."

"True," Lizzie said as she watched for someone who might be looking around for her. Just as the waitress returned her credit card, she saw a dowager type walk up the two steps into the tiki bar and look around. Lizzie left a 30 percent tip, then scrawled her name across the bottom of the charge slip. She jammed the receipt and card back into her bag as she stood up and walked over to the dowager, who was still looking around.

"Ms. Preston?"

"Yes. And you are?"

"The person you wanted to see. Please, I have a table over here." When they arrived Lizzie said, "This is my assistant," deliberately not mentioning Ted's name. "Would you like something to drink?"

"No. Thank you for asking. I'd like to get right to business."

"Do you think this location is a wise choice?" Lizzie asked quietly.

"Probably not. There are eyes and ears everywhere in this town. One place is as good as any other, I guess. That's just my opinion, of course. I wasn't sure if they would send someone. You're from . . ."

Lizzie interrupted her. "In a manner of speaking."

The dowager looked around. "Yes, yes, I understand."

Lizzie sized up the older woman within seconds. Rich but understated. Well groomed, pampered. Several face-lifts. One artificial hairpiece that was almost undetectable. Thin. She was probably into Pilates. She looked the type.

"Are you a . . . ?"

Lizzie interrupted again, and said, "Yes." She looked over at Ted, who had his cell phone in his hand. He mumbled something that sounded like *sorry,* as he turned away to take his fake call. Lizzie knew that he was actually taking a picture of Ms. Preston.

Beatrice-with-eight-other-names Preston was nervous. Suddenly her head snapped back, and she said, "I see you're almost finished with your drinks. I've changed my mind about staying here. My car and driver are outside circling. I'll call him to meet us at the entrance, and we can talk in the car if that's all right with you."

Lizzie shrugged, finished her drink with one swallow, then slipped on the gold suede jacket as Beatrice Preston made her phone call. Ted set his beer bottle back on the napkin and got up. Neither looked surprised at the change in plans.

Beatrice moved quickly as she led the way through the maze of people and rows of machines and tables. "They're everywhere. They don't look like security. See that person with the dreadlocks? He's security."

"How do you know that?" Lizzie asked as she trailed alongside the older woman.

"*I see things.* They know you're here. Now *they* know you're with me. We're already on video. Right now they're running facial recognition checks on the two of you. They already know who I am. Meeting here was a mistake. I should have known better," Beatrice Preston said fretfully. "I'm sorry, I'm usually more in control. This place, these people, they unnerve me."

Lizzie was relieved when they reached the front door. She turned around to take a last look at what was going on behind her. Everything looked exactly the way it had when they had first entered the casino. Maybe there were a few more people, but it was hard to tell. The casino's security people were *good.* She knew once they got outside it wouldn't be any different. In this day of satellites and microtransmitters, unseen eyes and ears could follow them everywhere, if what Ted said was true about security in Vegas being better than the technology Homeland Security had at its fingertips.

Within seconds, the trio was in a luxurious Bentley driven by an older man dressed in a spiffy uniform.

"Adam, just drive us around until I tell you to bring us back here." She turned to Lizzie, and said, "Please don't worry about Adam, he's been with me for over thirty

years. He's entirely trustworthy. He . . .
uh . . . sweeps the car several times a day.
We can speak freely and openly. A word
to the wise, young lady. If you're registered
at the Babylon, those people will be spying
on you. Adam tells me they slip something
called parabolic microphones and cameras under doors, or they have pinholes in
the wall that are almost impossible to
detect. In this town you are either part of
the problem or part of the solution."

Lizzie leaned back and crossed her
legs. She certainly was getting a lot of
information that was a tad on the worri-
some side. Maybe she should call Rena
Gold to secure other accommodations.
She smiled when she thought of Rena
and her role in the vigilantes' takedown of
the president of the World Bank. She'd
promised to help the vigilantes here in her
home base if they ever needed her help.
She rather doubted Rena would be
expecting a request from her benefactors
so quickly, but Lizzie knew she'd rise to
the occasion.

"I'd like to hire you to help my daughter.
The fact that you're here must mean
those . . . ladies have seriously considered

my request. You look so familiar to me. Have we ever met?"

"No, we've never met, Ms. Preston. My name is Lizzie Fox, and this is my associate, Ted Robinson."

Lizzie watched as the older woman mulled over the names but finally gave up when she couldn't place either name. "My daughter is in jail. I'd like you to get her out of there as soon as possible. Back there in the casino I told you that I see things. I mean that literally. My mother and my grandmother had the same ability. I think my daughter has the same . . . curse. I don't know for sure because . . . well, because I thought . . . What I did was estrange myself from her, literally from birth, hoping it wouldn't rub off because I . . . I don't understand any of it. My mother didn't understand it, either. We just have it, the ability to see things at times that other people can't see. I don't like to say we can predict the future, we can't. We see things a few seconds before events happen. Sometimes within the hour. I don't know what triggers those moments. Certainly not stress. Most of the time they happen when I'm at rest or just at peace with my life. I'm sorry to burden you with this, and I'm sure you think I must be demented. I'm not. I almost wish I was.

"While I am estranged from my daughter, it doesn't mean I don't love her or care about her. I have people who have watched her every hour of her entire life. Of course she doesn't know this. While most people wouldn't understand my reasoning, I say they don't have to live with this abominable curse, and if doing what I did for her meant she would escape being plagued with it, that's all that matters. Before you can ask, I've been all over the world seeking help. I've had every test known to man. I've seen every person in the field, and no one was able to help me. Experts are the ones who told me to remove myself from my daughter's life so, possibly, just possibly, she wouldn't be affected."

"And was she?" Lizzie asked. She couldn't help but wonder if the woman *was* demented. She looked at her in the dimness of the car and decided she was the real McCoy. Lizzie took great pride in her judgments of people and was rarely, if ever, wrong.

"I thought so until this gambling issue came up. But the gambling problem only came about after my daughter was mugged and suffered a head trauma. Her recovery was a long one. That's when she took up . . . gambling. Before then, in all the time she's lived here, she'd never once gone to a casino. She wins. All the time. Then she gives away the money. The casinos went after her, thinking she was cheating and beating the system, but they couldn't prove anything. They took her to one of their secret rooms, where they questioned her for hours and hours. They started following her, invading her privacy. Last year she was named Teacher of the Year by her school. Yet they managed to get her fired from her teaching job. These people are very powerful; they can do whatever they want. I'm talking about casino security when I say the 'people' are powerful. Marble Rose has been a victim several times. Someone hijacked her car. Another time someone broke into her house. The brakes on her car were tampered with, and yet those damn people never barred her from the casino. That's what doesn't make sense to me."

"Why didn't your daughter go to a lawyer?" Lizzie asked, as her agile brain sifted and collated what she was hearing.

"She did go to a lawyer. Actually she went to over a dozen lawyers, but as soon as they heard it was a casino problem, they either weren't taking on new clients or they flat-out refused to help her.

"She finally found one who asked for a twenty-five-thousand-dollar retainer, which she paid, and within a month he was gone. He put a sign on the door of his office and one on his house, saying that due to a family emergency he would be unavailable indefinitely. He took the time to assign all his other cases to other colleagues, with the exception of my daughter's case. She found out when she went to his office after her calls were not returned. The man prepaid his house bills and has not been seen since. It's over a month now that he's been AWOL. One would have to be a fool not to think the casinos' muscle got to him."

Ted leaned over and asked, "Can't you . . . tune in, or whatever you do, or however it works, to find out where he is?"

Beatrice Preston sighed. "It doesn't work

that way. I wish it did. I had one . . . vision of her sitting in jail. That's how I know she's there."

"Why is your daughter in jail?" Lizzie asked.

Beatrice Preston looked at Lizzie like she had sprouted a second head. "I just told you, they say she isn't in jail. Therefore, she isn't charged with anything."

Lizzie waited a full minute before she answered. "I have to talk to your daughter first. I'll go to the county jail tomorrow to see what I can find out."

"Fair enough. What about . . . you know who?"

Lizzie waited another minute before she responded. "That can't be true, Ms. Preston. Maybe she's booked under another name. If the police don't charge you, they have to release you. It's the law. It would help me to know what it is you expect, what it is precisely that you want me to do."

"Try telling that to the police. I'm sure casino security and the local police work in tandem. That's another way of saying the cops, at least some of them, are on the casinos' payroll. Everyone knows it, they just don't talk about it out loud. I want you to get me out of here and . . . take care of whomever is responsible for putting me here."

"What about the newspapers? Did you try going to them to ask for help? Did you file a missing person's report?"

"My daughter won a great deal of money at various casinos, but she doesn't come close to those math whizzes from MIT who reportedly took more than $10 million from the casinos in the nineties. They got away with it. My daughter just played slot machines," Beatrice Preston said defiantly. "When you have a gambling house, you are going to have winners, and you will have losers. She won, it's that simple, and those people are trying to . . . I don't know what they're trying to do, but she's in jail, so that has to mean something. Look, I'm desperate with nowhere to turn. I know that my daughter is in jail."

Lizzie's mind was racing. This was right up there with . . . no point in going there. No two cases were the same. If she took this case, assuming there was a case to take, it was going to be a challenge, she could feel it in her bones. "Like I said, Ms. Preston, I have to speak with your daughter, but I can't do that until I find her. Have you given any thought to speaking with your daughter? Perhaps the two of you could make amends."

"I think about it twenty-four hours a day, Miss Fox. My daughter refuses to speak with me. It's that simple. I cannot unring that bell."

Lizzie felt her eyes grow moist as she thought about Annie, and how she now had an official adoptive mother. Nothing in the whole wide world could replace a mother in a child's mind. Nothing. She said so.

"Yes, I know. I'm sure I will go to hell on a greased slide for what I've done, but I did what I thought best to spare my child what I had to go through. Perhaps some-day, after I'm gone, she'll understand. I plan to leave a letter with my lawyer to read to her. It's all I can do.

"So if there's nothing else, we should get you back to the hotel. You have my cell phone number. Please call tomorrow to tell me what is going on. Even if it's bad news. Bill me when you're ready and please remember what I said about securing other accommodations."

Beatrice Preston leaned forward, and said, "Adam, please take us back to the Babylon."

There were a thousand questions swirling around inside Lizzie's head. Out of the corner of her eye she watched as Ted text messaged someone. A satisfied expression was on his face. She looked down at her watch. She had five minutes before she had to flip her tape.

"Traffic in this town is atrocious. You need to leave a full hour ahead of time if you want to reach a specific destination at an appointed time," Beatrice said, as though they were friends and had just met.

"How long have you been here?" Lizzie asked.

"Tomorrow it will be a month. I'm staying with a friend. If you agree to represent my daughter, I'll leave so as not to get in your way or give my daughter a reason to balk. I think it will be better if I'm not a presence here."

"Do you love your daughter, Ms. Preston?" Lizzie was sorry she asked the question when she saw the naked longing on the older woman's face. She thought about Annie and Myra and how they'd lost their children.

"Only God knows how much I love my daughter and what a hell I've lived all these years, and yet if I had to, I'd do it all over again to protect her."

When the Bentley slid to the curb, Adam got out and walked around to open the door. Ted hopped out first.

Beatrice reached out to Lizzie and asked, "Could you please deliver a message for me to Myra and Anna? I don't know, does she still go by Anna—or Annie? As a child, I called her Annie. Tell them . . . tell them I'm sorry for their loss. I wanted to call so many times but was afraid to intrude. It had been so many years. And tell them their secret is safe with me. Can you do that for me, Miss Fox?"

"Yes, ma'am, I can do that for you."

Lizzie and Ted stepped out into the dark night and the Bentley pulled away from the curb. She looked up at the riot of stars overhead. Ted was still text messaging. She tapped his shoulder to get his attention. He finished his message and slipped his BlackBerry into his pocket.

"You said something about going to the newspapers. Is that still your plan?"

"Yep. Why? Oh, the walk we were going to take so I could clue you in on this Devil's Paradise. How about we do that later? We have all night. I should be back by midnight. If I'm onto something hot, I'll call you."

"I'm going to check out of here and secure other accommodations. I'll give you a call as soon as I nail something down."

"You going to be okay by yourself, Lizzie?"

"I think so, Ted. I'm a big girl."

"You know what, I liked the old gal. I'm a pretty good judge of character, Lizzie. She hurts. She's in pain. I think you and the vigilantes should help her. And the daughter. Don't look at me like that. I know, okay? So don't try feeding me any of that bullshit about being left holding the bag that day in court when you represented the vigilantes. From that day on you were one of them. Like the old lady said, your secret is safe with me. Hard to believe but true. Go get 'em, Counselor," Ted said, as a cab slid to the curb and he climbed in. "Call me."

Lizzie walked away from the entrance, then turned her back as she whipped out her cell phone and scrolled down until she found the number she wanted. She pressed in the digits and waited a moment to see if she'd get a message or Rena Gold herself. When she heard the soft-voiced greeting, she said, "This is Lizzie Fox. I need a place to stay while I'm in town. I have a male associate with me. Right now I'm outside the Babylon, but when I finish this call, I'm going to check out. Can you help me out?"

Without missing a beat the soft voice said, "Give me an hour, and I'll pick you up in front of the casino. How is . . . ?"

"Everyone is fine. They all send their regards. See you in an hour."

Lizzie powered down, then fired up a cigarette. She usually didn't smoke, and when she did light up, she never inhaled. Most times it was just a ploy until she got the lay of the land. Before she could even take one puff on the cigarette, three men were on her like stink on a skunk, asking her to put out her cigarette. She thought about giving them an argument but decided against it. They let guests smoke inside while they gambled, but they wouldn't let them smoke outside. She chalked up the encounter for use at some point in the future. She crushed out the offending cigarette and sashayed into the casino, a wicked smile playing around her lips.

Upstairs, in one of the secret rooms, three men stared at the monitor that covered the entrance. A man monitoring the huge front door of the casino stared at the picture of Lizzie sauntering through the casino. She turned at one point and stood perfectly still, as though she were posing for a photo shoot. She deliberately did a slow turn so that every camera in the casino could get her full face, profile, as well as her back. She offered up a megawatt smile and waved before she headed for the slot machine whose numbers had last read $188,311. The numbers now read $195,832. She stopped, rummaged in her purse, and slid a ten-dollar bill into the slot. Unlike Ted, there was no return on her investment. She walked away, her gaze everywhere.

The man staring at the monitor that

looked like it was featuring Lizzie Fox turned to his colleagues. "It's her! I knew it! She knows we're watching her. Gentlemen, this is one lady you don't want to mess with. She's the one who took on Renzo Savarone and lived to tell about it. There can only be one reason she's here. Dwayne, call the boss and arrange a meeting. I think he's out on the floor. I need to know how he wants to play this."

"Hold on, Mike, hold on. Looks to me like she's going to check out. That doesn't make any sense. She just checked in midafternoon. Yep, she's checking out. I can read the numbers on her credit card. It's a black one. The lady has resources. Okay, a bellman is going with her. You sure you want me to call the boss?"

"Hell, yes, I'm sure. What happened to the guy she checked in with?"

"He took a cab and was just dropped off at the *Las Vegas Review-Journal*. His name is Ted Robinson, and he works for the *Post* in Washington, D.C. He got real chatty with the driver. Told you it was worth it to put those cabbies on the payroll. Like you said, he checked in with the woman. I don't think they're an item—probably she's his boss or something like that. I assume she's checking him out, too, since they had a suite. We'll know when we see the bellman bringing down the bags."

Mike Oliver, one of the Babylon's best security agents, moved his 290-pound girth to the other side of the room to a monitor that covered the elevator Lizzie and the bellman were in. He watched, fascinated at the woman's boldness as she offered up a single-digit salute behind the bellman's back. The smile on her face made his blood run cold.

"Balls to the wall, boys," he muttered under his breath.

Chapter 8

Every bone in Elias Cummings's body ached. He moved gingerly in his well-padded chair as he kept his eyes on the colorful front page of the *Post.* He'd read every single word on the entire front page. Some of them twice. He probably could have recited the different articles verbatim if his feet were to the fire. Very clever of Maggie Spritzer to keep everything contained on one page, no flipping to the inside and searching for the end of an article.

He looked down at the picture of himself with Bert Navarro covering his body, a black-clad ninja hovering overhead. Thank

God the new EIC hadn't enlarged the picture. He shrugged. No matter, it showed Navarro in a good light, protecting his boss at great harm to himself. That should make the Senate sit up and take notice and vote favorably. The deliberately muttered comment by Bert that the press was supposed to hear worked well. Blaming Jack Emery and Harry Wong for the attack played out especially well.

Cummings looked to the left of the paper for Emery's short interview. It was cold and brittle and to the point. "Bert Navarro is no friend of mine. You know what you can do with your insinuations, don't you, Mr. Espinosa? You really don't want to know what I think about his proposed appointment as director of the FBI. Your paper is a family paper, isn't it?" The short interview went on to list numerous cases he'd won in court and also his prior engagement to Nikki Quinn, one of the vigilantes.

Cummings let his gaze go to the enlarged picture of the pile of ashes that had settled on the ground after the ninjas disappeared into thin air. He smiled, knowing full well that when analyzed, the ashes would prove to be human. He almost laughed out loud when he recalled the early morning news report of the break-in at the FBI lab during the night, where the only thing taken was the beaker of ashes that were being tested. The ninjas returning for their own so they could rise again. This time he did laugh aloud but sobered immediately when he saw Bert Navarro standing in the doorway.

"You okay?"

The tall, dark-haired assistant director just stood there, slouching. He had a scrape down one side of his face and two shiners. Navarro winced slightly as he straightened up and entered the room. "I'll live. I see you have the paper. The whole damn thing gave me a king-size adrenaline rush. And then the news this morning. Will you please tell me how someone broke into our lab? Goddammit, this is the FBI, and they infiltrated us. How the hell did that happen? Whose ass are we going to put in a sling over this?" Bert bellowed.

Cummings leaned back in his chair. "No one's. I thought you knew ninjas were invisible. What I mean is the myth is they can disappear, dissolve, whatever the hell it is they do. We have to ignore it because if we give any kind of credence to the news, it just makes us look worse. Thanks again, Bert, for saving my life. You know what I want to know is, where in the damn hell those Secret Service guys were while all this was going down?"

"They were there. Well, after the fact they were there. I remember lying on the ground and looking up at all those Brooks Brothers suits." Bert turned around and closed the door. On his way to Cummings's desk, he flinched a few times from the pain in his legs. He pulled a piece of paper out of his pocket and laid it on the desk. The words were simple and concise. *A setup, right?"*

Cummings nodded, then slid the slip of paper into the shredder.

"I'm on my way to the White House. No, Bert, you weren't invited. It's been a hell of a busy morning, I can tell you that. By the way, Martine Connor, our next president, if the polls are right, sent me a box, all tied up with a red ribbon, with seventy-two jelly donuts inside. I think that was her way of letting me know you're going to be confirmed tomorrow. You know how sneaky you have to be in this town, and if a box of seventy-two jelly donuts is what it takes, then so be it. I also think that's why I'm being called to the White House. Regardless, I'm outta here come morning. I'm going to Vegas."

"Seems like a lot of people are going to Vegas lately." Bert snickered. "Is there any truth to the rumor that you're traveling with Judge Easter and that you're getting married? Not just tying the knot but doing it in one of those Elvis chapels with the King singing at the nuptials?"

Cummings pretended horror, but it didn't quite come off, since he himself, on orders from Nellie, had started the rumor. "Who told you that?" he blustered.

"Aside from the fact that I almost got stomped to death by some fucking ninjas, then saved your life and still managed to come to work, I'd say it's because we at the Federal Bureau of Investigation are agents who are known to always get our man after we track down all the . . ."

"Enough!" Cummings growled. "Now will you get someone to carry these boxes down to my car?" The boxes contained the junk he'd accumulated during his tenure as director of the FBI. Junk, but still he couldn't leave it behind because one was supposed to exit with boxes of junk. As far as he knew, it was some kind of unwritten rule.

"What? You mean you aren't coming back here? No, no, you can't do that, Elias," Bert said. "The guys . . ."

"Screw the guys and the party they planned. Look, son, I'm no hypocrite. I know they can't wait to see me go. I remember the mutiny that almost happened when I replaced Mitch Riley. And, I don't need another gold watch. I'm walking out of here just the way I walked in, with *half* my dignity intact. Goddamn ninjas! You guys are never going to be able to live that down. Well, maybe you will." He grinned.

Bert's eyes burned. "Okay, okay, I can live with all that, but what I can't live with is you not wanting me to be your best man. How's that going to look when it hits the papers, you and Judge Easter being married in an Elvis chapel with Elvis lookalikes standing up for you?"

"Like we're two old fools having a hell of a good time. Give me twenty bucks, and I'll play one of those progressive slots for you."

Bert dug a twenty out of his wallet and handed it over. His eyes continued to burn as the director smothered him in a bear hug. He could feel the big man trembling.

Cummings was almost to the door, when Bert said, "What should I do about the ninja crap?"

Cummings turned around. "See that box of donuts the next president of the United States sent me this morning? Pick some guy you really hate and have him hand-deliver it to Harry Wong and make sure you put Jack Emery's name on the box, too."

It was the perfect exit line, and Bert burst out laughing as the director waved nonchalantly and walked through the door like he was going to lunch.

When Bert finally calmed down enough to speak coherently, he walked out to the corridor and bellowed at the top of his lungs the way Cummings did when he was pissed to the teeth. "Listen up! The party has been canceled, and Elvis has left the building. Jackson! Front and center."

A tall, handsome agent who believed he was the Second Coming of George

Clooney, a belief no one else shared, literally saluted, then waited. Bert hated his guts because he was a glory hound.

"The director's last order was for you, Jackson. He said you were personally to hand-deliver this box," he said, holding out the beribboned jelly donut box, "to Harry Wong's *dojo* and you are to get a receipt. He also said if Wong wants you to kiss his ass, you are to do it, and, know this, Jackson, the eyes and ears of the FBI are upon you, so don't screw this up."

John Jackson didn't look like George Clooney at that moment, he looked like a wet cat that had gotten tangled up in an electrical wire.

"Okay, back to work, everyone," Bert ordered, a smirk on his face. There was no way in hell he could have disobeyed Cummings's last official order.

Bert limped his way to his office and slammed the door shut. He wanted to cry so damn bad he didn't know what to do. He sat down and dropped his head into his hands. If he was smart, he would gather up his belongings and run after Elias Cummings. He thought about life in a federal penitentiary for what he'd been doing, which was aiding and abetting the vigilantes. He knew that, in his own way, Elias Cummings had been doing the same thing. But Elias was out now, and Bert had been passed the torch. Cummings had just walked out of the Hoover Building to start his new life, his tenure here at the FBI just a memory. Bert wondered if the memory would be a good or bad one.

Then his thoughts took him to Jack Emery and Harry Wong, his two best friends in the whole world, and what they'd just done for him so he could be appointed director of the FBI. He'd known in his gut the ninja event at the White House was a setup, but he was FBI through and through and needed Elias Cummings's confirmation to make him accept it 100 percent, which he now did. Jack and Harry would never give him up, just the way he hadn't given them up by refusing to sever his friendship with both men, even though the prize was taking over the FBI directorship.

Bert's thoughts switched over to the vigilantes, Kathryn Lucas in particular. He wondered if he was a fool. He believed he could separate his position at the FBI and still be a supporter and ally of the vigilantes. He bit down on his lower lip. Better men than he had probably thought they could play both ends against the middle. He'd made his decision the minute he'd allowed Elias Cummings to speak with the president about nominating him as director. Now he had to live with it. If he ended up in the federal pen, he'd have no one to blame but himself. He shivered inside his jacket.

Bert sat upright, his eyes clear and bright. It was time to think about a few things. Something was going to go down in Las Vegas. Why else would Elias and Judge Easter be going there? Duncan Wright, one of his best agents, had called him at home last night to check on how he was doing. After the amenities, Duncan had shared some information and asked what he should do with it. Bert remembered how he'd broken out into a sweat when Dunk, as the other agents called him, told him a source at the *Post* told him that Lizzie Fox and Ted Robinson had flown to Las Vegas in the *Post*'s private jet. Somehow or other, Bert had managed to mutter something—and he still couldn't remember exactly what he'd said—about filing a report and putting it on his desk in the morning.

He now shuffled through the stacks of papers on his desk until he found it. Dunk was concise and to the point. It was just the way he'd said it last night and not one word extra. That's when he noticed the sticky note on the back of the report that said Fox and Robinson had checked into the Babylon. And then they'd checked out. They had been met in the casino by a woman.

Bert tugged at his earlobe, something he always did when he tried to figure something out. Maybe this was some kind of cockamamie test. He reached for his phone to call the agent. "Get your gear together, Dunk. You're going to Vegas. Report in to me twice a day, every twelve hours. Pick up three agents, more if you need them, at the local field office in Vegas, and put a tail on Fox and Robinson. By the way, Dunk, in case you haven't heard the scuttlebutt, Director Cummings and Judge Easter are traveling to Vegas to get married. Don't say anything, Dunk, check it out and let me know what you find out."

No matter which way the wind was blowing, it always came down to CYA. And that's exactly what he was doing, covering his ass. He reached for a blank yellow pad and started to scribble—time, date, and the orders he'd just issued. Later, he'd transfer the notes to himself to a formal report on his computer.

Bert inched open the top drawer of his desk and propped his feet on it. In just a few days, if his confirmation came through, he'd be moving two doors down the hall to Cummings's old office. Maybe he'd assign Jackson the task of moving his things into the new space.

Bert closed his eyes and let his mind have free rein. He'd traveled a long, hard road. Being a minority had not been easy, but he'd hunkered down and played the game to win. If the announcement tomorrow was positive, as Cummings thought it was going to be, Bert had not only persevered, but he had prevailed as well.

But he had to revise his game plan.

An hour later, Bert was still working on his new strategy when John Jackson banged on his office door. Bert bellowed, "Come in."

The door opened and Jackson poked his head in. "I'm gonna get you for this,

Navarro. I don't care if you're going to be the new director or not."

Bert might have been discussing the weather when he swung his feet down on the floor with a loud, smacking sound. "You like working for the FBI, right, Jackson?"

"Just love it. Why?"

"'Cause I'm going to find a way to fire your sorry ass out of here. Where do you get off threatening me?"

The George Clooney look-alike blanched, knowing he'd stepped over the line. "Jeez, Navarro, can't you take a joke?"

"Not that kind. Get the hell out of here before I fire you now. I hate agents who whine. Reminds me of my niece, and she's only six years old."

The door to Bert's office closed quietly.

Bert settled back into his chair. *Now, where was I in my planning?*

Chapter 9

The dining hall, where Charles whipped up gourmet delights and where the Sisters took all their meals, was fragrant with the scent of cinnamon and freshly baked apple dumplings. The sideboard held other delectable delights: crisp bacon, plump sausages, fluffy golden scrambled eggs, and freshly squeezed orange juice.

The women all eyed the scrumptious array of food, trying to decide what to eat and what not to eat if they were going to focus on the apple dumplings that were taking center stage.

"Oh, who cares. I say we go for the

whole thing," Annie said happily as she waved her arm over the covered dishes. "In the next few days we'll be burning calories right and left." To prove her point, she loaded her plate with a little of everything.

Isabelle giggled. "Annie has a point. When we're on a mission, all we ever seem to eat is crackers and cheese except when Paula Woodley made us all those apple pies on our last mission. If I close my eyes, I can still taste them."

From the window in the kitchen that overlooked the dining room Charles watched his chicks—that's how he thought of the Sisters—fill their plates and take their seats at the table.

He'd spent the past ninety minutes cooking and baking, his second passion in life. His first had been serving as a covert agent in Her Majesty's Secret Service. Retired now, he relished his role as chief advisor to the vigilantes. He was still in the game and loving every minute of the time he spent with his chicks as they worked to help men and women whom the judicial system had failed, victims who had fallen through the cracks.

Piled on the kitchen counter and out of the Sisters' view, was a neat stack of unbound printouts. He scanned the papers as he tidied up the kitchen. He pretty much had everything he was looking at committed to memory, but still, he wasn't sure. He had spent the night in what the Sisters called his lair—otherwise known as the war room. He'd dispatched a small army of former agents to Las Vegas—most, like him, retired and only too happy to get back in action.

Las Vegas, the small corner of the world that never slept. He'd been amazed to find out that there were no clocks in any of the casinos. Sin City. "Land of lost dreams" was how one report had read. He'd scanned so many articles on gambling addiction, he got dizzy as he tried to fathom how people could gamble their homes away, just one step from gambling away their families.

Charles looked around the kitchen to make sure he was leaving it the way he wanted to return to it to prepare lunch— sparkling clean. The girls themselves would clear the sideboard and load the dishwasher.

He quickly shuffled his papers into a neat pile and slipped them into an accordion-pleated envelope. He walked into the dining room to pour himself a last cup of coffee, coffee he didn't need. His nerves were already twanging all over the place, and it was only eight in the morning. He knew he would consume another gallon of coffee before what promised to be a long day finally came to a close.

Following Charles's rule that no business was to be discussed until meals were over, they all made small talk when he took his seat at the table.

"The acorns are starting to fall," Nikki said. "I saw a dozen squirrels scurrying about hiding nuts. I think that means it's going to be a bad winter."

"The pinecones are falling, too," Alexis said. "I gathered two bushel baskets yesterday." The Sisters loved to add the pinecones to a blazing fire in the winter. "Remember how we all gathered the acorns last year and put them in baskets to make it easy for the squirrels? We worked for hours and hours, and those darn squirrels didn't want them. My back ached for days after all that bending."

"That's because we touched them," Yoko said. "If we had worn gloves, our scent wouldn't have been on them. I gathered two buckets yesterday and I saw this morning that they're all gone. Did you know that in the winter squirrels only find about ten percent of the nuts they have stashed during the autumn?"

Annie slid her chair back from the table. "Enough with the squirrels and pinecones. We have a mission to plan, and I'm in a hurry to get to Las Vegas. Look," she said, holding out her hands, "my palms are itching. That means I'm going to win some money."

The others laughed, but they, too, were just as anxious as Annie was to get down to business.

Within minutes the sideboard was cleared, the table was wiped clean, and the dishwasher was humming in the kitchen.

All eyes turned to Charles. He smiled. There were times when the Sisters allowed him to tease them, but their expressions told him this wasn't one of those times. "This is what I know at the moment. As usual, everything is ongoing and subject to change.

"As we speak, Elias Cummings and Nellie are winging their way to Las Vegas.

"Lizzie and Ted Robinson checked into the Babylon hotel and casino, then they checked out. Rena Gold has relocated them. Robinson has made contact with two of the local newspapers and struck up an alliance with a couple of very seasoned reporters.

"I received a call at four thirty this morning while you were all still sleeping. The call was to tell me that Bert Navarro's nomination will definitely be confirmed. The president will make the announcement at ten o'clock this morning." Charles fixed his gaze on Kathryn, and said, "Bert will be sitting this mission out. For his own welfare. Having said that, he can still work behind the scenes, and that's exactly what he's doing. Communication with Bert for the moment is iffy at best and will also have to be circuitous in nature.

"I am cautioning you very strongly, Kathryn, not to try to contact Bert. If you do, you could cause irreparable harm to him and to us. Do you understand what I just said?" Charles asked in a tone none of the Sisters had ever heard before.

Kathryn nodded as she looked around at her Sisters. She winced at their collective sigh of relief. The fine hairs on the back of her neck moved.

Murphy stirred, sensing distress in his mistress. "I can't believe any of you would think . . . You don't have to worry about me. All of you, relax. It's not like I'm joined at Bert's hip. We're . . . just friends," she lied, knowing they all knew she was lying. "I'm concerned for him just like I'm concerned about Jack and Harry. Like I said, you don't have to worry about me."

"We know that, dear. Sometimes we just have to say things out loud to make sure everyone is on the same page," Myra said soothingly.

"Myra is right, child," Annie said. "Now, Charles, can we please get to the good stuff? When and how are we leaving? Do we need to hurry and pack?" She looked around at the others and asked, "What does one wear in Las Vegas? Are we supposed to glitter and sparkle?"

"Never mind the glitter and sparkle, Annie. What are we supposed to do when we get there?" Kathryn asked. "What exactly is this mission all about?"

Charles cleared his throat. "Well, the current mission started out to be one thing, but with my people in place and reporting to me on an hourly basis, it looks like we might have inadvertently stumbled onto something else. Now is a good time to tell you that your payoff will come through Beatrice Preston. However, I may well negotiate another fee that could quadruple Miz Preston's fee. We'll get to that later.

"Lizzie had her face-to-face meeting with your new employer. With Las Vegas three hours behind us timewise, she will be getting ready shortly to head off to the county jail, where Marble Rose is being held. I have no idea what will transpire at that meeting. It's possible that if Marble Rose doesn't cooperate, the mission might well be scrapped."

"Why wouldn't she cooperate? Surely she can't enjoy being in jail. Why hasn't she engaged the services of an attorney?" Nikki asked. "The first thing a person does when she's arrested is to hire a lawyer. Is it possible she has been denied the opportunity?"

"At the moment, I can't answer that. All I do know for certain is that Marble Rose and her mother are estranged. The young lady is extremely bitter toward her mother."

"*If* we go, and *if* our mission isn't scrapped, what is the vigilantes' role in all of this? What exactly are we supposed to be doing once we get there?" Kathryn asked.

"Right now we're in a holding pattern, so let's use the time by me telling you what I have managed to learn about how Las Vegas works. I want you to store the knowledge away just the way those squirrels store their nuts for the winter.

"I'm told that the slot machines in Las Vegas pay the bills. The machines are referred to as 'beautiful vaults' because they bring in nearly three-quarters of the roughly $60 billion in gambling revenue at American casinos. That's billion with a capital *B*.

"Slot machines are the most popular form of gambling. The poker machines are a close second. Some serious gamblers, who like to play table games, consider slot machines not true gambling because they are programmed with a payback percentage and something they call a *hit frequency*.

"The machines contain a random-number generator, or an RNG, as they call it in the industry. It's a microcomputer that constantly, even when the machines are not in use, spits out numbers. Somehow or other the numbers are selected by using atmospheric 'noise,' but I don't understand that part at all. To continue, the random numbers correspond to positions on each of the reels in the machine. When you pull the handle or press the SPIN button, you are not really initiating anything except the spinning of the reel, which is merely for show. With the spin or handle, you are telling the machine to display the reel position that corresponds to the last set of random numbers that were generated.

"This is important because it debunks some long-held assumptions about slot machines. It all comes down to that precise moment that you pull the handle or push the SPIN button. Pressing that SPIN button or yanking the handle a hundredth of a second later would yield a totally different result."

"So can you beat the machines? And can the house fix them so they don't pay off?" Yoko asked.

"No and no, from everything that has been written about them," Charles said. "Unfortunately, I don't believe it."

"Then forgive me, dear, but I don't think any of us understands what's going on," Myra said. "Why are we going to Las Vegas? I thought, I think we all thought, that the casinos were somehow 'fixing' the machines to the benefit of the house, as opposed to the player."

Charles looked down at the ream of notes he had on the gambling industry. For some reason he'd thought his ladies would want to know all the nitty-gritty stuff he'd spent hours garnering. They'd just reduced all his research to two simple questions, to which he'd given two negatives in response.

"Obviously, none of you cares to hear the rest of my research on how it's impossible to beat the house or the odds. Having said that, there are always ways for something to slip through the cracks, as all of you know only too well. I have seen the *Las Vegas* series that played on television a while back, and I've also seen the *Oceans* movies, as you have. If I recall correctly, we watched those movies together.

You saw all the time, the effort, the planning that went into ripping off the casinos. Let me be the first to point out that they were *fiction.* This is *real.*

"My operatives, who at one time were the best of the best, and who I still think are tops, have been in touch with . . . let us just say, *people* in Las Vegas. It seems, aside from Marble Rose, the *people* in Las Vegas have been noticing that quite a few players have been winning large sums of money. The sums were not large enough to ring bells at first but still sizable enough that red flags went up. This strange occurrence began when Marble Rose hit her first jackpot. You all know I don't believe there is any such thing as coincidence. At the moment, this is just a gut feeling on my part, and we all know I pay little attention to gut feelings, since I have to deal in facts to ensure your safety at all times. But, those people, along with my gut, are telling my operatives that there is a definite undercurrent of unease among the casinos.

"Which now brings me to a rather bizarre message that came into our message board a little after midnight, seven minutes past twelve, to be precise. It seems"—

Charles paused and looked around at his chicks to see how they were taking it all— "the Nevada Gaming Commission has asked for your help. The message was not signed by anyone who works for the commission, I simply read between the lines. In exchange for your help, they're willing to let Marble Rose off the hook. And there is an offer on the table of a percentage of whatever was stolen/won and recovered." Charles smiled. "The percentage is, for want of a better word, awesome."

"What?" the Sisters whooped in unison.

"I'm not sure I understand," Myra said. "Is Lizzie to try and negotiate? Who is she going to negotiate with?"

"When Lizzie calls, we'll know more. If you journey to Las Vegas, these are the men you will be taking on." Charles held up several large, grainy photographs and slid them one by one across the table. Charles identified each picture as the Sisters passed the photos around the table and made comment after comment.

"Most of the action appears to be coming out of the Babylon casino. So I think we should assume that whatever is wrong started there. The Babylon is where

Marble Rose won most of her money; but she didn't discriminate, she gambled at just about all of the casinos, even going downtown to Fremont Street. She won a bundle at the Golden Nugget."

The pictures were back in Charles's hands. He sifted through them until he found the one he wanted. He held it up. "This man, Hank Owens, is head of security at the Babylon. He's been with the casino for over twenty years and is as good at his job as I am at mine. He knows every trick in the book. He's extremely well paid. He works twenty-three hours a day and gets by on one hour of sleep. I read that in some PR fluff in one of the Vegas papers. An exaggeration, I'm sure. His inner security ring—and that's what it's called, 'the ring'—is made up of four men. Mean men, ruthless men. Men who do exactly what Owens says when he says it. No deviations. The inner ring has been with Owens from day one. They work on the reward system. The 'rewards' are a mystery. They're only mentioned in whispers or behind closed doors. I believe that all the things that happened to Marble Rose prior to her arrest were a result of the inner ring. I think the Gaming Commission wants us to look into Owens and his little cabal. Like I said, this is all tentative and subject to change."

Kathryn jumped up. Murphy growled. "What are you saying, Charles? That we're not a match for this . . . inner ring? Ha!"

Charles smiled. "If you had allowed me to finish what I was going to say next, you would have heard me say, the inner ring is no match for *all of you.*"

"Oh. Okay, that's better."

"In addition, you will all have a secret weapon. Actually, four or five of them. I'm sending Harry to Vegas. I have a call in to some people I know who are arranging a martial-arts exhibition. Harry and his friends will be the judges. There might be a snafu or two since it's such short notice, but radio and television are wonderful tools. I'm sure we can come up with a good turnout, especially if it's a free exhibition. Las Vegas loves anything that's free."

"Charles, that is absolutely brilliant. How *do* you come up with such wonderful ideas?" Annie gushed. "Oh, I can't wait to attend. I love the blood-and-guts moves those boys make. That inner ring is toast if Harry takes them on."

Charles pretended to be embarrassed. Yoko virtually swooned at the anticipation of seeing her true love in Vegas.

"What about Jack? Is he going to go with Harry? What's his role?" Nikki asked. She didn't realize she'd been holding her breath until it exploded from her mouth in a loud, swooshing sound.

"I know you don't want to hear this, but Jack, like Bert, is going to sit this mission out. He's on the radar screen, just as Bert is. It could be dangerous for Jack to show up in Vegas and, in addition to that, he has no authority to do anything in that town except visit and gamble. Harry is different."

Nikki looked like she was going to cry. She bit down on her lower lip.

"I don't agree," Kathryn said coldly. "I think we should put it to a vote. Not Bert. I understand why he has to remain in D.C. I'm referring to Jack. Jack has always been our greatest backup. He and Harry always work in sync. I'm not saying either one can't operate without the other, I'm sure they can, it's just that it's better with both of them. Jack has a black belt, why can't he be one of the judges? I think we need to take a vote where Jack is concerned. It goes without saying that Jack would have to agree."

Nikki sent Kathryn such a grateful look that the former truck driver just smiled.

"Kathryn is absolutely right," the others agreed.

Myra looked at Charles, and said, "I think you've just been outvoted, dear. Personally, I always felt more confident when the boys were watching our backs. Jack must have some vacation days accrued that he can use."

Charles was gracious in his acquiescence. "I bow to the majority. I'll call both Jack and Harry to put them on alert."

The Sisters were hyped. "Tell us more about the inner ring," Isabelle insisted.

"The rumor is that if Owens were to turn his inner ring loose—*fire* them, if you prefer that term—none of the other casinos would snap them up. They don't like their methods. The other casino executives and their heads of security are businessmen. They operate by the book. Owens and his thugs play by different rules. The man does get results. The Babylon brings in the most money. Owens is credited with installing slots that give the best odds, and their video poker gives a 100 percent return—if you play long enough. In addition to all of that, his rewards program offers free slot play as well as cash back and comp dollars for being a good member. Before you can ask, everyone who walks in their doors is an instant member. Owens has a full-time staff working minimum wage plus tips just to take care of 'membership.'"

"I hate Hank Owens and his inner ring already," Annie said. Excitement rang in her voice when she said, "So, in addition to bailing out Marble Rose, we are going to . . . uh, take down Hank Owens and his inner circle. Oh, be still my heart," she cried dramatically.

Her outburst left the others smirking as they started whispering among themselves. Charles knew, just knew, they already had some wicked punishment in the works. He looked over at Myra, his true love, and winked. She nodded slightly, then laughed.

"All right, ladies, I have to get back to work. I'm going to leave this folder for you all to peruse. I will let you know the minute Lizzie checks in. In the meantime, Alexis, start thinking about disguises that will get you in and out of Las Vegas safely."

Annie clapped her hands in glee. "All rii-ight, kids, let's get to it!"

Chapter 10

It was early, dawn just breaking over the horizon, when Rena Gold tapped softly on the door of the luxurious condo she'd made available to Lizzie and Ted. When Lizzie opened the door, she smiled at the former showgirl, who was holding a tray with two cups of Starbucks coffee, two containers of orange juice, and a bag of sweet rolls.

"In my opinion, it's impossible to start the day without coffee. At some point today, I'll stock your refrigerator. A cleaning lady comes in once a week to freshen up the place. The girls and I just use this condo for . . . *other things,* and rarely keep food here. Like I said last night, it's not on anyone's radar screen. Nikki said ownership is buried very deep. You can stay as long as you need to. Is there anything else I can do for you, Lizzie? Just ask, and it's yours," Rena said breathlessly.

Lizzie smiled. "Not at the moment. However, I'd feel a lot better if you and your girls would go on vacation. Maggie and Annie authorized the use of the Gulfstream to take you and your friends anywhere you want to go. Today, Rena. Like this morning. Can you get it together and make it to the airport by ten?"

Rena pursed her lips for a moment. "Sure, but do you think it's really necessary?"

"Yes, I do. Don't think for one minute my departure from the hotel went unnoticed. They have those damn cameras everywhere. The valet parking attendants even have cameras on their lapels. They've undoubtedly already run your license plate. I don't want you anywhere near this place when our guests arrive. It's for your own safety.

Fear sparked momentarily in Rena's

eyes, but a second later it was gone as she squared her shoulders. "You know best. But I'm going to give you the number of a guy I know. You can trust him. He's lived in Vegas forever, and there's nothing he doesn't know about this town and the people who work here. That's another way of saying he knows where all the bodies are buried. He lives out in the desert, and if you think Hank Owens has security, you should see what this guy has. He's not much to look at, but he cleans up real good. Sharper than razor wire. He has his own posse. For all intents and purposes, ranch hands. No one really knows the backstory between my friend and the head of security at the Babylon, but whatever it is, it's deadly."

"So what you're saying is he's the go-to guy, and he has a hate on for the head of Babylon's security. What do people go to him for?"

"This and that," Rena said vaguely. "He takes care of things. His name is Little Fish. His friends call him Fish. He's full-blooded Shoshone."

"Just out of curiosity, how do you know this 'Little Fish'?"

Rena shrugged as she brushed at her thick red hair. "That's for another time, okay? If you need Fish, just tell him I told you to call. He won't question you because, as far as I know, only two other people besides me have this number." She walked over to a small desk set into an alcove and wrote the number on a Post-it. "It might be a good idea to memorize it as opposed to carrying the number around or listing it in your BlackBerry."

Lizzie nodded.

"I guess I should be going," Rena said. "I hope it all works out for you and . . . and the girls. Listen, Lizzie, that guy Hank Owens, he's bad news. I mean *really* bad news."

Lizzie smiled. "Understood, Rena. I'll call you when it's time for you to come back. Thanks for the juice, coffee, and rolls."

Rena just nodded.

Lizzie could see the worry and fear in her eyes. "Hey," she said softly, "this is a betting town. Who you putting your money on, that pissy Hank Owens, or me, the vigilantes, and Mr. Fish?"

In spite of herself, Rena laughed. "That's a no-brainer. See ya, Counselor."

"Yeah, see ya, Rena."

Lizzie bolted the door and was on her way to the kitchen with the coffee containers when Ted walked into the living room. "Did I just hear the door close?"

"You did. Rena dropped off coffee, juice, and some rolls." Lizzie carried the containers and the paper sack out to the state-of-the-art kitchen that looked like it had never been used. They sat down at the table and looked at one another.

"This town isn't what I thought it was," Ted said as he wolfed down two of the sweet rolls, one right after the other. He looked at Lizzie questioningly as to whether she wanted the other four rolls or not. She shook her head and sipped at her coffee. "You know, they bill it as a family place kind of thing. Family, my ass. This town is about money and nothing else. The only relationship this town has to family is it takes a family's money. Bottom line. The security is one step below the Mafia and the gestapo. Where the hell do they get off billing it as a *family* atmosphere?"

Lizzie swigged from the orange juice bottle. "And you didn't know this?"

Ted was taken aback. "And you did?"

"Of course. What time did you get here last night?"

"Around three. I took a cab. No, I didn't have any tails. I was shooting the breeze with a couple of reporters from the *Sun* and the *Review-Journal*. I wrangled an introduction from a buddy at the Old Gray Lady. The three of us hit it off, so we went off for a few beers. You were sleeping pretty soundly, or I would have woken you.

"I found out that reporters are pretty much censored, and they don't like it. It's not like back in D.C., where the only people you have to watch are the politicians— here you have to watch the casinos' security and the cops as well. One does not tread, even lightly, on their toes. No one knew anything about Marble Rose and her big winnings. At least that's what they said. They talked a lot about the celebrities who come here. And the guy from the *Sun* told me he'd just gotten a text message that there is going to be some kind of martial-arts exhibition at the Babylon in the next few days. The Babylon is the biggest draw here. Even the Wynn can't hold a candle to it. They talked quite a bit about the top-notch security and the guy—Owens—who runs it. They were telling me about his inner ring, but said they weren't allowed to write about it. They said those guys, the ones in the inner ring, live in mansions and drive Porsches. They wear five-thousand-dollar suits and handmade silk shirts, but they still look like goons. The reporters said they can't print that, either. The casinos own both papers. Those reporters make twice what I do. I might think about relocating here. They have unlimited expense accounts, too."

"Is there anything *else* going on that we should know about?" Lizzie asked as she checked the time on her watch.

"Yeah. But neither guy could put his finger on what it is. Something involving Owens and the Babylon. I asked a few pointed questions about the Gaming Commission, and they clammed up when I asked one too many. Suddenly they both wanted to call it a night. They did give me a little human-interest story early on if I want to follow up on it when I'm here. Seems there's some guy who lives out in the desert who's named after a fish. They said he has more money than God. He lives in the desert, but he's surrounded by green grass. They thought that was amazing. What I found amazing was the guy's got claymore mines all over his property. He has a major hate for Owens, but according to them, everyone in town has it in for Owens. The guy is supposedly lethal."

"His name is Little Fish and he's a full-blooded Shoshone," Lizzie said, a wicked gleam in her eye.

Ted sucked down that tidbit of information the way he sucked down his coffee. "Jesus! You didn't leave this place last night, so how do you know . . . Never mind, I don't want to know."

"That's a good thing because I wasn't going to tell you. You gotta love that old devil attorney-client privilege." Lizzie looked at her watch again. "Time to go, Mister Reporter. I ordered a car last night. It should be waiting out front just about now."

I ordered a car. It sounded like she'd just said she ordered Chinese. He could hardly wait to see what kind of car Lizzie had ordered. He made a bet with himself that it was something flashy, with a rocket engine that would start off at a hundred miles an hour. Lizzie was all flash. She wanted the world to see her coming. Probably a fire-engine red Porsche.

The only vehicle Ted saw when they went outside was a champagne-colored Range Rover. He just knew it was the latest model and fully loaded, not that he knew squat about four-wheel drive vehicles, much less fancy-dancy Range Rovers. What he did know was that the little baby sitting at the curb cost upward of a hundred grand, and Lizzie had just *ordered* it.

"Nice set of wheels," Ted said.

"I agree," Lizzie said, climbing behind the wheel. "Use that map on the dash. You're the navigator. Tell me where to go."

"What's the address of the county jail?"

Lizzie put the Rover into gear and pulled out onto the road, and without missing a beat said, "It's 330 South Casino Center Boulevard. Downtown. I would have thought they would lock her up closer to the Strip, but I don't really know where the substations are. There might be a reason for her being where she is. We'll know soon enough."

"Maybe they want to keep her away from the Strip and anyone who might get curious. Neither of the reporters I spoke with had ever heard her name. Let's face it, Lizzie, a name like Marble Rose Barnes is not a name you'd forget if you heard it. They didn't so much as blink."

"Hmmm," was Lizzie's only comment.

With the exception of Ted telling Lizzie where to turn and generally being a pain in the ass, as Lizzie put it, the trip to the Clark County jail was made with Ted doing all the talking as he discussed the front page of the *Post* and what would be on tomorrow's front page as a follow-up. From time to time, Lizzie said, "um," or "hmmm." It finally dawned on Ted that Lizzie was *thinking,* which meant she was *working,* so he clamped his lips tight and stared out the window at the horrendous traffic she was battling. On second thought, he decided, he wouldn't live here even if they gave him his own personal slot machine.

Out of the corner of his eye, Ted watched Lizzie. She looked blissful, serene. For some reason he felt scared witless at what he was seeing. He jerked his gaze back to

the road and the snarl of cars all around
them. While Lizzie looked serene and blissful, her attire shrieked *look at me!* So, like
any other red-blooded male, he had looked.
He'd even taken a second look, and wondered what was wrong with him that he
wasn't attracted to the woman driving the
vehicle he was sitting in. Any woman as
beautiful, as perfect, as intelligent as Lizzie
Fox should have every man in the universe
lusting after her. He felt proud of himself
that she didn't turn him on. Only Maggie
Spritzer turned him on. It was either the
second or third time he'd had this discussion with himself. He wondered if he was a
fool.

"Lizzie, make the next left and that
should put us right where we want to be.
Listen, can I ask you a question on the
personal side?"

"Go for it. I might answer, I might not."

"Do you . . . do you dress like you do for
a reason? I mean, is it the real you? Or do
you dress . . . like, you know . . . to play a
part?"

"That's three questions and my answer
is, what do you think?"

"I think you play to your strengths, which

in your case are beauty, brains, and lust. I
don't mean that you're the one doing the
lusting. What I meant . . ."

"Well, there you go. I can see why
you're the *Post*'s ace reporter. I have two
rules, Ted. Rule number one is: *Never
explain.* Rule number two is: *See rule
number one.*"

Ted laughed as Lizzie swerved into a
parking space that was labeled VISITOR
PARKING.

The Clark County jail was a busy place,
since it was attached to a police station. So
police officers were milling around, getting
ready to hit the road for a new day of protecting the citizenry of Las Vegas. A small
group of people, who looked like they were
in no hurry to reach the front door, hung
back as Lizzie and Ted walked around
them and marched toward the door with a
purpose. Ted held it open, and Lizzie sailed
through, head up, lip gloss shimmering.

Lizzie sniffed. For an instant she let her
nasal passages remember the scent. All
police stations smelled the same—sweat,
burnt coffee, and Pinesol being the pri-
mary contributors.

Lizzie wore a lavender suit whose skirt had a slit up the side that revealed a generous expanse of thigh with every step she took. Ted wondered if she was wearing panties, then mentally slapped himself for such an outrageous thought. The waterfall of silver hair cascaded down to her shoulders. Ted made a mental note to tell Maggie that Lizzie shimmered and glimmered. Maggie loved to hear stuff like that.

All activity ground to a halt when Lizzie walked over to the desk sergeant. Oblivious to the approving stares she was getting, Lizzie was all business when she offered up her credentials, and said, "I'd like to see Marble Rose Barnes, I'm her attorney."

The desk sergeant leaned down over his desk so he could ogle Lizzie's cleavage, and said, "I wish I could help you, Miss Fox, but we don't have a Marble Rose Barnes in lockup and we don't have a Marble Rose Barnes in detention, either."

Lizzie managed to offer up a look that said her world had just come crashing down, and this buffoon was the reason. "Oh," was all she said. Lizzie waited, knowing that, at times, silence was the better part of valor. Sooner or later, the Keystone Kop would want to make her world right side up and say something enlightening.

She made a pretense of stuffing her credentials back into her designer bag when the sergeant said, "But we do have a Jane Doe in lockup. When she was brought in six days ago, she had no ID on her and she refused to give us her name. If you want to see if our Jane Doe is your whatever you said her name is, I can arrange it."

Lizzie cooed her response. "Why, you dear, sweet man, how kind of you. Yes, I would like to speak with your Jane Doe if it isn't too much trouble."

The desk sergeant offered up a sappy grin as he bellowed to someone named Simmons and instructed him to fetch Jane Doe to the visiting area. He then looked down at Lizzie, and said, "You know the drill, Counselor, leave your handbag, your cell phone, your keys in this basket. They'll check your briefcase when you go through security." He looked over at Ted, and said, "If you're not a lawyer, take a seat over there."

Lizzie nodded to Ted as she dropped

her belongings into a tattered wicker basket and followed an officer with a Michelin Man waistline as he waddled down the hall and around a corner, where he picked up a phone and spoke into it.

"You can sit over there," Simmons told her, motioning to a grungy steel table that was bolted to the floor with an equally secured bench on either side of it.

The benches were stainless steel like the table but a deadly shade of pea green. Lizzie felt nauseated when she sat down and opened her briefcase. She had no clue what she would do if the Jane Doe she was about to meet wasn't Marble Rose Barnes.

The door opened, and a young woman who looked to be about thirty walked over to the table and sat down. Lizzie studied the woman for a full minute, taking in pale blond hair that the lawyer guessed was normally lustrous. Right now it was stringy and in need of styling. Her eyes were clear blue and intense. She looked to weigh about 120 pounds. She was dressed in an outfit that resembled hospital scrubs.

Lizzie held out her hand. "My name is Elizabeth Fox. I'm an attorney. I'm here to represent you if you want. By the way, they have you listed as Jane Doe. Is your real name Marble Rose Barnes?"

"You look familiar. Do I know you?" the young woman asked, avoiding the question as to her identity.

"I don't think so. I live in Washington, D.C. Are you Marble Rose Barnes?"

The young woman still didn't answer the question. Instead, she asked a question of her own. "Who sent you here?"

"A Ms. Beatrice Preston contacted . . . some people I work for. I met with Ms. Preston last evening but did not commit one way or the other as to representation. I told her I had to speak with you first, and the decision would be yours. This might be a silly question, but why haven't you engaged the services of an attorney?"

The blue eyes sparked. "Because I'm safer in here as Jane Doe than I am on the outside. Go back and tell *Ms. Preston* I don't need her help. Tell her I can pay an attorney on my own. You can also tell her to stay out of my life."

Lizzie tossed her yellow legal pad and her Montblanc pen into her briefcase and snapped it shut. "If you change your mind in the next twenty-four hours, call me."

"How would you suggest I do that? I have no money in here. I did ask for an attorney, and they ignored me. I'm not even sure why I'm in here."

"They told me up front that you had no ID when you were brought in here."

"That's a lie. I had a wallet in my pocket. I asked for an attorney more than once. They didn't read me my Miranda rights, either. I'm not stupid, Miss Fox."

Lizzie absorbed what she was hearing. She leaned across the table. "Do you want to get out of here if I can guarantee your safety?"

"Yes, but how are you going to do that? I don't want my mother involved in my life, certainly not *this* part of my life."

"I'm a lawyer, remember. Leave it up to me. I guess that means you are Marble Rose Barnes. Right or wrong?"

The young woman nodded. "Yes, I am Marble Rose Barnes, and I just remembered how I know you. I don't mean personally. I just remembered where I saw you and why you are so familiar. I sent money for *their* defense. I'm not just saying that, I did. Two hundred dollars."

Lizzie smiled. "Why don't we agree to keep that knowledge to ourselves for the time being? Deal?"

The bright blue eyes sparked again. A matching smile tugged at the corners of the young woman's mouth. "Deal."

Chapter 11

Lizzie signaled to the officer standing near the door that she was ready to leave. Marble Rose stood up, and the two women shook hands. "This might take a while, so be patient, but you will be out of here as soon as I can arrange it."

"And my mother?"

"Since you're retaining me, your mother just ceased to be part of the equation. I will have to call her and tell her. It's the right thing to do. You signed a legal, binding contract with me. Once you're home, you can write a retainer check. Everything has to be legal, Marble Rose. By the way, if you want, I know a law firm that can chase down that lawyer that took off with your twenty-five-thousand dollars. The Nevada State Bar Association frowns on things like that, as does the legal community in every other state. I'd do it myself, but I think I'm going to be a little too busy to take on any side issues."

Lizzie thought the desk sergeant looked uneasy when she presented herself in front of his desk. "Your Jane Doe's name is Marble Rose Barnes. She said she had a wallet on her person when she was arrested. I'd like to see it. And my client was not given her Miranda rights. I want to talk to the arresting officer, and I want my client released in exactly ninety minutes. You should be able to process the paperwork in that length of time. If you can't, we are going to have some serious issues to deal with. Just out of curiosity, what was Jane Doe charged with?"

"Well now, hold on here, Counselor."

"No, you hold on, Officer Dewberry. What was Jane Doe charged with?"

"Assault and battery, resisting arrest, and inciting a riot, and there was no wallet on her person and no ID."

Lizzie knew a lie when she heard one.

"And the location where those incidents allegedly happened? My client denies all charges."

"They always do. Never had anyone come through here who said, *Yeah, I did all the things you said I did.* It all went down outside the Babylon casino. There were witnesses," he said defensively. He damn well hated smart-assed lawyers who looked like the woman standing in front of him. His ears started to ache with what he knew was going to happen in the next few hours.

"I bet there were," Lizzie drawled. "I'm on my way now to see Judge Logan McPherson to get a warrant for the Babylon's security tapes. You might want to pass that along to whomever you pass things along to. Ninety minutes, Officer Dewberry. By the way, see this guy?" she asked, pointing to Ted. "He's the *Post*'s star reporter. That's the *Post* in Washington, D.C. The nation's capital. They love stuff like this. The AP will pick up on it, and it will be global within hours. You know how fast the Internet works. I'll be sure to spell your name correctly."

Without another word, Lizzie turned on her heel and followed Ted to the door. Two cops tripped over themselves as they rushed to hold the door for Lizzie while Ted stepped to the side. Lizzie offered up her megawatt smile and sashayed through the door.

Outside, Ted said, "We won that one, right? Who the hell is Judge-whatever-his-name-is?"

"Oh, yeah, we won that one. The judge is a friend."

"Oh." Ted decided he really didn't need more details. He watched as Lizzie worked her cell phone while he started to text message Maggie. Then Maggie called him for more instant information. He tried to listen to Lizzie's end of the conversation, but with Maggie jabbering in his ear it was hard. He closed his cell and started to text message.

"I would love to have a drink while I'm here," Lizzie said, "but I'll have to get back to you on the time and place. I appreciate your offering to have the warrant delivered to me. The Silver Horseshoe. I'll be there. I'm sure anyplace you recommend is top-notch. What a darling man you are."

Ted looked down at the message he was sending and was chagrined to see he'd typed in the words *darling man.* Maggie would raise her eyebrows at that one. He deleted the message and started over. His nose was twitching, a sure sign that something was about to pop. He said so in his message to Maggie.

Lizzie unlocked the door of the Range Rover and climbed in. At least one of Ted's questions was answered. Lizzie Fox was wearing panties.

Lizzie settled herself in a booth done up in faux cowhide. Everything in the Silver Horseshoe was cowhide—the walls, the booths, and the bar stools. She looked around. "They should have called this place the Silver Cow. I wonder why they call it the Silver Horseshoe?"

Ted pointed toward the bar area. Hanging from the ceiling on fishing wire, directly over the bar, hundreds of horseshoes dangled. "This place is known for horseshoe contests. Some famous people participated in those contests. Even a few presidents." When Lizzie looked at him with an unbelieving expression, he just shrugged his shoulders and laughed. "I keep telling you, I read a lot."

"The judge said the food here is the best," Lizzie said, flipping open the menu. She looked up at a pretty young man and gave her order. "White wine spritzer, house salad, dressing on the side, along with a wedge of goat cheese. Two éclairs for dessert."

Ted tried not to laugh when he gave his order: "A beer, steak, a loaded baked potato, skip the salad, and a piece of pumpkin pie."

While they waited for their drinks and food, Lizzie spent the time on her cell phone, and Ted continued to text message Maggie.

When a second pretty young man set down their drinks, Ted looked up. Then he looked around for a moment. "Is this a gay establishment?" he asked.

"Uh-huh."

"So does that mean Judge-whatever-his-name-is . . ."

"Uh-huh."

Ted returned to his BlackBerry.

He almost fell out of the booth ten min-

utes later when his food arrived. He looked
down at the turkey-sized platter that held a
steak almost as big. The loaded baked
potato was nestled in something that
looked like a soup tureen. He looked over
at Lizzie's skimpy salad and the sliver of
goat cheese. Even the éclairs were mea-
ger, no bigger than the holes some donut
shops sold. It was obvious the male
appetite was king here. He shrugged. When
in Rome . . .

Thirty minutes later, Lizzie looked over
at Ted's empty plates. All she could see
was a bare bone. Her expression was full
of awe. "I cannot believe you ate all that
food. What good are you going to be to
me if you're sluggish all afternoon?"

"This? Don't worry about my being sluggish. My body doesn't know that word,"
Ted said, pointing at the empty plates.
"This was just an appetizer." He looked at
Lizzie's salad plate, which looked like it
hadn't been touched. The goat cheese had
one corner missing. The éclairs and the
wine spritzer, on the other hand, were just
memories.

"So, what's our next move?"

Lizzie looked up to see a handsome young man approaching their booth. "Miss Fox?"

"Yes."

"Judge McPherson asked me to deliver this warrant. Is there anything else I can do for you while I'm here?"

"No, this is fine. Thank you for coming all the way over here from the courthouse. Tell the judge I owe him a big favor."

The attractive young man smiled, showing an incredible array of glistening white teeth that were bright enough to light up a dark night. "The judge said you would say that. He said to tell you he can never repay you for what you did for him."

The young man left, and Lizzie smiled as she slipped the warrant into her handbag.

Whoa, Ted thought. This woman was going to drive him to his grave. "I suppose that favor is none of my business."

"Right, it's none of your business. I told you I know people who know other people who know still other people. Don't even go there, Ted."

"Yeah, right."

Lizzie looked down at her one-of-a-kind Patek Philippe. "Time for a little repair work, then I'll meet you out at the car." Lizzie tossed the Rover key to Ted, who caught it in midair.

He felt smug as he sauntered out to the parking lot. He knew what repair work meant. Lip gloss, a little tweak with the mascara brush, a spritz of perfume. Then what women did was to lean over and shake their hair so it looked wild and sexy. He was certain he was the only man in the world who knew what women did in restrooms when they were preparing to slaughter some unsuspecting guy.

Sure enough, Lizzie had fresh lip gloss on those kissable lips, and her eyelashes, which were like little feathers, glistened with fresh mascara. Her wild mane of silver hair looked even wilder when she climbed into the car. He was again rewarded with the knowledge that the all-powerful Lizzie Fox wore panties. He felt smug all over again.

The car in gear, Lizzie asked, "What is Maggie saying?"

"Judge Easter and Elias Cummings

should arrive this evening. Wong and Emery are coming to judge a free martial-arts exhibition to be held at the Babylon. Your . . . uh . . . Sisters are preparing for their trip out here. Someone broke into the FBI lab and stole the beaker of ashes that were being tested to authenticate whether they were human or not. They were. Those guys at the Bureau are a bunch of clowns. Navarro has a lock on the nomination, and the announcement that he will be installed immediately is imminent. Espinosa is working on my stuff as I feed it to Maggie. I have to share a byline, but that's okay. The media, with the exception of the *Post,* has suddenly gone low-key on the ninja activity. Orders from the White House is the scuttlebutt.

"By the way, where are you going to stash Miss Marble Rose?"

"What makes you think I'm going to stash her anywhere? She has a home. She strikes me as a very independent kind of gal. She can stay with us if that's her choice. Okay, we're here," Lizzie said as she pulled into the same parking slot in the marked VISITOR PARKING that she'd used before. She looked over at the car parked next to hers. Her brow knitted in a frown.

"What?" Ted asked, an edge in his voice.

"See this car parked next to me? It's a Bugatti Veyron. It costs $1,700,000. There's a guy that lives here in Vegas who's a car freak. He owns the ten most expensive cars in the world. He built a special climate-controlled warehouse to store them. He has armed guards who live on the prem-ises to monitor his cars."

"And I need to know this . . . because?"

"Because the owner is on his way into the police station. Do you see him?"

"You mean that human tank whose feet are as big as canoes?"

"Yes."

Ted sucked in his breath. "Who is he aside from being the owner of that fancy set of wheels?"

Lizzie turned to look at Ted. She smiled, and Ted shivered. "He's the mouthpiece for the Nevada Gaming Commission. I think he's here to see me."

"No shit! Are you saying he's the eight-hundred-pound gorilla?" Worry crept into

Ted's voice. "You can take him, can't you, Lizzie? You know what I mean, you can outlawyer him, right?"

Lizzie smiled again. Ted started to shake all over. His fingers kept hitting the wrong keys as he valiantly tried to text message Maggie with the new information. After he sent his message, he looked over at Lizzie, and asked, "Are we deliberately sitting here so you can make an entrance, or are we sitting here because you don't want to go up against this guy?"

Ted got the evil smile again. His stomach tied itself into a knot when Lizzie asked, "What do you think?"

"What I think is you can take that big guy down just by batting your eyelashes. Good thing you smeared more of that stuff on back at the Silver Horseshoe. What's his name?"

"I can't believe you don't know his name with all that reading and researching you do. His name is Cosmo Cricket."

Cosmo Cricket. "You shitting me, Lizzie? No one would name a kid Cosmo Cricket."

Lizzie laughed again. "His parents did. Close friends and associates call him Kick."

The knots in Ted's stomach tightened as he climbed out of the Rover. "Just tell me one thing, Lizzie, do you know this guy?"

"No, never laid eyes on him before today. Never spoke to him. I know people who know him, if that's your next question."

Lizzie slid out of the Rover and looked at herself in the side-view mirror.

"You look great, Lizzie. Your lip gloss is shimmering." Maggie was absolutely going to love this. "I think you're good to go. Let's just get in there and fry that guy's ass, Lizzie Fox style. What the hell is he doing here, anyway?"

"That's a good question, Ted. I'll make sure I ask."

"Do you know anything about the NGC?" Ted asked.

"Probably as much as you do. It was founded in 1959 by the Nevada legislature. It's involved in the regulation of casinos throughout the state, along with the Nevada Gaming Control Board. They're responsible for administering regulations, granting licenses, and ruling on disciplinary matters brought before them by the Nevada Gaming Control Board. It's made up of five members appointed by the governor. Commission members serve for four years in a part-time capacity.

"Their big gun is Cosmo Cricket. One has to wonder why the NGC would send someone like him to deal with little old Marble Rose Barnes. She must be more important than we originally thought. I think we can make our entrance now." Lizzie looked down at her watch. "Being fifteen minutes late is quite fashionable, even in police stations. You ready, Teddie?"

"Hell, no, but I'm game."

"Your recorder set? Camera ready? Flex your fingers, and let's take this show on the road."

"Yes, ma'am."

Chapter 12

With one exception, nothing much had changed since their exit almost two hours earlier. The walls hadn't been repainted, they were the same ugly shade of puke green, the smell was the same, Pinesol gagging. The slight difference was that the room appeared to be more crowded. Not with people but with one person, who seemed to be taking up all the space in the room. There were other people in the room, but at first glance they all seemed to be hugging the sickly looking walls, staying well out of the way of the big man who was chatting up a tall, lanky, bespectacled gent carrying a briefcase. Another lawyer.

Seated at his high platform desk, Officer Dewberry looked anxious. His gaze went from one man to the other, then to Lizzie and Ted and what was happening in his station.

"He looks like a goddamn tank," Ted mumbled under his breath.

Lizzie ignored him as she waltzed up to the platform and tilted her head to the side as though to say, *I'm here, what's our delay?* What she said was, "I'm here to pick up my client. I said ninety minutes, Officer Dewberry. I didn't mean 120. Time is money."

A husky voice from behind her said, "You're late, Counselor, we've all been waiting quite patiently."

The cadence in the big man's tone was almost hypnotizing. At least Ted thought so. The lanky man standing next to him cleared his throat, but he didn't say a word.

Ted saw everything in slow motion as Lizzie turned, the skirt separating to reveal her shapely thigh. And then time stood still as Lizzie gazed intently on the man standing in front of her. To Ted's eye she looked like a beautiful Greek goddess—maybe Nemesis, a goddess of vengeance. Cosmo Cricket stood frozen in his boat-sized footwear, his mouth open, but no words were coming out.

Shit! Shit! Shit!

Ted's fingers hit the keys on his Black-Berry, not knowing if they were the right ones or not. Maggie would have to figure it out. He watched as Lizzie's come-hither eyelashes danced. Cosmo Cricket closed his mouth. And then the goddess spoke.

"When one is having lunch with the leaders of the free world, one does not rush."

Ted pounded the keys. He felt like he was at a tennis match.

Cosmo Cricket stared at the beautiful woman standing in front of him. A smile tugged at the corners of his mouth. Everything he'd heard about the Silver Fox appeared to be true. He tried to take a deep breath but couldn't. For the first time in his long, illustrious career, he was totally speechless. He wasn't sure, but he thought he might be falling in love. The man standing next to him cleared his throat again. Cosmo's canoes shuffled as his hand moved in greeting.

Every nerve ending in Lizzie Fox's body twanged as she stared at the ugly man. His broad face looked like a slab of concrete full of cracks and craters. A honker for a nose more or less dominated the chiseled chin, with its dimple in the middle. But it was his ears, shaped like minipancakes, that drew her attention. He was so ugly he was beautiful. She looked down at hands that were bigger than catchers' mitts. Everything about him was custom-crafted—from his suit to his extralong tie, to his shirt, big as a tent, and the shoes. No way could this man buy off the rack. Ted was right, the man was as big as a tank.

A worthy adversary? *Easy does it, Lizzie,* she cautioned herself. *Just remember, it's you versus him. You play to win, remember that. This isn't the time to let emotions come into play. Besides, every woman in the world knows the man hasn't been born you could trust.* Just another man smitten with her? At that precise instant, she couldn't decide, so she smiled, and the room suddenly became lighter.

Ted kept hitting his keys, really pounding on them when he heard a strange noise that sounded like it was coming out the tank's ears. He recognized the sound because he'd uttered it too many times not to remember. A groan of pure pleasure. He relaxed as he continued to relay the real-time action to Maggie. Lizzie had it in the bag. Beauty and the beast. Like he had one iota of doubt which of the two was going to be the underdog. Not Lizzie. No way, no how. The guy was toast.

Finally, finally, the tank decided to speak—to the relief of everyone in the room. "I know what you mean, I had lunch with those same leaders yesterday. You just can't rush them when they're sharing their secrets. Cosmo Cricket. My friends and colleagues call me Kick." He held out his hand.

Lizzie laughed, the musical sound bouncing off the walls. It was the evil laugh Ted recognized and feared. *Shit! Shit! Shit!* He kept punching the keys as fast as he could. Another point for Lizzie. The eight-hundred-pound gorilla was never going to know what hit him when the

canoes gave out under him and he was flat
on his ass.

"Elizabeth Fox," Lizzie said, a smile in
her voice.

Whoa. Whoa. Elizabeth? Maggie was
going to salivate over that one.

Lizzie knew the pile of granite in front of
her was going to give her a bone-crushing
handshake. She braced herself and gave
it back to him until his eyes narrowed, and
he nodded to show she'd one-upped him.
Cricket wanted to suck on his closed fist
to make the hurt go away.

The devastating eyelashes fluttered.
"And you're here . . . because?"

The canoes moved backward a step,
then another. He felt dizzy from the scent
of the woman's perfume. He'd never had
trouble with his vocabulary before. Ordi-
narily words just flew from his lips. Important words. Profound words. Right now he
felt like he was in the third grade and
unprepared for the make-or-break year-
end test. Lizzie's feathery lashes continued to go up and down like window
shades. Her lip gloss shimmered as her
tongue flicked out, then went back in. She
looked amused.

"To make sure Miss Barnes's release goes off on schedule and to apologize for any and all inconveniences suffered by your client. My colleague here, Alvin Lansing, is chief counsel for the Babylon. He's prepared to drop all the charges against your client. I'm here to write up a summary for the NGC. End of story."

Ted looked up at the fussy-looking attorney. He was no gunslinger. He had *nitpicker* written all over him.

Lizzie wagged her finger playfully, the wicked smile still on her face. "No, it's not the end of the story. The end of the story is a long way down the road," she said in a singsong, lilting voice that sent chills up and down Ted's spine.

Lizzie turned to Officer Dewberry and snapped her fingers. "My client, please. *Now!*"

The tank moved forward. Lizzie's arm shot out for him to keep his distance. The finger went up again, wagging in warning as her left hand reached into her bag. She held out her business card. The tank reached for it, his face hard, his slate-gray eyes hooded. "Hold on here!"

"What does that mean?" Lizzie

murmured. She sounded like she didn't care one way or the other what it was about.

The tank's lips thinned to a straight line. "It means the Babylon is dropping all charges against your client. They're prepared to be *reasonable*."

"The word *reasonable* is not in my vocabulary, *Mister* Cricket." Out of the corner of her eye, Lizzie detected movement. Marble Rose Barnes was walking toward her, still dressed in her hospital-type scrubs.

Ted's fingers continued to dance on his BlackBerry. He stopped long enough to step backward and snap a few pictures.

Cricket's canoes moved suddenly. "Who is that guy?" he demanded.

Panic rippled across Ted's face, but he continued jabbing at the keys. He wondered if it was possible to get carpal tunnel syndrome of the fingers. Lizzie allowed her eyebrows to shoot upward. The lashes were working overtime, as were the glistening lips. Ted rather thought it was time for a fresh application. He held his breath while he waited for Lizzie's response to the question.

"He's whoever you want him to be, *Mister* Cricket."

Perfect response, Ted thought as he tapped more words down the line to Maggie.

"Come along, dear," Lizzie said, taking Marble Rose's arm and leading her toward the door. "These gentlemen will take care of all that nasty paperwork."

"Who . . . who was that monster?" Marble Rose asked as she took one last look over her shoulder.

Lizzie laughed. "Isn't the circus in town, Ted?"

"Jesus, Lizzie, that took some balls," Ted said, getting into the front passenger seat. Marble Rose climbed into the back. Lizzie slid behind the wheel, gunned the engine, and turned the wheel a little too hard to the left. Ted almost blacked out at the loud crunching sound.

"Ooops, did you see what I just did?" Lizzie powered down the window and stared at the mess she'd just created. She shifted gears, moved forward, then shifted into REVERSE. A second loud crunching sound boomed in the quiet morning. She hopped out and stuck her business card under the windshield wiper, but not before she scribbled down her insurance information and snapped a picture on her cell phone. "Damn, I just can't seem to do anything right this morning." She was back in the Rover a second later and dialing the number of the office she'd just exited. She made a breathless report and ended up with, "Call me anytime, I will cooperate fully." A second later she barreled out of the parking lot.

"That was pretty ballsy," Marble Rose chirped from the backseat.

Ted almost got whiplash as he craned his neck for a better look at the damage Lizzie had done to the 1.7-million-dollar car. Oh, man, the tank was going to be one pissed car owner. Then he started to laugh. His money was definitely on the woman racing down the road.

"You think? Where to, honey?"

Marble Rose looked out the window to get her bearings and started to give directions.

Officer Dewberry scrunched his eyes in concentration as he copied down the information one Elizabeth Fox was calling in. Sooner or later the owner of the car would come storming through the door. And he had just ten more minutes until it was time to go off duty. Let Mitchelson, his replacement, deal with it. He was so relieved to see the two lawyers leave, he skedaddled to the men's room.

Forty minutes later Lizzie pulled into a residential neighborhood, took two left turns, then pulled into a driveway next to a small brick house with a front porch and tons of flowers everywhere. Lizzie got out of the truck and looked around. It all looked so very normal. Out on the street, two little girls wearing helmets were riding their bicycles, their mothers hovering nearby. Somewhere a dog barked, another barked in return.

Marble Rose frowned. "I don't have a key. It was in my wallet. Do you think you could call a locksmith for me?"

"I can do better than that." Lizzie rooted around in her purse until she found what she wanted and went to work. The door opened, and she led the way inside. "*Now* you call a locksmith to change the tumblers, Miss Barnes."

Marble Rose walked out to her kitchen to look for her address book.

While her client called from a landline, Lizzie called her insurance company and reported the accident. "Yes, Mr. Richardson, it was my fault, but the owner's car was parked over the white line so I didn't have enough maneuvering room. I really don't know who the owner is. I left my card and your number. I also called the police and reported it. I was in their parking lot but was late for an appointment, so I couldn't wait. Fine, you know how to reach me."

Ted thought Lizzie was going to start to purr at any moment.

Lizzie sat down in a deep sofa that was so comfortable she sighed. The room was pleasant, with no clutter at all. The floors were oak and polished. The sofa and two chairs were covered with a nappy material that had little nubs all over it. A vase of wilted yellow flowers sat in the middle of the coffee table. The only other color in the room was in the three oversize lemon yellow pillows and the two watercolors that were so vibrant they made her blink. She did notice that there were no photographs, no junky mementoes on the mantel or on any of the little tables. The ficus tree in one corner looked like it needed to be watered, as did the other plants.

From her position on the sofa, Lizzie could see into the dining room. The table was loaded with books, folders, and legal pads. Teaching materials, she thought. Or else her study materials for a dissertation.

Marble Rose walked into the living room. "I don't want to sit down, if that's all right with you. I want to burn this outfit and wash the stink of jail off me. Do you understand?"

"Of course. This won't take long. I just need to ask you a few questions. We'll set up a meeting for tomorrow morning."

"Okay, fire away," Marble Rose said.

Lizzie looked at the attractive woman standing in front of her. "Who are you, Marble Rose Barnes?"

Marble Rose Barnes sat down in the middle of the floor and crossed her legs. Floors could be buffed and polished. No stink would stay on the floor, as opposed to the fabric-covered furniture.

"I'm an orphan. But that's just my opinion. I was abandoned early on. Again, that's my perception of my early years. Oh,

I had a mother and a father, but I never knew my father. I never really knew the woman who calls herself my mother. The name on my original birth certificate says my name is Ann Marie Barnes. I had this imaginary friend—actually, she was my only friend—as a child, and I called her Marble Rose Epsom. I got the name Epsom from a jar of Epsom salts that was in my bathroom. The day I turned eighteen I changed my name to Marble Rose Epsom. I had my lawyer send the woman who says she's my mother a letter to that effect. Since I have no contact with her, I don't know if she acknowledged the Epsom part of my name or not. My lawyer tells me she accepted the Marble Rose part, and in any correspondence, she refers to me by that name. Does that answer your question?"

"It certainly tells me who you are. Now, I want you to tell me everything that happened and don't leave anything out, no matter how inconsequential you might think it is. I'm going to record our conversation, with your permission. This way there are no problems later on, and it makes it easier for me to refer to this conversation,

as opposed to calling you every ten minutes to clarify things." Lizzie flipped open
her recorder, turned it to the ON position
before she looked meaningfully at Ted,
who gave a slight nod to show his recorder
was also turned on.

"Who were those two guys back at the
police station?" Marble Rose asked.

Lizzie smiled. "Two men who are going
to have a few sleepless nights for a while.
The rather large . . . gentleman is Cosmo
Cricket. His friends call him Kick. He's chief
counsel for the Nevada Gaming Commission. The tall, thin man who didn't say a
word is chief counsel for the Babylon. His
name is Alvin Lansing. Mr. Lansing
showed up to drop all the charges against
you. Mr. Cricket was there to make sure it
happened so he could report back to the
NGC. I'm not clear on how they knew we
were there, but we'll find out. If you need
an immediate answer, then my guess
would be Officer Dewberry notified them. I
simply do not believe in coincidence. Now,
let's get down to business."

Outside, Cosmo Cricket looked at his
car and wanted to cry. The entire driver's

side of the door looked like a freight train had sideswiped it and come back for a second hit. "Son of a fucking bitch!" he roared.

Alvin Lansing looked at Cricket's pricey car, winced, and scooted off to his own Volvo three spaces down. Nobody ever hit a Volvo.

The only thing on Cricket's mind was murder. Slow murder of the person responsible for what had been done to his prized car. At least the son of a bitch had the good sense to leave a card under the wiper blade. *How in the damn hell did this happen? This is the police parking lot, for Christ's sake. Where were the fucking cops?* He looked around and didn't see a soul. He grabbed the card. He blinked. Squeezed his eyes shut, opened them, and blinked again. He began cursing, making up obscenities as he went along. And then he started to laugh. He was still laughing when he struggled to open the door. He was howling with rage when he fished around in the trunk for the tire iron. He broke a sweat as he gouged and dug at the sleek door. He finally got it open.

He tossed the tire iron on the floor below

the passenger seat and leaned over to close the door, only it wouldn't close. He continued to curse and laugh all at the same time. Well, he'd just have to drive with one hand on the door and the other on the wheel. He did take a moment to wonder what would happen when he had to shift gears. The goddamn door would probably blow off and hit some high roller on his way to a casino, who would then sue his ass off.

Some days it simply did not pay to get out of bed.

Chapter 13

Charles Martin sifted through a stack of e-mails he'd just printed out. He smacked his hands in glee at what he was seeing. His immediate problem was solved. He literally ran to the front porch of the main house and rang the bell, the sound reverberating over the mountain. When the bell rang, everyone dropped what they were doing and raced to the war room. The ringing bell could signal good news or bad news.

In this case, the girls decided it was good news.

"Come, come, I have something to show

you all. I think we can do this, but your window is going to be very tight," Charles said as he led the way. The women took their seats at the round table while Charles pressed buttons, and all the plasma TVs came to life. As always, Lady Justice surrounded the room. Charles pressed more buttons. The picture of a group of softball players appeared on the huge screen. According to the sports announcer, it was the bottom of the ninth inning in an exhibition game for the benefit of breast cancer research, and the Southwestern team known as the Paiutes was leading with a score of 2 to 1. There was a runner on first and second when Hickam's star batter sauntered up to the plate, swung the bat in a nonchalant manner, looked around, and took the time to give a thumbs-up to the local television audience and the fans in the stand, who were whooping and hollering.

"It's a baseball game," Isabelle said.

"But it's an all-girl team, and it's softball, not baseball. There's a difference," Charles said.

The pitcher, a long-legged blonde, looked in, got the sign from the catcher, wound up, and tossed a sidearm fastball that just caught the outside corner of the plate. On the next pitch, the star hitter swung and missed, and the crowd in the bleachers went wild. Finally, the pitcher wound up one last time and threw a pitch that had the batter salivating as it slowly made its way to the plate, seemingly as big as a beach ball. But when the batter swung with all her might, the ball dipped as if it were falling off a table, and the batter nearly wrenched her back as her bat met nothing but air.

Fans and players converged on the field to congratulate the Paiutes. The blonde was suddenly hefted up and onto the shoulders of the first baseman and the catcher and doused with what the sports announcer said was sparkling apple cider.

Off the field, the announcer inched his way to the tall blonde. "Dr. Loganberry, tell us how you feel right now."

"I'm very happy. We played a good game but so did Hickam. We might be rivals here on the field, but off the field we're doctors, recovering patients, and medical person-nel trying to raise money for breast cancer research."

"And that, ladies and gentlemen, was Dr. Candice Loganberry, an oncologist who practices here in Las Vegas. Let's all give her a big hand, and don't forget to dig deep and give them a donation when you leave the ball field."

"Wow!" the girls said almost in unison. They grew silent as they looked at Charles, then at Annie.

"Well, we were wondering where to send our fee. I think we just decided," Annie said. The women clapped in approval.

"Wait, there's more," Charles said. The women waited again while he slipped in a new CD and pressed PLAY.

At the Babylon, four men walked to the podium in what looked like a conference room. A tall, athletic-looking man who looked like he was ex-military, with his iron-gray hair and ramrod posture, introduced himself as Hank Owens, head of Babylon security. Then he introduced the casino's attorney, Alvin Lansing, and the owner of the casino, Homer Winters. He turned to the left and motioned for a large man to come to the microphone.

"That guy looks like they glued sixty-seven fireplugs together, and he's what they got," Kathryn said. Charles smiled when she said, "He's got to be the ugliest man I've ever seen. Poor thing, he must have fallen out of the ugly tree and hit every branch on the way down."

Charles laughed out loud at her comment. "That's Cosmo Cricket. He's the NGC's attorney and the man Lizzie is going to go to war with. Listen."

Hank Owens patted Cricket's arm in a show of friendliness. The women blinked and leaned closer when they saw Cricket shake off the man's hand.

"I saw that," Annie said. "Those two are *not* friends."

Owens never missed a beat as he continued as though the little byplay had never happened. "As all of you here in Nevada know, the Babylon and its employees are keen to help all charities, and today, in honor of the Paiutes winning the exhibition game, we here at the Babylon pledge one million dollars to be donated to Dr. Loganberry and her research team. In addition to that donation we will be donating a million dollars to the Austin-Hatcher Pediatric Cancer Foundation. We will also be hosting a gala to honor both teams here at the

Babylon. We're inviting the public and all the guests who are registered here at the time for a free evening of dining and entertainment, Las Vegas style. At this moment I can tell you we are in talks with Wayne Newton, Joan Rivers, and Barry Manilow to perform at our gala. No one has turned me down so far.

"We promise a star-studded night with Cordon Bleu chefs who will prepare the same food they make for the Academy Award parties in Hollywood. All we ask is that you all bring your checkbooks so we can try to match outside funds with our donations. And now, Mr. Cricket has something to say."

Cosmo Cricket moved to the microphone. His voice was a husky baritone as he thanked everyone for coming to what he called "this impromptu news conference . . ."

"The members of the Nevada Gaming Commission wish to donate $5 million to Dr. Loganberry and her research team. We'd like to thank Mr. Winters for agreeing to host the gala Mr. Owens just spoke about." He stepped back and to the side.

Owens reached for the microphone, and said, "Unless there are any questions, we need to get to work to plan the gala."

"It would help if you'd tell us when it is," a reporter shouted from the back loud enough to be heard all the way in the front of the room.

Owens laughed self-consciously. "I guess that would help, wouldn't it? I think I just got carried away with the moment. A week from today. Okay, then, that's it. You can contact our PR office if you need more information. Thanks for coming, and I hope you'll all get the word out so our guests can match the funds we're going to be donating to these worthy causes."

The girls watched as the men trooped off the stage. The camera went dark as Charles removed the disk and turned off the CD player.

"So we're going to be softball players?" Annie gurgled. "I do love those pink ball caps."

Charles rapped on the table to get their attention. The girls stopped buzzing. "Personally, I don't know how he's going to pull all that off in just seven days. There are female softball leagues all over the country who play for breast cancer research. They're going to want to attend."

Alexis clucked her tongue and wagged her finger. "Charles, what you do not know about women would fill a book. I can guarantee just about every one of those women will be there even if they have to walk cross-country to get to Vegas. They're dedicated, and there's nothing more important to women than breast cancer research."

"You're absolutely right. I bow to your knowledge, Alexis," Charles said magnanimously. "If you're right, and I have no reason to doubt you, then all of you will fit in just perfectly. All you're going to need will be those special pink caps, and I have no doubt you know exactly how to get them."

"You're such a dear, sweet man, Charles," Annie cooed. "Now, how do we get to Vegas undetected? The joint is really going to be hopping with the softball gala and Harry's martial-arts exhibition. Guys to the guys and girls to the girls. Oh, this is beyond exciting, isn't it, girls?"

It was hard not to get caught up in Annie's enthusiasm. Even Myra, the most conservative of them all, was laughing at what was going to happen once they all arrived in the gambling mecca.

"A tour bus? Is that our game plan, Charles?" Nikki asked.

"Oh, Nikki, driving cross-country to Nevada will eat into our days," Myra said. "We need to come up with something better than that. When we get there, we can hire a tour bus," the ever-practical Myra added. She fingered her pearls, a sure sign she was worried about something.

"I can have the pilot bring the Gulfstream back," Annie said. "Airport security is a little too tight for comfort these days. I worry about using false IDs regardless of how good they are."

"Annie's right," Charles said. "But to bring the Gulfstream back at this point in time, even though it's now leased to the *Post,* just might raise a few red flags."

Annie nibbled on a nail. "Do we have time to buy a new one?"

"No, Annie, we don't. But I do know someone who might agree to lend me one for a short period of time. Of course it will have to come across the pond, but that's a mere six hours. If my friend is agreeable, plan on leaving late tomorrow afternoon. I have to make a few calls now, girls. I'll ring the bell when I have confirmation."

The women looked at one another. Across the pond could only mean one thing. They all looked at Myra, who only shrugged.

Annie was jubilant. "Sir Charles does have friends in very high places. I assume it's a done deal. So, girls, let's make a plan. You're going to get those pink hats just right, aren't you, dear? Will we have numbers or names on them? What about jerseys?" she asked of no one in particular.

Nikki fished her cell phone out of her pocket. She'd set it on vibrating mode when she entered the war room. Charles frowned at cell phones ringing when he was conducting business. She looked at the number of the caller. "It's Maggie.

"What's up?" Nikki asked.

She listened without saying a word. Ten minutes later, she powered down and repeated everything Maggie had told her. The room turned electric at her words.

They whooped in glee when Nikki said, "Ted thinks Lizzie is in love with that guy who looks like a Mack truck. Mr. Cosmo Cricket." Then she told them what Lizzie had done to Cricket's one-of-a-kind car.

"Oh, she's smitten all right. However, I'm not sure *love* is the right word. But I do think our Lizzie was definitely making a statement."

Annie gurgled with laughter. The others joined in.

"I just want to know one thing. Who the hell is our client, and what are we supposed to do when we get there?" Kathryn asked. "What's Lizzie doing except checking out the slot machine princess? Is she part of whatever is to come, or is she coming back here?"

"I guess we'll find out when we get there. Charles will coordinate everything. Since we're probably going to be leaving momentarily, I suggest we finish our outdoor work. Whose turn is it to make dinner tonight?"

"Mine," Yoko said. "Charles said everything is ready, I just have to cook it. He didn't say what it was, though."

"It's meat loaf and baked potatoes. And broccoli and some kind of mess that looks like stewed tomatoes," Kathryn said. She looked at the others. "What? I was in the kitchen looking for some cookies, and I saw everything on the counter. I really don't like meat loaf but I can eat it, and I absolutely loathe stewed tomatoes."

Yoko laughed, her eyes twinkling. "How about some Wasabi Prawns, sesame rice noodles with a nice sesame-and-Wasabi sauce mixed with water chestnuts, shaved broccoli, and carrots? A side order of ribs with burn-your-mouth sauce and fortune cookies for dessert. Will that suit you, Kathryn?"

"You bet, but I'd like something a little more substantial than a fortune cookie for dessert. What are the chances of you whipping up a coconut cream pie?"

"One in a million." Yoko laughed. "I'll give it my best shot, but I'll have to keep Grady and Murphy in the kitchen. They will be the culprits I blame for snitching the meat loaf."

"Whatever it takes," Kathryn said as she pulled on her work gloves and left the house with the others.

Murphy and Grady stayed behind when

Yoko enticed them into the kitchen with the promise of chew bones.

While the vigilantes went about their business, back in Washington Maggie Spritzer eyed Joe Espinosa in disbelief. "Tell me you're making that up!"

Espinosa grinned. "I swear on Ted, Maggie, and here's the proof!" He held up his minicam and flicked a switch. Maggie blinked and then burst into chuckles when she saw six ninja figures standing on the steps of the Lincoln Memorial. One of them started to jabber in either Japanese or Chinese. Then they disappeared in a puff of smoke.

"What'd they say? What'd they say?"

Joe just grinned from ear to ear. "They said their work here is done. They just came to say good-bye." Joe couldn't help himself, he guffawed. "They're taking the ancestor's ashes they heisted from the FBI lab with them and will never darken Washington again, and the residents of D.C. can go about their lives. But, they said, if the politicians raise their ire again, they'll be back."

"What?"

"Hey, Maggie, you can't make this stuff up. I don't know who wrote their dialogue, but that's the translation I got. I have no idea what their work is/was, nor do I know what raised their hackles, but they're gone, and we can all sleep peacefully in our beds tonight. How do you want to go with this?"

"Can you put a spin on it that will work for Bert? Then lay it to rest. We have other things to decorate our front page. Get back here as soon as you finish up with . . . uh, the ninjas. Does it go without saying you were the only reporter at the Lincoln Memorial?"

"Yeah, I can make it work for Bert, and, yes, I and about fifty tourists and two cab drivers were the only ones to see all the action. I got their comments. You gonna run with this below the fold, right? The tourists aren't going to forget that experience for a long time."

"You got it. Don't go heavy on the wording, do it with the pictures and reduce the comments to one-liners. You have thirty minutes, Joe."

Maggie loved the word *diversion*.

Back at her computer, she stared at the

crazy-looking words Ted had sent her at the speed of light. She was probably the only person in the whole universe who could decipher Ted's mishmash. She understood every symbol, every letter. All she had to do now was figure out how best to use the information to the vigilantes' advantage.

Maggie stared at the picture of what Ted had called a human tank with whom Lizzie might or might not be smitten. She studied the figure from all angles and finally saw what might attract the lawyer. "Go get 'em, Lizzie. But make him sweat first," she mumbled.

Her e-mail pinged. She moved her mouse and saw a download from Charles. As she read she got excited all over again.

Chapter 14

Retired Judge Cornelia Easter handed her small carry-on to Elias Cummings the moment they stepped off the plane. She wondered why she didn't feel nervous. Probably because her old and dear friend Elias was with her. For some reason, a man always seemed to make a difference. She corrected the thought. Sometimes they made a difference. Then again maybe she was calm because she just didn't give a tinker's damn about anything anymore.

As she walked along with her companion, she thought about the last time she'd been in Las Vegas. At least twenty-five years ago. Then it had been ricky-ticky, sleazy and decadent, and the mob ruled. Today, it was a whole different world, if you believed what you saw on television. She did wish, though, that she knew more about why Charles wanted her and Elias to come here. And maybe get married in the bargain. She couldn't decide if that was a good thing or not. An old shoe and an old sock getting together. There were worse things in the world, she decided. She liked Elias, and he liked her. They could be companions.

She looked over at Elias when he veered to the side to speak to a man who could have doubled as a soccer ball. Her brows knit into a frown when she realized the two men seemed to know one another. As the outgoing director of the FBI, Elias knew a lot of people. She waited for an introduction that didn't look like it was going to happen. Elias cupped her elbow in his big hand and steered her toward a door that said CROWN ROOM.

Inside, people milled around while drinking and eating. Laptops were open, others watching a big-screen TV. Elias handed his credit card and airline ticket to the girl in

Reception, waited a minute, then stuffed both back in a jacket pocket.

"Nellie, get some coffee and a sandwich or a drink. I won't be long."

Nellie's head bobbed up and down. She moved off, knowing she was not to interfere. Otherwise, there would have been an introduction. She knew she'd never seen the man before. Who was he? Was this an accidental meeting or had it been arranged by Charles? She debated a moment about calling Charles to ask but decided to wait it out to see if Elias would confide in her once the meeting, if it was indeed a meeting, was over.

Nellie carried her sandwich and coffee over to a table and sat down. Every newspaper known to man was on the table. At least she wouldn't be bored. And the sandwich was actually rather tasty. The coffee was delicious. The only problem was she couldn't smoke, and that irritated her.

Across the room in what looked like a small alcove, Elias sat down and stared at Peter Udal, the president of the NGC. "It's been a long time, Peter."

"Yes, a very long time. I did send you a Christmas card."

"And I believe I sent one in return. Let's cut to the chase, Peter. Why this urgent meeting?"

"The casinos are in trouble. A delegation came to my office about a month ago, hell, maybe it was six weeks ago, and told me some pretty bizarre tales. We got right on it, but so far we can't pin anything down. Elias, do you know *anything* about how this town operates?"

"Only that the guys who run those casinos make boatloads of money every single day of the year, and that includes Christmas. I thought NGC was on top of things. Is this FBI business, or are you talking to me as an old friend? As of Friday I am no longer the director of the FBI. I can pave the way for a meeting with Navarro if you think it's advisable."

The roly-poly man worked his lower lip as he pondered the offer. "It might come to that, but for the moment, talking to you might help me make my decision. I'd like to start off by saying we're rather desperate, and because of that, we might have done something really desperate. Time will tell."

"How about a drink, Peter? I'll fetch it. What's your poison?"

"Whiskey straight up."

"Be right back."

At the bar, Elias ordered the drinks and added two sandwiches to a plate. At the last second he snatched up a half dozen cookies because they looked ooey-gooey good, and he did like his sweets.

Back at the table, Peter Udal reached for his drink and downed it in one long gulp.

Elias knew the man was deadly serious.

"I'm going to give you the short version, Elias. If I give you the long one, we'll be here till Elvis returns. It came to our attention a while back that a young lady was winning big in the casinos. On the slots. The biggest wins were at the Babylon. She was checked out and, as the saying goes, she's squeaky clean. I can't prove this, but she says the security at the Babylon roughed her up. She's a schoolteacher. She went to Harvard and is a Rhodes Scholar. She's working toward her PhD. She seems genuinely to love kids and is considered an excellent teacher. When we ran the check on her we found out she'd been very badly mugged, and her recovery was long and painful. There are no blemishes on her record at all. She's just your all-American kid from next door. I say *kid* because she's thirty-one. To me that's a kid.

"Her first day back at work, a fellow teacher takes her out to dinner to celebrate, and they decide to stop at the Babylon and take in one of the shows and play a little on the slots. There is absolutely no sign that this young woman had ever frequented any of the casinos before. Or the friend, who is married with three little kids. She's as clean as Marble Rose Barnes. By the way, that's her name. I forget the friend's name.

"Then Miss Barnes started going to the casinos on her own, maybe once a week, sometimes twice. We have video of her walking up and down the slot aisles as she looks for just the right machine to play. She eventually picks one and plays no more than fifty bucks in one night. She won every damn time except once, and she probably would have won that night, too, but she was rousted and kicked out. The lady won *millions*. The executives held meetings. They complained to us. We went to her, and she was very cooperative. I'd stake my life on it that she's just who she says she is, the luckiest damn woman in the world. The casinos aren't buying it. Especially Hank Owens at the Babylon because his place was hit the hardest. Owens is head of Babylon's security and meaner than a snake.

"One night about three weeks ago, Miss Barnes showed up, and they did a snatch and grab. That's a lawsuit in the making. They did the wand thing, made her strip, with a female attendant in charge, of course, gave her new clothes to wear, made her wash her hair, remove all her jewelry, then sent her out on the floor with an army of security. She walks around for about twenty minutes before she finally settles down to one of the progressive machines. She had come in with a fifty-dollar bill. They confiscated her bill and gave her another fifty. You following me so far, Elias?"

"Yes."

"She plays an hour on the same bill. She wins a little, she loses a little. At the end of the hour, she's down forty-three bucks, then she hits. Big! To the tune of $487,345. The floor goes nuts. She's scared, you can see her fear on the video. Hank Owens is like a caged lion. You can see that, too. The little miss takes her check and goes home.

"That same night up and down the Strip people are winning like crazy. Everyone is beating the house. I formed a special committee, and we went back to the night Miss Barnes won her first jackpot. That's when the Strip started losing money. From then until now, the casinos are out a billion bucks. That's a lot of serious money, and they aren't taking it lightly."

Elias washed down the last of his sandwich and reached for a cookie. "You must have a theory. I thought you guys had better protection than Homeland Security."

"We do, goddammit. The girl's legit. She's just damn lucky, and the casinos have to suck it up. By the way, the girl's winnings are not included in the billion. That's an inside job. Believe it or not, this town is tighter than a duck's ass, and nothing goes unnoticed. So the casinos banded together, put out the word in the industry, and there's a million bucks sitting on the table for information leading to the arrest of whoever is responsible for the loss of the billion. So far no takers and no information.

Every hour this continues the casinos are losing money. To be honest, Elias, we don't know what to do. Understand, I'm not proud of the fact that I'm coming to you. We should be able to contain this ourselves. I'm going to brag here and tell you we have the best of the best as far as legal counsel goes. I'm sure even you've heard of Cosmo Cricket."

Elias frowned at the name but couldn't place him immediately. Finally, it dawned on him. "Ah, the big gentleman. The one with an addiction to cars. I did read something about him not too long ago. He bought some fancy car and paid almost $2 million for it. It made the papers in Washington. No one in his right mind pays that kind of money for a car. You're over-paying him, Peter."

Peter Udal laughed. "Let me tell you about that special car. Actually, I think it made the front page of the paper this morning. Seems some hotshot female attorney from back East rammed into it. Right in the police parking lot. Not once, but twice. According to Cricket, the car is totaled. I think it just needs a new door, but what do I know? I drive a Jeep. It takes me where I need to go. Fancy cars are not something I have time to deal with."

Elias felt his antenna go up. "Who was the attorney, do you know?"

"Oh, yeah, her picture was in the paper. A real looker. Fox. Yeah, Fox was her name. She said the owner didn't know how to park and was over the white line. She even has a picture of Cricket's parked car and damn if it wasn't parked over the white line. Looks like his insurance company will be the one sucking it up. Why are you laughing, Elias? Oh, you know her, right?"

Elias finished his drink. He wondered if Nellie was reading in the paper about Lizzie's foray into playing bumper cars. "In a manner of speaking. She's to the East Coast what your Mr. Cricket is to Nevada. If you're a betting man, put your chips on Fox."

"That good, huh?"

"That good, Peter."

"Let me finish this so your companion doesn't get irked at you for letting her sit so long after a long plane ride. Over the past few weeks, Miss Barnes has filed numerous police reports. Her house was broken into. Her car was vandalized. She was fired from her job. And seven days ago there was an altercation outside the Babylon when she won another $300,000. This time she fought back and was arrested. Her attorney as of yesterday is the lawyer that smacked up Cricket's car. So, I guess she's in good hands."

"The best."

Udal took a deep breath. "Look, Elias, you can see how desperate I am here. I went so far as to try to contact those vigilantes, that's what I meant when I said we did something desperate. I know you had them on the FBI radar screen, so I was hoping you could . . . intercede for us. You must know with all your resources at the Bureau how to reach them or know someone who knows them. I offered a percentage of the recovery plus a flat ten-figure deal. That's a lot of scratch even for this town. Plus we don't want word getting out about all of this."

Elias snorted. "And you think having the vigilantes invade Vegas won't somehow *get out?* What planet have you been living on, Peter? Just for the record, and as much as I hate to admit it, those damn women are smarter than our best agents.

Jesus, they took down the acting director of the FBI, they went head to toe with the president of the World Bank, who has never been seen or heard of since they went after him. Those women are a legend in their own time. They have more money behind them than Fort Knox. They have people helping them from all over the world. I heard not too long ago they're guns for hire these days. I can't help you, Peter."

"Oh, Christ, now I remember. That Fox woman. She's the one who defended the vigilantes before they skedaddled. They're like those goddamn ninjas that invaded your space. What's up with that, anyway?"

"Some kind of publicity stunt would be my guess. Yeah, yeah, they broke into our FBI lab and stole some ashes. Yeah, yeah, we were asleep at the switch. I admit it. Let's not beat a dead horse here, Peter."

"So you won't help me."

"Not won't. Can't. Is there more, something you haven't told me?" Not that he cared one whit, he just wanted to get away before he tripped himself up somehow.

"I suppose. Homer Winters is the sole owner of the Babylon. For the past few years he's been living on Chesapeake Bay near his two daughters. He was hands-on 24/7 until his twin daughters gave him an ultimatum. They want nothing to do with the gambling industry; they say it's sinful and unhealthy. For a few years they wouldn't allow Homer to see his four grand-children. They told him to give it up or to get out of their lives. It was a hard decision for that old bird, but he buckled. He's eighty-six, time for him to retire, anyway. His two sons-in-law wanted nothing to do with the business, so what the old gent did was pretty much turn it over to Hank Owens and his inside ring to run. There was a condition, though, and that was that Owens had to put the Babylon on the map by doing things for the community. That was to appease the daughters.

"You probably don't know this, but yes-terday Owens made an announcement that the Babylon was going to host a gala to celebrate the Paiutes winning an exhi-bition softball game. The whole world is invited, and he pledged a million dollars for breast cancer research. The teams that compete are all made up of doctors, nurses, patients, and medical personnel.

The members of the NGC pledged $5 million. This morning the Babylon stepped up to the plate and changed the amount and met our pledge. Stuff like that makes Homer and his daughters happy.

"The Babylon is also hosting a martial-arts exhibition. I'm not sure where the entry fees go. I think some children's organization. The Babylon gives out free space, food, drinks, and publicizes it. They seem to do something every week. The NGC thinks it's all a cover-up. It's my personal opinion that all good deeds are a smoke screen when it comes to Vegas.

"Hank Owens is ex-military, Delta Force is what I'm told and, like I said, meaner than a snake. His inner ring is just as ruthless. The man runs a tight ship. We have an expression out here that pretty much sums up what we're all about. We're on him like stink on a skunk, but we can't get him. We tried sending a couple of our guys up to see Homer, but he was clamming with his grandkids and wouldn't give us the time of day other than to say we should take it up with Hank Owens. There wasn't anything we could do after that. Personally,

I think Homer is senile. But, that's just my opinion."

"So you think Owens is the one ripping off the Strip and using Miss Barnes as a cover? I didn't think it could happen again after those MIT card counters walked away with $10 million, but maybe it is."

"Nothing else makes sense. Cosmo is on it, but he's coming up dry. Now do you see why I need to reach the vigilantes?"

Elias pretended to look thoughtful. "Best-case scenario, Peter, what do you see those women doing to Owens and his inner ring?"

"Cutting off their dicks and jamming them up their asses." Peter shrugged. "I didn't get that far in my thinking. Hell, look what they did to the national security advisor. Who were those guys with the dynamite up their asses? Christ, I can't remember anything these days. So, you aren't going to help me, then?"

"Do you want me to ask Navarro to come out here on the Q.T. with a team of agents? That I can do. He's had run-ins with the vigilantes. It's the best I can do, Peter. Listen, I have to go. Good luck."

Udal nodded glumly.

Then Elias leaned over, and whispered, "You didn't hear this from me, okay?" Udal nodded. "Your best bet is to get to Lizzie Fox, and when you do, you better have a very *HIGH* dollar amount in mind. Play straight with her, and I can almost guarantee the vigilantes will be in your sights in a heartbeat."

Udal looked up, and whatever he saw in Elias's expression seemed to satisfy him. All he could say was, "How high? You got a phone number?"

Elias laughed. "High enough so you don't embarrass yourself, and high enough so you and your commission lose sleep for a very long time. Your mouthpiece, Cricket, has the phone number. Get it from him."

"That high, huh?"

"Yep. See ya, Peter."

"Yeah, see ya, Elias."

Peter Udal walked over to the bar for a fresh drink after Elias and the lady he was with left the room. He sat back down and did some people-watching, his mind on other things. What kind of number would embarrass him and cause him to lose sleep for a very long time? Elias had said to play straight with Fox. Just for the barest second he wondered *how* straight was straight. Damn straight, he decided. He jerked at his cell phone, powered up, and when the gruff voice said hello, he replied, "Give me the Fox woman's phone number." It wasn't a request, it was an order, and Cosmo Cricket recognized it as such.

Cricket rattled off the numbers. "Peter, I think I'm capable of handling my car problems. I don't need you to intercede on my behalf. I am, after all, a lawyer."

"So is she," Udal barked. "Who said anything about intervening on your behalf? If you're stupid enough to spend that kind of money on a car, you need to cover it in bubble wrap before you take it out on the road. Is there anything else I need to know at the moment?"

"No, Peter, not at the moment." Cricket wondered if he was being aced out by the long-legged, silver-haired woman. His eyes narrowed to slits as he contemplated his options if that was to happen.

"Good." Udal clicked off and dialed the number Cricket had given him. He waited while his heartbeat kicked up a notch. The voice that greeted him was soothing, light, and almost musical.

"This is Lizzie Fox. What can I do for you?"

"Miss Fox, this is Peter Udal. I'm the president of the Nevada Gaming Commission, and I'd like to speak to you as soon as possible, like within the next hour. I'll be more than happy to pay your fee, whatever it is. Before you can ask, this meeting has nothing to do with our chief counsel and his fancy car."

"I think I need to know a little something before I make a decision. Time is money, Mr. Udal."

Udal cleared his throat. "How does a billion dollars sound for your intervention?"

The melodious voice turned brisk and professional. "What kind of intervention?"

"I'd rather not discuss something like this on the phone. Right now I'm at the airport. I can be back in town in forty minutes or so. There's a little place downtown called the Rabbit Hole. No one will pay attention to either one of us, and the food is very good—they don't serve rabbit. Rabbit is the owner's name. He used to be a prizefighter before he got knocked silly. His wife does the cooking. He watches."

"An hour, then," Lizzie said before she hung up.

Udal felt sick to his stomach when he got up to leave his comfortable chair in the Crown Room. Maybe he'd gone too high. He wished Elias had been a little more specific. He hoped to hell the casinos wouldn't balk.

Udal spent the forty-minute drive back to the city hitting his speed dial and talking to one after the other of the casino executives. A few complained but in the end agreed to his outrageous demand.

He felt a little better when he spoke to the owner of the Crystal Palace, who said, "Jesus, Pete, I'd agree to double if you can guarantee to get rid of Hank Owens and his gang. Count me in. If you need me to talk it up with some of the other execs, be glad to do it."

"Thanks, Jerry, I got it covered."

"Is it a guarantee, Pete? Are they *that* good?"

Udal forced a laugh. "Money-back guarantee."

"Hey, Pete, heard your main guy had a little fender bender." He started to laugh and couldn't stop. "You guys are paying Cricket way too much. Moreover, he was over the white line."

"Yeah, I'm buying him a moped for Christmas."

"Damn, I'd pay to see that guy riding one of those. See you around, Pete. Call me if you need help."

"Thanks, Jerry. I'll stop by when we have this all locked up, and we can have a drink and shoot the breeze."

"I'll look forward to it."

Udal looked at his watch. Right on time. He wondered if Lizzie Fox was one of those women who liked to make an entrance or to be fashionably late or whatever the hell it was women did to keep men on their toes.

He pulled up in front of the Rabbit Hole, double-parked, stuck a bright blue NGC sticker on his windshield, and got out of the car. No one looked at him. No one even glanced his way. For the first time he noticed that the day was bright and shiny. He hoped it was a good omen.

The Rabbit Hole was a dismal place

with cracked linoleum on the floor. The tables listed and had cardboard under the legs to keep them steady. The vinyl on the chairs was covered with strips of gray electrical tape. He wasn't sure, but he thought the vinyl might have once been turquoise in color. Dark green pull-down shades graced the windows. There were nine tables in all and a counter where lone customers sat so as not to take up an entire table. With all the stainless steel and mirrors it looked like a diner.

The Rabbit Hole had four things on their menu. Beef stew, chicken noodle soup that was loaded with actual chicken, fresh bread, and honest-to-God home-made apple pie that was served with ice cream whether you wanted it or not.

Udal looked around. There was no one in the Hole who looked like she might be a high-powered attorney. He felt a tap to his arm.

"By any chance are you Peter Udal?"

"I am. And of course you are . . ."

"Elizabeth Fox. This is my associate, Ted Robinson. He goes where I go. Please don't let it become a problem."

Udal sucked in his breath when he

looked up at the striking woman standing next to him. Her hair looked like spun silver. He wilted a little when he stared at her mouth. But it was her outfit that really drew his eye. The vision in front of him was wearing painted-on red leather pants with matching vest, and he knew in his gut there was nothing under the vest but *her.* She was wearing what his oldest daughter would call slut shoes, outrageous heels with a few tiny straps across the toes. He almost felt sorry for Cosmo Cricket.

Udal looked up at Ted and made an instant decision. "I won't let it be a problem. Follow me, and we can get down to business."

"Are we going to eat?" Ted asked.

"Of course. The menu is limited, but once you eat here, you'll go out of your way to come back again and again."

"Works for me," Ted said as he sat down on one of the lopsided chairs. He wagged back and forth before he reached for a wad of napkins to put under the legs.

They ordered stew all around. "The pie comes with the stew even if you don't want it, so don't make a fuss. The hot bread is to die for. I always take a batch of everything home when I manage to come here to eat. My wife loves it.

"Since this is my gig, I guess I should get right down to business and since, as you say, time is money. Here's my deal, but before I get to that, I want to assure you I have the full cooperation of every casino in this town. We want to engage the services of the vigilantes and are prepared to pay them a billion dollars. That's with a *b*. I'm not going to beat around the bush here. We need to take out, I think that's the phrase that's used these days, the security team that manages the Babylon. We're losing billions, so agreeing to pay the women that much will save us in the end. No killing, that's an absolute. No way, no how. We just want Hank Owens and his inner ring to disappear off the face of the earth so we can get back down to business. And, of course, whatever your fee is."

Ted was busy clicking away on his BlackBerry as he mumbled and muttered to himself. *Holy fucking shit, a billion dollars. The guy rattled off the number like he was agreeing to pay a fiver at Starbucks.*

"What if I say I want some perks?" Lizzie asked.

"Name them."

"Miss Barnes gets reinstated at her school and gets paid her lost wages plus reinstated benefits if they were terminated."

"Done."

"Miss Barnes is compensated for her six days in lockup. A generous compensation."

"Done."

"And she needs extra compensation for the humiliation she suffered at the hands of those goons at the Babylon. That comes out of the Babylon's coffers."

"Done."

"And you tell your gunslinger I call the shots. I don't want Mr. Cricket cramping my style."

"Done. So when can I . . ."

"I'll be in touch. Be sure you understand, Mr. Udal, I have not agreed to any of this. Yet. We are talking about a contract, are we not?"

"Absolutely."

"And your eight-hundred-pound gorilla is not to interfere."

"I'll see to it."

"And the money is to be paid in

advance. I can set that up in the Nether-
lands Antilles. Do we agree?"

"We agree," Udal said, a rock the size of
a dinner plate settling in his stomach.

"Then I suggest we eat this fine fare,
and I will get back to you around four this
afternoon. Is that acceptable?"

"It is."

Ted's fingers had blisters. He wondered
if he'd be able to hold a fork to eat.

"There is one thing that you will have to
agree to, Miss Fox. It's coming from the
casinos, not me, but I have to say, I agree.
Miss Barnes has to agree to relocate far
away from Nevada. If she's as good a
teacher as you say she is, she can get a job
anywhere. That one little point is not nego-
tiable."

Lizzie smiled, and the room was suddenly brilliant with light.

"Done. But she must still be reinstated,
with an apology, so that her record does
not show a dismissal."

Chapter 15

It was almost dark when the bell rang once, a loud, booming sound that shook the mountain. Murphy let loose with an earsplitting howl, throwing his head back and pawing the ground. Grady, his companion, not to be outdone, did the same thing as flocks of birds emerged from the trees and took wing.

The women, who were just finishing their yard work, stripped off their work gloves and headed for the main house, jabbering as they ran. One bong of the bell meant *hop to it, NOW.*

Yoko looked down at all the ingredients

that were ready to be cooked. She took a quick look in the oven at the coconut cream pie with the luscious topping that was browning. It needed another minute. Her eyes raked the unusually large prawns, then she sighed. One bong meant *now,* not one minute from now. She quickly removed the pie and slid it onto a hot pad on the counter with one hand, turning off the oven with the other. The luscious-looking pie slid off the trivet and onto the counter. She shrugged as she sprinted for the door, then across to the compound. She was the last one into the war room, arriving breathless. She was about to explain about the pie when Charles held up his hand and got right to business.

"Time, girls, is of the essence. Your mission has been confirmed. Lizzie just nailed down all the details. The money brokers in Las Vegas have agreed to pay you, the vigilantes, a whopping billion dollars to . . . uh . . . take care of some rather unpleasant individuals, five in all. Lizzie will brief you on your arrival. I have on loan a British Airways Red Cross jet that will be setting down at Raleigh-Durham International Airport in exactly three hours. That means you need to change and get dressed and head out immediately. A van will be waiting for you at the bottom of the mountain to take you to the airport, where you will be met by seven male nurses who will assist you onto the plane. You will be arriving by . . . wheelchairs. When you arrive at McCarran International Airport, you will be taken in your wheelchairs to an as-yet-undecided location. There is no time for questions at the moment. Go! Don't worry about dinner, I'll force myself to eat my delicious meat loaf all by myself. There will be packaged food aboard the plane for all of you and, of course, drinks."

"Billion!" was all he heard, as the women hastened to follow his instructions.

Yoko was about to open her mouth to explain about the dogs eating the meat loaf but decided to let Charles find out for himself.

The women jabbered and babbled about having $1 billion to donate to charity. They scattered, ripping at their work clothes as they ran back across the compound to their quarters.

Fifteen minutes later they were at the bottom of the mountain and climbing into a large white van with a huge red cross on each side.

While riding down in the cable car, Yoko had explained about the pie, the first pie she'd ever baked in her life, sliding off the trivet. "Charles will have to eat it with a spoon. I'm sorry, Kathryn."

"No, no, no. I'm so . . . honored that you even tried to bake me a pie. I hope Charles chokes on it. No, I don't wish any such thing, I just said that. I don't know why I even said it," Kathryn babbled.

"Charles didn't say when Jack and Harry were going to Las Vegas," Nikki said fretfully. "I wish I knew where we're going to be staying."

"I don't think it matters, dear. One place is as good as another," Annie said cheerfully. "I brought money. Did any of you?"

The women looked at Annie as much as to say, *Money, what's money?*

"To gamble with." Annie reached in her pockets and pulled out wads and wads of folded-up bills. "I even have some stuck in my bra. Don't worry, I have enough for all of us. We want to win. Big. Really big!"

"What's bigger than a billion bucks?"

Kathryn demanded. "I can't believe our services are worth a *billion* dollars."

"Well, I can!" Annie said. "We're worth every penny. It isn't ours, anyway, dear. We have to give it away. I'm talking about winning for ourselves. If we win, we get to keep the money. We can buy some of those fancy sparkly clothes they sell in Vegas. The kind the showgirls wear when they go off duty. I can't wait to buy my first pair of rhinestone cowgirl boots! We need to get some leather, too. With lots of *fringe.* Lizzie can help us, she has such exquisite taste in clothes."

"But the catch is, we won't look like Lizzie," Alexis said, giggling.

"And to think, Annie, you were wearing a god-awful white sheet when I came to that mountain in Spain. Now you're a clotheshorse," Myra said. "I knew I should have pushed you over the mountain that day. I am not wearing rhinestone cowgirl boots!"

"Want to bet?" Annie asked.

Myra worked her mouth into a grimace. She started to finger her pearls. She knew she'd be wearing cowgirl boots with rhinestones before the mission was over, and she'd probably be singing the dreadful song that went with the boots. Something about a rhinestone cowboy.

Ninety minutes later, the white van roared across the tarmac and came to a full stop near the British plane. The doors to the van slid open, and white-clad figures pushing wheelchairs appeared out of nowhere.

"Oh, this is sooo exciting. I've never been in a wheelchair before. I've seen people playing basketball in them and doing that wheelie thing," Annie said, as strong arms lifted her out of the van. "I'm absolutely loving this," she said to no one in particular.

Just as the British Red Cross plane hit a cruising altitude of thirty thousand feet, Lizzie Fox was sitting once again in Marble Rose Barnes's comfortable living room. Ted was busy punching words into his BlackBerry, but his ears were tuned to the conversation surrounding him.

"I have what I think is good news and a little of what you might perceive as bad. Which do you want to hear first?"

Marble Rose looked like she was back to normal. She wore khaki slacks with a lemon yellow T-shirt and camel-colored loafers. Her shiny blond hair curled around her face. She looked like the girl next door with her intelligent blue eyes and an oh-so-subtle shade of lipstick. Curled in her lap was a pure white Angora cat with startling green eyes. Marble Rose explained that after her arrest a friend who had a key to her house had come in and taken the cat to care for. The cat was purring loudly as it burrowed in her lap.

"Just tell me," she said as she stroked the cat's head.

"Well, we started out with me demanding you be reinstated in your job with full back pay and, of course, all your benefits. They agreed. By *they,* I mean Mr. Udal, who is the president of the Nevada Gaming Commission. He speaks for the casinos. I received a call from him, and he said the Babylon is falling into line. You will be compensated for your . . . false arrest, all the pain and suffering you endured. Handsomely compensated. You could donate everything you've won at the casinos to charity, plus what's in your trust fund, and still live very handsomely on your compensation if you so desire."

Marble Rose smiled. "I guess that's the good news. What's the bad news?"

"The bad news is you have to relocate. I know, I know, that's not what you want to hear because first he said he would make sure you got your old job back, but as we negotiated, he turned a little stubborn. If you stay, you will be banned from all the casinos on the Strip as well as those in town. I took some liberty and said you'd take the deal. I can always go back and say you changed your mind. I wouldn't recommend it, Marble Rose. You're a good teacher, from everything I've heard. You can get a job anywhere. Some . . . things are going to happen here, and I don't want to see you become part of the problem or the solution. Oh, the casino is going to buy your house at fair market value. We can close this out, and I can deliver checks to you by tomorrow morning. You should plan to leave right after breakfast tomorrow."

Ted looked up and watched the young woman as she pondered what she must perceive to be her options, when really there weren't any choices open to her.

Would she take Lizzie's advice or not? He hit the BlackBerry again.

"And my mother?"

"Your mother is not part of this equation."

Marble Rose licked at her lips. "I suppose you wonder . . ."

Lizzie held up her hand to stop whatever she was going to say. "Nothing is ever totally black or totally white. There are always, always, gray areas. Growing up without a mother is . . . well, it's the worst thing in the world. My mother died when I was seven. Suddenly there was no one to brush my hair in the morning, no one to tuck me in at night and sing to me, no one to tell me to eat my vegetables. My father didn't know how to iron, so I was always wrinkled. He wasn't much of a cook, either, but he did his best. One of our neighbors bought me my first bra. That same woman explained everything to me about 'that time of the month.' My prom dress was all wrong, my peers said it was slutty. I just loved the ruffles and sparkles and thought I looked like a million bucks. I cried for days when I heard what they said about me. There was no one to share it with but the dog. I missed my mother every day of my life, and I still do.

"The reason I'm telling you this is because just a few days ago, a very wonderful, kind lady adopted me. She adopted *me.* I now have a mother. This wonderful lady was the first to say she would never, ever, try to take my mother's place because that was impossible. She said she would just be a stand-in mom."

Marble Rose chewed on her lower lip as she twirled her hair between her index finger and thumb. Lizzie smiled to herself. She used to do the same thing when she didn't know what to decide. Hell, she still did it when no one was watching.

"You don't understand . . ."

"I understand more than you realize. You have absolutely nothing to lose by talking to your mother one-on-one. I'm willing to go out on a limb here and say when you walk away it won't be final. You'll make your peace and be happy about it, but the best part is you'll have a mother you can call on the phone, a mother you can visit, and, in time, open your heart to. This is just advice, Marble Rose, and now I'm off my soapbox. Tell me if you accept the offer."

Marble Rose took so long before she finally spoke, Lizzie was about to scream in frustration. "All right. So, what, I just get in my car tomorrow and . . . drive off?"

"That about sums it up. Where you go is up to you. You have your whole life ahead of you. Make wise choices, and you won't go wrong.

"Believe it or not, Marble Rose, you set this town on its ear. By next week it will never be the same. Be proud of the fact that in some small way you're part of what's going to be made right. So, if there's nothing else, I'll see you tomorrow morning."

The huge white cat leaped to the floor and meandered over to Ted. Putting down his BlackBerry, Ted dropped to his knees and whispered to the cat, who yawned, then slapped at Ted's hand with one of its paws.

Marble Rose laughed, a genuine laugh of amusement. "That means Lily likes you."

Marble Rose walked to the door and opened it. "Thank you hardly seems adequate. Will it do?"

"It will do," Lizzie said.

"Miss Fox . . . where does my mother live?"

"California. Land of sunshine. Here, take this," Lizzie said, handing her the card Beatrice Preston had given her. "Good luck." She reached out to hug Marble Rose.

In the car, Lizzie settled herself, and said, "I love happy endings."

"Was that true what you told her, about your mother and all that? Now, where are we going?"

"Ask yourself why I would lie about something so sacred. We're going to the Babylon to a meeting, so please be quiet and let me think."

Ted always followed orders.

"It looks to be a slow evening," Mike Oliver said to those seated at the long table affording them a view of one of the monitors that covered all the casino's entrances and exits. "I think we should lie low for a few days. Udal is on our ass, and . . ."

"You aren't paid to think, Mike, so shut up. Did you forget who runs this operation?" Hank Owens asked.

The 290-pound blimp, as Owens called Mike Oliver, his right-hand man, was not intimidated. "It's my ass on the line, and I'm worried. There are too many damn people here all of a sudden. The goddamn outgoing director of the FBI suddenly shows up with some retired judge. Tell me that's not something to be concerned about. And suddenly we have to have this martial-arts exhibition, right-now-or-else thing. Don't you think that's a little suspicious?"

"The outgoing director is here to get married. People do that, you know. For some asshole reason, they think it's romantic to have some overweight clown with sideburns pretending to be Elvis marry them. This isn't the first time we've had spur-of-the-moment events. It happens all the time, and you damn well know it. Don't go blowing this all up into something that is nothing but a pimple on your ass. I'm on it, Mike."

Dwayne Richards, the second member of Owens's inner ring, was a muscular-looking thug with a pockmarked face that scared little children. He tilted his head to the side and stared up at his boss. He was soft-spoken, which made him seem all the more deadly. "If there's nothing to worry about, why did you switch up this morning and raise the ante from $1 million to $5 million to that breast cancer research? And why is our glorious boss and owner of the Babylon, Homer Winters, on his way here from the airport?"

"I'll tell you why," Leon Quintera, the third member of the inner circle said. "Because Udal told him to get his ass here ASAP. Even people like Homer Winters jump when Udal tells them to."

The fourth member of the inner ring was an ordinary-looking guy named Stu Franklin, who had curly sandy-brown hair and a boyish smile. Under his five-thousand-dollar Hugo Boss suit he was all muscle and sinew. He was also an ex–Navy SEAL. He liked to think of himself as the voice of reason when his fellow goons were ready to go off half-cocked. "If you think Alvin Lansing is a match for Cosmo Cricket, then I have a rocket launcher ready to fire up your ass. The meeting that's supposed to take place an hour from now is not your run-of-the-mill get-together, Hank, and we all know it, so don't go blowing smoke. Something is happening, or something is going to happen. Cancel tonight with your people, and we'll all rest a little easier."

Owens leaned back in his chair as he thought about Franklin's words. He could afford to take a hit tonight and maybe for the next few nights until everyone settled down. He looked around at his inner ring and knew they were jittery, and jittery was not a good thing. He nodded to show he agreed with Franklin.

"I don't like it that Winters is on his way here," Mike Oliver said.

"He owns the frigging place, Mike," Hank said. "We're just his hired guns, who work for a salary. We're overworked and under-paid."

The others laughed, recognizing the joke.

"Just be respectful. Ask after the family. Make sure you remember the grandkids' names. You can sidetrack the old geezer real easy. The only thing he's interested in is the bottom line, his charities, and how clean this place is. I don't see one com-plaint finding its way to him."

"Udal . . ."

"Will you stop with the Udal thing already. He's not God, you know," Hank snapped. He couldn't let his men know he was get-ting more pissed by the minute as he, too, wondered what was going on. Christ, how he hated Peter Udal and that monster Cosmo Cricket.

Stu Franklin pointed to a monitor covering the main entrance, where a bright red Corvette had just roared up and come to a stop. They all stared at the gorgeous set of legs that swung out of the car. He whistled to show his approval. "Now, that's one classy-looking woman."

The men watched as the valet held a whispered conversation with the owner of the Corvette. The watchers saw a look of alarm spread across the valet's face, then he laughed as the woman pressed some bills into his hand.

"Ah, she's just telling him to be careful with her wheels. Women are fussier about cars than men are," Mike Oliver said.

Down below at the entrance, Ted held the door for Lizzie. "And what was that all about?"

Lizzie was humming under her breath, a tune Ted more or less recognized but couldn't quite put his finger on. Then it came to him, and he laughed out loud. A Kenny G song, "What A Wonderful World."

He was still laughing as they walked around the casino.

Lizzie stopped humming long enough to say, "I don't think you want to know. When we leave, that particular valet will not be working here."

"And you know this . . . how?"

"Are you sure you really want to know?"

Ted wasn't sure if he did or not, but he knew damn well Maggie would want to know. "Yeah," he said.

Lizzie, aware of cameras and all things security, whispered in Ted's ear. He stopped in midstride and burst out laughing all over again. Lizzie smiled and looked upward and waved and mouthed the words, "See you in a bit." To Ted she said, "I play to win, I told you that."

"Wait, wait. How do you know Cricket is the owner of that car?"

"I saw him drive into the garage. He's not going to let some kid park a car like that. Not to worry, it was Cricket. Look, Ted, I'm not as evil as you think. This morning I went out for coffee to bring back and there, in the parking lot of the condo, was this guy from Edison, New Jersey, staring at a red Corvette he won in a crap game. He was drunk as a skunk and worrying about how he was going to explain the Corvette and being here in the first place to his wife. Seems he came here with a few friends, who disappeared on him after the crap game and headed back to New Jersey, and left him high and dry. There he was, clutching the title to the car and I said I'd give him ten grand for it, and he said okay. End of story. So, no, it is not a rental, no, I will not claim any damage to it, and when we leave here tonight, I will turn the car over to the valet, who is now working at the Venetian. Win-win, Ted."

"But who is going to pay for the damage to Cricket's car? Not that I care."

"When this is all over, I'll step up to the plate or negotiate a settlement. Don't worry, Ted, I got it covered."

Ted was laughing again as Lizzie went back to humming "What A Wonderful World."

In the underground garage, Julio Valencia, known to his friends as Doc, was having the time of his life as he scooted around the ramps in the red Corvette looking for a silver Enzo Ferrari whose price tag was a mere $1 million. He knew because he was a car buff. He looked down at the two thousand dollars the silver-haired woman had pressed into his hand. He laughed when he recalled how she'd whispered, *"Check the video cameras, then just back into it and smash in the front. You might want to give it a second crunch. Don't worry about my car, then park the Corvette, nose out. You have a job waiting for you at the Venetian. Three bucks more an hour. Just tell them Mr. Udal recommended you. Remember this number and call me if you have any problems."*

Hot damn, the valet thought. *Now I can take my girlfriend to Jamaica.*

He loved and hated the sound of the Corvette smacking into the Ferrari's front end. He swung the Vette around and had another go at it. He got out to assess the damage and was satisfied the car was probably totaled. He climbed back into the Corvette and roared down a level to another floor, where he did what he was told and backed the candy-apple red machine in. He climbed out and walked up the ramp to the outdoors. He walked down the street, hailed a cab. His thoughts were on his girlfriend, Lucinda, and the two grand in his pocket.

Chapter 16

"My treat, Joe," Maggie said, paying for two coffees and two bagels. She carried the tray over to a small table in the coffee shop in the lobby of the *Post,* and set it down. Joe had two copies of the morning edition of the *Post.* Both of them were grinning from ear to ear as they stared down at the headline. It wasn't a WAR headline in big bold letters. It wasn't even a medium War headline. The fine italic heading was a statement: *Mass Exodus From The Nation's Capital To Las Vegas.* Underneath the startling headline it read, *Does anyone in Washington really believe what happens*

*in Vegas stays in Vegas? This paper thinks
NOT.*

The printing was so finely scripted
readers either had to put on their glasses
or bring the paper to within eight inches
of their faces.

"Great teaser!" Espinosa said.

"I can't take credit for it. It was Ted's idea.
That's why I gave him the byline. I'll bet you
five bucks the phones at the paper are
jammed."

Espinosa grinned. He shook his head.
"That's a sucker bet. It's like old times, eh,
Maggie? Do you miss all the digging and
the running, the adrenaline rush?"

"Yeah, old times," Maggie said wistfully.
"Of course I miss it, but being the EIC has
its moments, like right now. I have to admit,
give this town a nugget and they'll run to
hell and back to get to the nitty-gritty. Who
the hell ever ran a headline like that with no
story, just two pictures, some red arrows,
and a question? No one that I can recall. I
made the decision to double our print run
tomorrow."

Seasoned reporter that he was,
Espinosa agreed with his boss. "And we
did it in color!"

Maggie looked down at the picture of the White House and next to it a full aerial shot of Las Vegas with a large arrow running from the White House to what looked like a particular casino. A second arrow ran from Vegas to the White House. A particular casino with no name.

"Joe, neither you nor I pretends to be a fashion maven, so I want you to take my printouts Ted has been feeding me via his BlackBerry to Mavis Riley and have her do a write-up of Lizzie Fox's wardrobe. That lady is so into fashion I want every woman in D.C. salivating when they envision the Silver Fox's clothes. Tell her I will allocate a full three inches of space above the fold. Four if she absolutely needs it but no more. Be sure you give her credit, the socialites in this town follow her fashion advice. You always want to keep them wanting more and more and more."

"What went down at the meeting last night?" Espinosa asked. "Did Ted fall asleep at one of the gaming tables?"

"Nothing that exciting. It was canceled at the eleventh hour. Seems the owner of the Babylon flew in, got his jockeys in a knot, and said he was too tired to conduct business at that hour of the night. It's on for this morning. All the players were in place, but nothing went down. Ted won two hundred bucks and Lizzie lost forty-five dollars. But something interesting is on the front page of the *Sun* this morning. Seems someone has it in for Mr. Cosmo Cricket. His Enzo Ferrari, which set him back a cool mil, was pretty much totaled in a parking garage. That's two cars in two days. Seems the guy is chewing nails and spitting rust."

Espinosa laughed. "Don't they have security cameras in those garages?"

"Well, yeah," Maggie drawled. "Vegas is the land of security, but for some reason the cameras were short-circuited last night. That's what happens when you're dumb enough to take up *two* spaces. Ticks off the next guy who can't find a space. Shit happens, Joe. Listen, I have to get up to the office. Find out who else is bugging out of here. You sure you don't want to take that five-dollar bet?"

"Nah. Are you sure Ted doesn't need my help? I can do there what I'm doing here. Ted might need me, Maggie."

Maggie gathered up her paper and trash and stared at him for a long minute. "It might come to that, Joe. I think I can guarantee that there will be no available flights to Vegas out of D.C. today or tomorrow. I'll let you know. Get me everything you have on Homer Winters and his family. *Everything,* Joe. Call in on the hour."

Espinosa saluted smartly. "Yes, ma'am." He started to text message Ted until he realized the time difference between D.C. and Las Vegas. Ted was probably still catching his *z*'s and might not have his BlackBerry set on vibrate. Espinosa slipped his own BlackBerry into his pocket and sauntered out of the coffee shop. At the last second he turned around and went back to get two coffees to go. Maggie liked it when people brought her coffee. So what if he was brownnosing the new EIC? So what?

The inner ring were munching on jelly donuts and drinking vanilla-flavored coffee as they viewed the night's security films. The only thing of any interest was live video of Homer Winters stomping his way toward his chauffeur-driven car, which was blocking the entrance to the casino. They all shrugged, as much as to say, *He's old, and if he wants to be a curmudgeon, let him.* He was the owner in name only as far as they were concerned. Hank Owens, although he'd never admit it aloud, considered the Babylon to be *his.* He knew how to keep Winters in line.

"Nothing else?" Owens asked.

"I picked up the airport video before I came in this morning," Leon Quintera said.

"Anyone look at it yet?"

"No, Boss," the men said in unison.

"That's it, then?" Owens's tone of voice clearly meant there better not be anything else.

"Unless you count the morning edition of the *Washington Post,*" Oliver said.

Owens bent over to stare down at the online headline. He started to curse. "What the hell does that mean? Who the hell is 'flocking' here? I want names.

"Now, look alive, gentlemen, we're in the security business here. Let's see who's arrived in our fair city in the dark hours of the night. Maybe if you guys put your

glasses on, you can identify the Washingtonians who are invading our fair city."

Airport tapes were usually on the boring
side, grainy and poor quality but still good
enough to make out the features of those
the camera captured. You could always tell
the high rollers and the movie stars
because they held their heads up so the
cameras could capture them full face. It
was the travelers who wore caps, sunglasses at night, or big hats, and kept their
heads down, that interested the security
team.

"Jesus, look at that!" Owens said as the
camera caught a British Airways Red
Cross jet sitting on the runway. "How come
all handicapped or sick people come to
Vegas?" he grumbled.

A string of obscenities flew out of his
mouth when he saw the portable stair-
case wheeled up to the jet's door, which
was standing open. Seven white-coated
attendants descended the steps, each
one carrying a wheelchair. An airport
worker opened the collapsed chairs and
lined them up. Minutes later, the same
attendants carried frail-looking patients

down the steps and carefully placed their charges in the waiting chairs.

"Jesus Christ, tell me those people aren't registered here at the hotel. You know what hell wheelchairs cause in the gaming rooms. First they block the aisles, then the people sitting in them start to complain about the cigarette smoke and the watered-down drinks. They demand instant service, and they want smiles and hop-to-it-ness. They send their goddamn food back six times, and want to-go bags. And they damn well don't tip, and they tie up the elevators. Well, where the hell are they staying?"

Mike Oliver was busy tapping away on a computer. "No one is showing seven British handicapped guests. Probably staying someplace private. I think we're in the clear, Boss."

"Okay. Keep everyone on their toes. Who the hell knows when old Homer will decide to show up. I'll be in my office. I have to deal with that shit about Cosmo Cricket's fancy set of wheels. He thinks he's going to walk out of here with a check for a million dollars.

"Richards," he boomed, "find out what

the hell went wrong with the garage cameras. I'm not going to authorize a million-dollar payout if Cricket doesn't know how to drive. I don't give two shits if Udal is his boss or not. You, Oliver, find out where those handicapped people are staying. Something is not sitting right with me about that jet and its passengers. Check the hospital and see what reason, if any, they might have to be going there. If they're here for fun and games, nail it down."

The inner ring rolled their eyes, then sat down together to decide if they wanted to waste their time on handicapped people or sit and finish the donuts and the coffee.

"Screw it," Quintera said. "A private ambulance picked them up, which means someone has money, and people with money pay for privacy. End of story."

The others agreed. They went back to their food.

Down the hall and around the corner, Hank Owens stomped his way into his private office. He settled himself behind his desk and bellowed for coffee, which appeared like magic just as Cosmo Cricket walked through the doorway. As always, Owens was struck by the sheer size of the man. He sighed and motioned for the lawyer to enter and take a seat. "Coffee?"

"Sure, why not?" Cricket asked.

Owens bellowed again, and within seconds a young woman carried in the coffee on a silver tray. Guests always got a silver tray, another one of Homer Winters's cockamamie rules.

Owens decided to take the initiative. "What do you want from me, Cricket? The cameras were down. It happens, we both know that. You parked the damn car yourself, we have you on video. You buy a car like that, you buy enough insurance to cover it. And you took up two fucking spaces! Jealous crackpots abound. We both know that, too. I just don't see where our liability is. Lansing said you need to fight it out with your insurance company." It all sounded real good to Owens's ears, but he knew that in the end the Babylon was going to pay *something* to the man sitting across from him. That was another one of Winters's cockamamie rules—step up to the plate and take responsibility. "That's Lansing's opinion and mine as well." The lie didn't bother him one little bit.

Cricket leaned back and crossed his legs. "You see, Hank, that's a problem. Opinions are like assholes, everyone has one. Pony up, or I'm going to have a chat with Homer. I bet you thought I didn't know he was in town. Well, I do know. So, we can do this the easy way or the hard way. Just send the check to my office. Thanks for the coffee." At the door, he turned, an amused expression on his face. "Have you met Elizabeth Fox yet? No? You're in for a treat, then."

Hank Owens's eyes narrowed to slits as he listened to the big man's laughter wafting back into his office. His gut instinct kicked into high gear as he heaved himself out of his chair. He marched down to Alvin Lansing's office, which was screamingly neat, just like the wimpy man sitting behind the polished desk. Lansing was a Homer Winters's appointee; otherwise, Hank would have gotten rid of him a long time ago, Harvard Law School or not.

"I want everything you have on Elizabeth Fox, Alvin, and I want it right now." Even though he was speaking to Lansing, his gaze swept to the left, to a marble table where two leather check registers rested. His gut churned at the control the man sitting behind the desk had.

Alvin Lansing leaned over and plucked a folder that was at least an inch thick from a pile of color-coded documents on the corner of his overly neat desk. He handed it over.

Lansing absolutely detested the man standing over him. "Read it and weep." He wanted to add the word *asshole,* but he wouldn't lower himself to Owens's level. He would have the last laugh when he wrote out the check to Cosmo Cricket, knowing the million dollars would come off the top of Owens's bonus at the end of every month for the next ten months. Owens and his little posse of thugs would be going through some serious dollar withdrawals in the months to come. If Lansing had been a boisterous kind of guy, he would have gotten up and danced a jig.

He was looking forward to his luncheon date with Homer Winters, the man who had plucked him from his graduating class and given him, a skinny kid from the wrong side of the tracks, a job. He owed everything to Homer Winters and the way the old man had set him up for life. He could walk away right now, right this minute, and would never have to worry about money ever again. Even his four children and their children would never have to worry about money. All he owed Hank Owens was a good swift kick to his posterior. Maybe when he related the current events as he saw them to his boss, Homer would tell him why he kept Owens on the payroll. Then again, knowing Homer, it might not happen.

Maybe it was time to put a bug in Homer's ear, time to get out, time to let the sharks and barracudas do each other in. Time for him to let go and enjoy his remaining years in the bosom of his family.

Lansing looked around the office that his wife had decorated for him. It was a restful suite of rooms, and he had his own sparkling-clean bathroom complete with shower and a small dressing room. The two-office suite was done in soft earth tones, with just splatters of color on the walls and a few cushions. The green plants were healthy and glossy, plants he himself watered twice a week. The small fish tank built into the wall, filled with colorful fish, was so mesmerizing it often lulled him to sleep. The long sofa was made of down and easy on the eye besides being comfortable. The armchairs were just as lush. On the bookshelf behind his chair was an array of his own family pictures and a like number of Homer and his family.

In his own way, Lansing knew he was insidious when it came to Hank Owens. Because he was, he kept two large leather-bound checkbooks strategically placed on an inlaid marble table to the left of his desk, containing checks only he could make out and sign. Each time Hank Owens came into his office, his eyes invariably went to the marble table and the checkbooks. Lansing always enjoyed the naked envy in the man's eyes.

One of Hank's favorite sayings was, "There are more ways to skin a cat than the one staring you in the eye."

Alvin Lansing got up and closed the door to his office. He walked back to his chair and sat down. Then he started to laugh. The sound was squeaky but so full of mirth he couldn't stop as he envisioned Owens reading the contents of Elizabeth Fox's folder.

Chapter 17

Jack Emery looped the strap of his carry-on over his shoulder and followed Harry Wong off the plane. Harry was muttering and mumbling to himself as he strode along. "We're not dressed right."

Jack looked around at the Stetsons and cowboy boots everyone seemed to be wearing. Even here in the airport, slot machines were ringing and chiming, at some times deafening, as customers won a handful of nickels or quarters. "What gave you your first clue?" Jack snapped. "This is like Hollywood, land of make-believe and shattered dreams. Everyone wants to be Western. It's the new buzz-word."

Harry continued to gallop along. "Eat shit, Jack."

Harry could be so surly sometimes. "Ah, that's the Harry I know and love. I bet you ten bucks if you showed up in cowboy boots and a Stetson, Yoko would scream and drag you off to her lair, assuming, of course, she's been able to set up a lair here.

"Listen, Harry, remember what I told you. This town is known for its eavesdrop-pers. Either we talk in code or we don't talk. Always assume we are going to be watched and spied on. Charles told me this whole damn town is wired, and there is no such thing as privacy." Jack decided to jerk Harry's chain. "Which shouldn't be a problem for you since you are so tight-lipped and only grunt. What the hell Yoko sees in you is beyond me. You need to lighten up and have some fun. All you do is worry and stew and fret. That's no way to live."

Harry stopped in midstep. Jack bumped into him. "You do know I could kill you with my little finger, right? I could do it right here in this damn airport. Or I could stick my other finger in your ear, and you'd just topple over, and I'd say you bumped into me and dropped dead. Oh, well, too bad, too sad, boo-hoo. How's that for conversation?"

"Well, it wasn't exactly what I had in mind, but I am getting your point. We really have to stop having these little love fests in public, or people are going to start to talk."

In spite of himself, Harry burst out laughing. "Do we know where the girls are staying?"

"Someplace out in the desert. As soon as we get settled in at the Babylon, I want to go out there. Hold on, Harry! Wait, wait! I want to get a paper."

Jack literally dragged Harry over to a gift shop that had newspapers piled high on a counter. He looked them over until he found the *Post*. He slapped a bill down on the counter and moved off. "Holy shit, Harry, look at this! I wonder if we're part of the 'mass exodus' out of Washington." He looked up at Harry and grinned. "This is pure genius," he said, pointing to the headline. "Good old Maggie."

The two men gave each other a high five

as they continued their trek through the airport. Even Harry's step seemed a little lighter.

"You worried about Ted Robinson, Jack?"

"No, I'm not. Ted's an okay guy. Down deep he's really decent. He stepped off the road there for a while, but that was because of Maggie. Guys do crazy shit when their women screw them over. We should have brought him in earlier, and our lives would have been a lot easier. He was a good friend for a lot of years. We'll take it one step at a time. Maggie will keep him in line. Does that make you feel better?"

"Yes and no. We had our issues. Well, if he goes off the straight and narrow, I'll just kill him."

"And Ted knows that. Ah, look, there's the Babylon guy with his little sign. And that's your name on the card he's holding up, Harry Wong. Guess he's got our wheels."

"Wiseass," Harry said, as he lined up the limo driver in his sights and waved his hand. "I'm Harry Wong," he called out.

"Welcome to Las Vegas, Mr. Wong." He

ignored Jack and offered to take Harry's bag but Harry declined the offer.

Jack almost laughed. One of these days he was going to take a peek in Harry's bag to see what the hell he was lugging around. Probably secret ninja shit like his disappearing capsules and a hundred power bars and that crappy tea he drank by the gallon. But not the morning stars that he tossed with such deadly accuracy. Not with the security procedures in place at airports these days.

Outside, just as Harry was sliding into the backseat of their stretch limo, Jack's cell phone rang. He stepped away from the car and brought the phone to his ear. "Talk to me, Charles, and tell me where the girls are." Jack listened carefully, then said, "We just bought a copy of the paper. Tell Maggie she's a genius. Yeah, I know she knows it, but tell her anyway." He continued to listen as Charles rattled on. "Tell me you're making that up, Charles. No one in their right minds would agree to pay out that kind of money. Well, I understand it's easier to pay it out now than risk losing ten times that much. Okay, okay, they write it off. You want me to . . . what? Yes, Charles, I heard you. Okay, okay, I'll do my best." Jack powered down and stepped into the limo. He looked over at Harry and gave him the high sign to keep quiet but at the same time letting him know he had news.

Harry started to jabber in several different languages, to Jack's amusement and the driver's chagrin. Somewhere in Vegas he was sure there was an interpreter who would try to dissect Harry's verbiage. Jack tried not to laugh because Harry made up words as he went along when he wanted to be ornery. Jack knew just enough Cantonese and a smattering of Japanese to grunt a few words in reply. Wouldn't that interpreter be surprised to find out they were talking about manure and topsoil. At least that's what Jack thought they were talking about.

They rode the rest of the way in silence, both men stretched out, their eyes closed. They looked like two weary visitors who didn't have a care in the world.

While Jack and Harry were pretending to snooze, the vigilantes were pacing the confines of what at one time had been a nursing home. Now it was just an empty building out in the desert. On the long ride from the airport, the only things they could see for miles were a few straggly trees and some unhealthy cactus even taller than the trees. The driver had pointed out an oasis a mile before he brought the car to a stop at the empty building.

"Some Indian named Little Fish owns that spread. It's like the marvel in marvelous. All that green grass. A couple acres of it. The owner has an ongoing war going on with the Strip. The Babylon in particular. No one knows exactly what it's about, but it must have some weight and some teeth to it because none of the owners have ever bounced him. Every so often he will mosey into town with his posse and take the Strip by storm. I read somewhere that his property is mined. To keep people out," he added, as though the women might not know what *mined* meant.

"He's also very rich, and he got that way by playing poker. These days he plays just to get enough money to buy water that he trucks in from Arizona to water all that grass. The casinos go crazy when he comes to town. That might be more than you need to know, but Charles did say I was to apprise you of any and all details. Just to be certain we're all on the same page, we will be leaving one of these vans for you. There are assorted decals in the back along with four different license plates."

Then they were alone staring at one another.

"I knew it! Just crackers and cheese and bottled water," Kathryn said.

"Are we just supposed to sit here and wait?" Alexis grumbled.

"This is the most depressing place we've ever been in," Isabelle said.

Nikki stared at Annie, and said, "Do not even think about suggesting we play word games. This place gives me the creeps. I can't believe Charles had us dumped here with no plan of action."

"I'm sure Charles has his reasons, dear. As you know, and as you point out to us on a regular basis, the devil is in the details."

Nikki flounced over to where there stood a long line of hard blue plastic chairs stacked up against the wall. She yanked at one and sat down. "Will someone please open the door so we can get some fresh air in here before we all die of suffocation?"

Yoko ran to the door and opened it. She hated it, absolutely hated it, when any of the Sisters was unhappy. Not that she was exactly happy, she wasn't. But they'd always worked together to overcome discomfort. She turned around when Annie started to bellow.

"Little Fish! Ladies, we are slipping, and that is not a good thing! Am I the only one who knows who our neighbor is? Charles told us before we left about a man Rena told Lizzie about in case we . . . uh . . . needed help. Rena even gave Lizzie his phone number."

The women looked at Annie as though she'd sprouted a second head, each of them running Charles's last words over in her mind.

"Annie's right. We are slipping. How did that get by us?" Kathryn demanded.

No one answered.

Nikki was off the chair a moment later. "I hear a car. A car means we have company. Scatter, ladies!"

"Myra and I will stay here, dear. Go, hurry, and stay out of sight."

"Is the car stopping?" someone shouted.

"Yes, and whoever it is knows we're here since the door is wide-open. It's a man, and he's walking up to the door. Everyone relax, I can handle this," Annie said, confidence ringing in her voice.

Annie walked to the door and stood in the center, her eyes bright and curious. Myra stood to her side, both hands on her pearls.

Annie stared at the tall man, who had skin like worn shoe leather. His eyes were piercing blue, and they looked angry. His hair was iron gray, at least at the sides. Some sort of old army hat was crunched down on his head. He wore old, comfortable clothes that looked like they might have been army issue at one time, and stout combat boots encased his feet.

This was indeed a man. She almost smacked her lips in glee at the possibilities she now might have in regard to her sadly lacking social life.

A sun-bronzed hand snaked out. "Fish."

"Ah, no thanks. We won't be here that long. Fish goes bad rather quickly." She used both hands to grasp his. It was a rough hand full of callouses. The nails were cut short and clean. She absolutely loved the holstered gun at his waist. Annie almost swooned.

The man standing in front of her looked disgusted. "It's my name." When Annie just stared at him he said, "Little Fish. It's an Indian name. What's your name? Why are you here? It isn't safe out here in the desert for a woman. I don't have time to be watching out for a gaggle of females."

Annie threw her hands up in the air. "Well, Mr. Fish, I don't recall asking for your help or your opinion. I'm more than capable of taking care of myself, and what gaggle of females are you talking about? And, what's it to you what my name is? It's none of your business why I'm here. Your turn. Just for the record, I can shoot a snake's eyes out from five hundred feet."

Myra let go of her pearls to hang on to the door frame. She wondered if anyone but her knew this was Annie's version of flirting.

"And you expect me to believe that?"

There was such outrage in the man's voice, Myra found herself smiling.

Annie bristled. "Obviously, Mr. Fish, you have me confused with someone you think cares what you think. Read my lips. I *can* shoot a snake's eyes out at five hundred feet, and that's the end of it unless you want to bring it to a test."

Fish stepped back for a better look at the woman who was giving him what he called *what for*. She had spunk.

"In case you don't know it, Miss No Name, that building you're standing in is full of rattlesnake nests. The desert is full of them, so I hope for your sake that you aren't lying about your marksmanship, and I also hope you have a gun. There's no electricity in that building. It's doubtful the plumbing works. It gets pretty cold out here at night."

Myra's gaze skittered around as she looked to see if anything was slithering across the floor. She knew the others would be doing the same thing.

"I'll be leaving soon. Before it gets dark. Not that it's any of your concern."

"Lady With No Name, I just came by to warn you about this building. They've been trying to sell it for ten years. And I don't want you trespassing on my property and getting yourself blown up."

Annie decided to show this person she did indeed have some spunk. "You flatter yourself that I would trespass on your property. You, on the other hand, are a nosy old grouch who wants to know what's going on close to that mined property of yours, which then brings the question, what are you hiding over there with all that green grass?"

Fish blustered a bit, and said, "Women like to run barefoot through grass."

Annie drew herself up to her full height and glared at him. Then she laughed. "And ruin a fifty-dollar pedicure? You don't know much about women, do you?"

The man turned defensive. "I know enough. Well, I tried to warn you. Don't show up at my door with a snakebite."

"Don't you worry about me, Mr. Fish. I'll be sure to tell Rena Gold you said that."

Then she slammed the door so hard one of the front windows cracked down the middle.

The knock on the door made Annie smile. Myra was just shaking her head. She opened the door.

"What did you say?"

"I said go away." Annie slammed the door a second time.

A second knock sounded. Annie opened the door again. "What? Do you need me to escort you to your vehicle? Go home and trip through your land mines." She slammed the door shut again.

"Annie, I don't think that's any way to snare a man. I might be a little rusty, but I'm thinking a few kind words would maybe get you . . ."

"Is that what you think, Myra? You think I was flirting?"

"Oh, yeah," the others said in unison.

"You need some lessons," Nikki said. "Now, if you really want to get that Fish person interested in you, you're going to have to do a little sucking up. Now get out there and say something nice before he leaves."

Annie frowned. She opened the door and shouted, "Yoo-hoo, Mr. Fish, wait up a minute." She tripped down the cracked walkway and smiled. "I was . . . uh . . . wondering if you might know where I could find a pair of white boots with rhinestones?"

Little Fish looked like he'd just fallen

through the rabbit hole. "Come to think of it, Miss No Name, I do know a cobbler. Walk out to the car with me, and I'll write down his name. I have to warn you, he's expensive."

"That's okay, I'm rich," Annie babbled. "And I do have a name. It's . . . it's Honoria. My friends call me Ria."

Fish grinned. He hadn't had this much fun in a long time. "How do you know Rena?"

"That's NTK. It means need to know."

"I know what it means. I used to be in the military. You look familiar. You from around here?"

"I think I'd remember you if we'd met, you being so cantankerous and all. I don't usually associate with curmudgeons. Life is just too short. I live in New Jersey."

"Nobody lives in New Jersey," Fish said.

"Well, after I left, the state did kind of fold up. Thanks for this," Annie said, waving the piece of paper back and forth. "What's the other phone number?"

"It's mine. That's in case you ever want to call me, Miss Anna de Silva."

Annie's jaw dropped. She stared at the man who was staring at her. Should she panic and run, or should she brazen it out and hope for the best?

Fish climbed into his car and leaned out the window. "Rena called and explained. Your secret is safe with me. I was funning with you. The guy's a great shoemaker. You being rich and all, you should give some thought to maybe making an offer on one of the casinos in town. Maybe we could partner up financially and give it a whirl. I kind of feel drawn to you, and you got some grit to you."

Grit! Panic bubbled up, but she managed to ask, "Which casino? I didn't know there were any for sale. I don't even know you."

"Well, you know me now. There aren't any casinos for sale right this minute, but one will be going on the market in the next day or so. You have my number. Call me if you're interested."

"Which casino?"

"The Babylon."

Annie turned around and ran as fast as her legs could carry her. She slammed the door again, and the other front window cracked down the middle. "Oh, my God! That man knows! He called me by my name! He wants to go into business with me! We have to get out of here right now! Wait till I tell you . . ."

The women clustered around and demanded to know if aside from *knowing about them,* through Rena, the leathery menace who had darkened their door had asked her for a date.

"Oh, it's better than that. Listen up, girls."

Chapter 18

Ted Robinson sat on a high stool in the condo's kitchen, his fingers working his ever-present BlackBerry. Lizzie was standing in the doorway talking on her cell phone, taking one call after the other. He wasn't sure, but he thought she looked . . . He grappled for the right word, not exactly worried, maybe apprehensive or concerned. He looked down at a message that had popped up from Maggie:

What's she wearing?

Not, *What's going on and why is she worried?* But, *What's she wearing?*
Ted's fingers flew over the keys.

A washed-denim bomber jacket and a kind of skimpy T-shirt underneath with lots of cleavage showing. A short skirt with strings hanging off the bottom. I mean short. I guess she's wearing panties. Do you want me to check? I think she went to a tanning bed somewhere during the night. She's bronzed. Looks like all over. Makes her hair sparkle like diamonds. No makeup that I can tell except lipstick.

The incoming message read:

Not necessary to check out panties. What's on her feet?

Ted's fingers tapped away.

Shiny black boots with heels that are at least four inches high. She looks like an Amazonian Aphrodite.

Maggie's response:

Any jewelry?

A set of headlights in her ears. I don't know much about diamonds. Hers are *big.*

Maggie's response was:

Diamonds are a girl's best friend.

Then she clicked off, and Ted was left staring at Lizzie, who looked like she was finished with her cell phone. His eyebrows rose in question.

"A small change of plans. It seems Marble Rose wants to go with us to the casino to accept her payoff. And, she wants one more crack at those slot machines. Since nothing has been signed, I see no problem with her coming along. I also think she has every right to take another crack at those machines for what she went through. We'll know soon enough if there's a problem when we get there.

"The vigilantes are on their way to somewhere. It seems they were temporarily located at an abandoned nursing home out in the desert, that one Little Fish said was infested with rattlesnake nests. It also seems that Rena Gold confided in Little Fish about the vigilantes. That does not make me happy. The flip side of that is, according to Rena, the man is not stupid and has his own agenda where the casinos are concerned. He might have secured the information on his own and just attributed it to Rena. I will check that out. Regardless, Little Fish, according to Annie and the others, is on our side."

"I'll check him out. He's the guy who has green grass, and his property is mined, right?"

Lizzie nodded. Ted immediately started hitting the keys to his BlackBerry. He knew that within the hour, Maggie and Joe would have the skinny on Little Fish.

"Lizzie, what's our bottom line here? What exactly is going on? I'm usually pretty quick on the uptake, but I seem to be out in left field on what exactly is happening. I thought we came here to spring Marble Rose, which you did, and to make the casino assume liability, which you did. Then all of a sudden there is dirty work afoot, but I'm not clear on what it is. Suddenly the owner of the Babylon is here to attend the meeting we're about to have. The NGC is up to its eyeballs and is willing to pony up beaucoup bucks to have the vigilantes do *something.* A martial-arts exhibition is arranged on the fly, and suddenly Harry and Jack are en route but only after Elias Cummings, the outgoing director of the FBI, and Judge Cornelia Easter arrive here to get married. Helloooo.

"The *Post* is stirring up some kind of wasps' nest that's driven the presidential election to page three. Something I never would have believed could happen. Washington is the land of politics. By the way, Martine Connor is experiencing cash flow problems as they approach the finish line. She's in desperate straits."

Lizzie frowned. "How desperate?"

"Maggie said there's no money for the television blitz they planned for the last three weeks of the campaign. On Annie's orders, she's taking IOUs for full-page ad space every single day, and she's got Joe doing below-the-fold coverage. Millions, to answer your question."

"We can deal with that after we finish up today. Anything else?"

"Bert Navarro is on his way here. Seems the official explanation is that Elias Cummings wants him to be his best man. Maggie thinks otherwise. Hell, *I* think otherwise. So that makes a rather long list of Washingtonians who are in town. If you're counting, which I am, it's Cummings, Judge Easter, Jack, Harry, Bert, you, me, and—of course—all seven vigilantes. All heavy hitters except me. What are you all going to do, and why exactly are you doing it, whatever the hell *it* is?" Ted felt so frustrated he wanted to bang his head on the kitchen wall.

Lizzie sauntered over to the counter and hoisted herself onto one of the stools. Yep, she was wearing panties. Her legs were so long her feet rested on the floor. Ted tried not to look at the shimmering thighs. He swore to Maggie that Lizzie's thighs sparkled. Maggie responded by saying there was a sparkly something or other that came in a spray can that women sprayed on themselves. He rolled his eyes at this information. Who knew?

Lizzie looked at her watch. She decided she had time for a brief catch-up chat with her newest associate. "Marble Rose was our initial case, but she was a diversion. Yes, she won a boatload of money, and, yes, they put the screws to her, but she was still a diversion. Her . . . uh . . . winning streak, for want of a better word, happened just as Owens and his team were taking on the other casinos and the Babylon and winning big. I don't know as of this minute how many people are involved in what they orchestrated. Greed, as I've always said, is the most powerful motivator in the world. I guess to people like that, no amount of money is ever enough. I do know that the Babylon, like most casinos, has a bonus program. Whatever the head of security saves the casino by being on top of things factors into his monthly bonus.

"I'm thinking that guy Owens has a small army of gamblers who hit a casino once, then they're replaced with others in the crew. That's why they haven't been caught. Mr. Udal says this has been going on for a year, but even with all their high-tech security, they couldn't nail anyone. Then in comes Marble Rose and her big winnings, which brought it all front and center.

"I guess the casinos have their own code of ethics. What they do behind the scenes is something else. That slogan *What happens in Vegas, stays in Vegas* has some truth to it. Bottom line is they want the entire security team at the Babylon taken care of. And they are willing to pay for it.

"Everything is a smoke screen. To put them on edge so they might make a mistake. They know something is up, but they don't know what it is. I got a phone call late last night from Peter Udal, and he said there were no big wins anywhere on the Strip in the last two days, which means Owens and his people are lying low because they can smell trouble. We have to flush them out.

"We're a temporary fix until the vigilantes take over. Another distraction, if you will."

Whatever Lizzie was going to say next was cut off when her cell phone rang. "I'll be right down." Then she said, "Our taxi is here, Ted."

"No fancy cars today, Counselor?"

"No, no fancy cars."

Kathryn Lucas drove the white van, with Nikki riding shotgun and the other women sitting secure and buckled up in the rows of seats in the back. A mile down the road and past Little Fish's spread, she pulled over to the side of the road. The girls hopped out, removed the Red Cross decal and license plate. The new decal, a decorative bouquet of brilliant-colored balloons, graced each side of the van. Matching three-inch letters raced across the top of the balloons and spelled out the words THE PARTY STORE. The current license plate was replaced with an Arizona plate. "Make sure the paperwork matches the plate," Kathryn said as she slipped behind the wheel again.

"Where are we going? I think we'll all feel better if we have a destination in mind," Myra said.

Nikki turned around and said, "I think until Charles locates a nest for us, we should check out the Babylon. All we have to do is put on our padding, our serviceable shoes and wigs, and hit the ground running. We'll park somewhere on the Strip, get out and, one by one, walk up to the Babylon. We can all use the exercise. We'll meet back at the van at a designated time. If anyone has a better idea, let's hear it."

Alexis spoke for the others when she said she agreed. She immediately started to dig into her Red Bag.

Fifteen minutes into their drive, Kathryn broke into their chatter. "I can't be sure, but I think we picked up a tail. Either that, or whoever is driving that big SUV is just out for a joyride."

"Oh, it's probably that Fish person," Annie said airily as she plopped a Shirley Temple wig on her head and gave it a good tug. "I think you should pull over, pretend you're having engine problems, and when he stops, we take him out."

Myra's hands flew to her pearls, and she grasped at them like a lifeline.

"Good idea," Yoko, who now looked like a dumpy little Chinese lady with short black hair and bangs, said. She looked over the top of her granny glasses and winked at Annie.

Kathryn yanked at a baseball cap that said she was an Atlanta Braves fan. She appeared to be twenty pounds heavier, almost as dumpy-looking as Yoko. "Okay, let's do it!" For five seconds the van swerved, then swerved again, before it slid to the side of the blistering road. She said, "That was a tire-blowout simulation. How'd I do?"

"Just perfect," Annie said, as though she were an expert on driving an obstacle course.

"Okay, I'm going to be looking at the right-front tire. Yoko, Nikki, get out and start waving your arms all around. Let's see if the SUV stops to help three women."

"What if there are more than three people in that SUV?" Myra asked anxiously.

"Well, there are seven of us, so I think it might be a crapshoot," Annie said, her hand on the door handle, ready to slide it open if her help was needed. "If you don't want to be part of the action, you just sit in here and play with your pearls."

"That hurt, Annie."

"It was supposed to *sting,* Myra. Ah, look, they went right past, but now they're backing up. Get ready, girls. Oh, dear, those men look like lean, mean fighting machines."

"How many are there?" Myra demanded, her voice now ringing with confidence.

"I see four," Annie hissed.

"Piece of cake," Myra shot back.

Annie turned around, and said, "Myra, my dear, you rock!"

Myra beamed. Alexis and Isabelle clapped in approval.

The three dowdy-looking women were bent over poking at the tire when four strapping men, Little Fish in the lead, approached. Yoko was jabbering a mile a minute in Japanese as she kicked out at the tire with a shoe that looked like it belonged to a longshoreman.

"What seems to be the problem, ladies?" Little Fish asked.

Yoko straightened up to her four-foot-eight height and said, "You are the problem!" She pivoted, her right leg swinging out like a piston, felling the man nearest Little Fish, while her left hand, fingers like steel rods, jammed into the man on the other side of Fish.

Nikki took the third, while Kathryn did a lightning pirouette and had Fish in a neck vise as Yoko reached for the gun on his hip.

Kathryn dusted her hands dramatically. "Guess that takes care of that! What should we do with them?"

The door to the white van slid open on well-oiled tracks. Annie held up her hand for silence. "Trouble," she hissed.

"I think the question is, what should we do with you?" a voice said from the SUV, where three men stepped to the ground, guns drawn.

Quicker than lightning, Yoko had her foot on Little Fish's neck. "Make a move, and I crush his throat." She bellowed for Annie and the others, who raced to the scene.

Myra and Alexis reached for the new-comers' guns and tossed them into the desert. Her foot still on Fish's throat, Yoko handed the gun to Annie.

"Get over there and sit down with your friends while we decide what to do with you," Isabelle shouted.

Kathryn looked over at Yoko. "You didn't kill those two, did you?" She sounded like she was asking if Yoko had picked up eggs at the grocery store.

"I don't think so." Yoko shrugged to indicate it didn't matter one way or the other.

"You," Myra said, pointing to the three newcomers. "Come over here, sit down, and put your hands over your heads."

Annie had Fish's gun and was waving it around. "Move, and I'll shoot you. Ask Mr. Fish here how good I am with a gun."

Yoko stepped away from Fish.

He started to cough and sputter. "Okay, okay, you took us. But, my dear lady, I'm afraid that I cannot vouch for your proficiency with firearms since I have never seen you do more than wave one around. But in case you haven't noticed, there happens to be a rattlesnake sitting up just about a hundred feet to your right."

Annie spun around, raised the gun, and fired, all in one motion. The rattlesnake dropped like a ton of bricks. Annie calmly walked over to the dead snake, picked it up, brought it back to Fish, and asked, "How about that? Have you ever seen a three-eyed rattler before today?"

"Can't say that I have. Look, we were just following you to make sure nothing happened to you. We were trying to protect you, for God's sake."

"Oh, how sweet of you, Mr. Fish," Annie cooed. Then she snarled, "Does it look like we need protection? Maybe you should think about hiring us."

"What makes you think we need protection?" Nikki asked.

"Because you're going into a snake pit, that's why. I can only guess why you're here and who hired you. You think those bad boys at the Babylon are going to let you take them? Get real."

Nikki laughed. "We took *you,* didn't we? Not that it's any of your business, but we have backup in town. It's time for *you* to get real. I say we take these guys back to that empty building, tie them up, and get on with what we came here to do. These wusses are amateurs and not worth the effort we're expending on them. Let's vote."

"Seven to zip to go back to the abandoned building," Alexis said, after all seven hands shot into the air.

"Ladies, ladies, please. We need to be reasonable here. I've known for two days that you were coming. Rena . . . well, let's just say she's a very good friend. She was worried about you and wanted me to . . . watch over you. If I had an ulterior motive, I would have called the cops day before yesterday and sat around to wait to collect the massive reward that's on your heads. I didn't do that, I won't do it, and neither will my men. For whatever it's worth to you, I cheered you on when you . . . uh . . . were in your active mode. I can see now why you're in such demand, but again, you don't know the people you're dealing with. When big money like this is involved, there are no rules."

"Why should we believe anything you tell us?" Yoko asked.

"Because I'm telling you the truth. And because Rena asked me to watch over you because she said she owed you, but there was nothing she could do personally. Rena saved my life a long time ago. There was a bad car accident, and I was part of it. She pulled me out of my truck just minutes before it exploded. She's been like a daughter to me ever since. Call her, for God's sake, ask her."

"Can we put our arms down now?" one of the men asked.

"Only if you fold your hands in your laps and behave," Kathryn said.

The big, burly men did as instructed. They lowered their heads in shame that a bunch of women had taken them on and reduced them to begging.

Nikki walked away and pulled out her cell phone. She scrolled down until she found Rena Gold's number and pressed the autodial. Rena answered on the first ring like she was holding her phone and just waiting for Nikki's call. Nikki spoke quickly. "Yes or no will do it. I don't need a dissertation."

"Well, you're going to get one. Everything Fish probably told you, and I can guess what he said, is true. And it can only mean you have them captive. It wasn't that I didn't have faith in you, I do, but I also know how those goons at the Babylon play the game. I didn't want anything to happen to you. Backup in any language is always a good thing.

"You can trust Fish with your lives. Nikki, I'm sorry if I stepped over the line."

Nikki heard and understood the anguish in Rena's voice. "Okay, but if you're lying to me, we'll come after you. You know that, right?"

"Of course I know that. Your secret is safe with Fish and with me."

Nikki slipped the cell phone back into her pocket. She walked over to the little group and leaned over to reach for Fish's hand and helped him to his feet. The others did the same for his men. "Rena said you were okay. We didn't go into details. Just stay out of our way."

Annie walked over to Fish and handed him his gun, butt first. He holstered it and looked sheepish. Annie smiled.

"You need to fix that crazy-looking wig you're wearing," was all Fish could think of to say.

This was where she probably should have said something corny, like, *Thanks for the tip,* and then fix the damn wig. But she yanked at it and said, "Up yours" before she walked back to the white van. The others followed her.

Fish's laughter followed them until the van doors closed.

"That was real romantic, Annie," Kathryn said.

"Shhh, I'm thinking," Annie retorted.

Chapter 19

The security room at the Babylon was swimming in testosterone as Hank Owens and his posse of goons watched the monitors.

"Looks like they're all here, Boss," Mike Oliver said out of the corner of his mouth. His voice was pitched low so as not to aggravate a man who was already pissed to the teeth. "Looks to me like they're just milling around until it's time to make their way up to Lansing's office."

"I don't see Homer. Did he get here yet?" Owens snarled.

"He's been in his office since eight

o'clock. He ordered breakfast and is now reading the morning edition of every newspaper that's printed. He didn't look happy when he got here. He usually shuffles when he walks, but this morning he stomped his way up to his office. He's been focused on the *Post,* since that's what he reads when he's at his home on the Chesapeake. I gotta tell you, Boss, the guy don't look too happy," Oliver said.

"And I give a good rat's ass if that old bastard is happy or not!"

The inner ring went mute. While Owens confided in them on some things, they all knew they were not privy to the really important workings of the casino. None of them ever made an issue of it, but it rankled. It was their asses on the line when Owens wanted something done on a wink and the sly while he sat up in his office staring at the monitors.

The inner ring knew Owens was outraged that he hadn't been invited to the meeting in Lansing's office that was due to take place in forty minutes. Even though he wouldn't be physically in the room, he would still know what was going on, thanks to the miniature cameras Quintera and

Richards had installed at four thirty in the morning. Homer's office had been bugged a little after midnight. Hank Owens wasn't the head of security for nothing. When he said he wanted to know everything that went on at *his* hotel/casino, he meant *everything.*

Hank Owens leaned closer to one of the monitors. His clenched fist banged on the desktop with such force, the monitor teetered and almost came loose from its fittings. "That bitch is back! Son of a bitch, she's walking around trying to pick a machine. Of all goddamn days, she picks today, with Homer here." He banged the desktop again, then he moved away, his back to his men, and spoke into his sleeve the way the Secret Service agents did when they were guarding the president.

Down below on the main floor, Lizzie felt the air stir around her. Security. She looked over at Ted. She could tell that he, too, had felt the atmosphere and knew exactly what it meant as he trailed behind Marble Rose and the Silver Fox.

Lizzie looked at the startling numbers flashing on the progressive slot machines.

The amounts were dizzying. Which one, she wondered, would Marble Rose pick? Would she home in on the $906,000 one or the one that clanged away with flickering numbers that read $1,111,111? All those 1's. Totaled, they numbered seven. Wasn't the number seven considered lucky in gambling circles? She didn't know. She held her breath when Marble Rose stopped at the million-dollar-plus machine. The air around her stirred, but Marble Rose moved on.

Lizzie looked away from the machines and saw Cosmo Cricket staring at her from across the aisle. He winked at her. *Winked?* Suddenly she felt flustered. She knew she was supposed to do something, but she felt like she was in a time warp. She wanted to respond to the wink, but she had to keep her eyes on Marble Rose. The hell with Marble Rose. She let a seductive smile play along her lips and made a kissing/smacking motion. She wiggled her index finger in Cricket's direction. The sudden realization hit her that she was flirting with the big man. She tried to remember the last time she'd genuinely flirted with anybody, but no time or date would come to mind.

Marble Rose stopped at a machine whose flickering numbers read $7,202. To Lizzie's stunned surprise, she sat down and pulled a twenty-dollar bill out of her pocket and fed it into the machine. The air stirred again, and the phalanx of security moved off.

Lizzie looked down at her watch. Twenty minutes until she had to head upstairs to the meeting. The slot machine was whirring and singing its own song as cherries, bars, and something called SECRET BONUS appeared, then disappeared. The machine chirped—a sound that indicated Marble Rose had won forty dollars. She continued to hit the SPIN button and won another ten dollars. Within seven minutes she'd gambled away her fifty-dollar winnings and was still down twenty dollars of her own money. She pressed the SPIN button again and three SUPER BONUS symbols appeared. She leaned back and waited for the machine to quiet down. She'd just won the $7,202 jackpot. She cashed out her winnings and headed to the cage, where she would redeem the slot machine slip for real money.

While the teller counted out the bills, Marble Rose turned to Lizzie and said, "I'm ready to go now."

"Where would that be?"

"My car is loaded, and I'm headed east to New York. I'm going to bunk with a friend until I can find a place of my own. They need teachers up there. I did call my mother, Ms. Fox. We talked and are going to get together over the Christmas holidays. It didn't feel right, my going there now. I need some time to think about it. I don't want to make a mistake."

Lizzie nodded in approval. "It's a start. I hope good things come of your meeting. Just be open, Marble Rose."

Marble Rose nodded. She rooted around in her purse for a slip of paper. "I'm a little nervous about traveling with a lot of money. She handed Lizzie the envelope containing her winnings. Can you wire the monies to the account number I wrote on the envelope? I hate this place," she blurted.

"Yeah, me, too," Lizzie said, leading the way to the elevator. She looked around for a sign of Cosmo Cricket but couldn't see him. Her face suddenly felt warm at the thought of the big man.

When they left the elevator and entered Alvin Lansing's office, introductions were made, then Lansing suggested they all move to a larger conference room where he said they would be more comfortable. He stepped aside to allow the two women to precede him. He made small talk with Homer Winters on the walk down a narrow hall to the larger room. Noticeably absent from the group was Hank Owens.

After five seconds, Lizzie decided that this particular conference room had been decorated so people would relax and doze off. The walls were a soothing misty green. The carpet was one shade deeper, the upholstered chairs on wheels were evergreen in color. The long conference table had a soft, muted, watery-green marble top. Trees that looked like weeping willows nestled in the corners. Underneath one of them was a small decorative waterfall almost concealed by the dangling fronds from the tree. The sounds of trickling water over polished stones was beyond restful. The misty green walls were covered with children's art, bright in color. All were signed. Homer Winters was pointing them out to the room at large, saying it was the children's way of thanking him for the pediatric wing he'd donated to the local hospital.

At the end of the table was a huge silver coffee urn with a waiter ready to serve croissants, coffee, and fresh fruit. As tantalizing as the coffee smelled, and as luscious as the croissants and fruit looked, everyone declined and sat down. The waiter shrugged and left the room.

The lawyers got down to business while Homer Winters carried on a conversation with Marble Rose about children and their art. Ted Robinson discreetly tapped out messages on the BlackBerry on his lap. Peter Udal was listening intently to both Winters and the lawyers as they bickered. He turned, his ears picking up the change in Lizzie Fox's tone.

"Look at me, Mr. Lansing!" Lizzie commanded. "Do I look to you like I talk just to hear myself? Those are the numbers, and they are not going to disappear if you blink. Wire the money *now* or this meeting is over. Make me wait one more minute, and the price goes up by $50,000 for each minute you make me wait. This establishment is guilty of everything I've outlined for you. One more minute, and I will be filing so many lawsuits your head will spin. The clock is ticking."

Lansing looked flustered at being dressed down by a woman in the presence of Homer Winters.

Winters waved his arm. "Do what the lady says, Alvin. She's right, and everyone in this room knows it. You wasted almost four minutes so add $200,000 to the total. This young lady can use the money."

Cosmo Cricket fixed his gaze on Lizzie and discreetly gave her a thumbs-up. Lizzie felt warm all over again. Ted pecked away at warp speed.

Alvin Lansing excused himself and left the room. He returned ten minutes later with a wire transfer slip and three extra copies, which he handed to Lizzie. Lizzie swiveled around and handed one of the slips to Marble Rose.

The room was quiet as they waited for the young woman to look down at the confirmation wire. There was absolutely no expression on her face when she folded and slipped the paper into the pocket of her jacket. She didn't say thank you, she didn't say good-bye. What she did was stand up, lean over, and whisper in the old man's ear. He nodded and patted her hand.

Winters stood up and walked over to where Lizzie was standing. "You're a hell of a lawyer, young lady. I checked you out after I got here. I wonder if I might have a private word with you and Mr. Udal. You can come, too, Cosmo, if you have nothing else to do," he said in his reedy voice. The spring in his step as he moved around belied that elderly sounding voice. His blue eyes were brighter than stars as he looked from one to the other.

Lizzie offered up her dazzling smile and accepted. "And my friend?" she asked, nodding at Ted.

"Of course, we'll make it a regular party. What shall it be, Peter? The Rabbit Hole?"

Ted's fingers continued their frenzied tapping.

In the security room, Hank Owens was ready to foam at the mouth. "That goddamn old goat is up to something, and he's smart enough to take it out of the Babylon. What the hell did that mean, he researched that woman? Then telling her she's a hell of a lawyer! Goddammit! There's no way we can put someone in there to listen. Udal and Winters would pick up on it in a heartbeat."

His minions knew they weren't expected to respond. Owens was simply venting the way he always did when he got his knickers in a knot.

Owens started to pace, his face full of rage. Something bad was going to go down, and he knew it involved him and his people. "Richards, find a hooker downtown, one who doesn't look like she practices her profession. Dress her down, promise her anything, but get her to the Rabbit Hole before that crew gets there. Tell her to find some old lady to take with her so it looks legitimate. Now, Richards! Not tomorrow. Quintera, see if you can pick up anything on the tapes where that chick was whispering to the old geezer."

Stu Franklin leaned back in his chair. His brain was spinning wildly as he mentally added up his portfolio. With what he had stashed in the Caymans and his portfolio, he could walk away and live very nicely, not luxuriously, for the rest of his life. He'd committed to one more year before getting out of Vegas. One more year would allow for a luxurious lifestyle. But sometimes careful plans just weren't in the cards. Any gambler knew when to hold and when to fold. His gut was telling him it was time to beat a strategic retreat.

"What's wrong with you, Franklin?" Owens snarled. "You look like you're up to something. What?"

Stu uncrossed his legs and stood up. "Actually, Hank, I was wondering what you'll do with whatever information you can get from the Rabbit Hole. It looks to me like there are a few too many people here who can cause trouble. Believe it or not, what happens in Vegas does not always *stay* in Vegas."

Owens stopped his frantic pacing to look down at one of the monitors. *Today must be Fat Lady Day.* Dumpy women wearing the kind of shoes his grandmother used to buy. Floppy hats and shapeless dresses. All old people wore sweaters because of the air-conditioning. These women weren't wearing any kind of wraps. Old people always wore sweaters. Some even wore shawls like his grandmother's. They came in with twenty dollars in free chips, got a free lunch, and left with the same damn twenty chips. He counted the dumpy women milling about as he listened with half an ear to Stu Franklin. Stu usually made sense.

"No one can prove a thing. This *will* stay in Vegas. We're in the clear. Our plan from the beginning was two years. We're acing it. Don't tell me you're turning into a Nervous Nellie."

"No, Hank, I'm not turning into a Nervous Nellie." He wanted to say he'd turned into a Nervous Nellie a week ago, but he wisely kept quiet. Hank Owens was a snake, and Stu didn't trust him out of his sight. He made his decision right then and there. When he broke for lunch he was going to get in his car and head for God knew where. In anticipation of what was happening, he'd packed some of his belongings and stowed them in the trunk of his car. A week ago his plan had been to drive to California, then cross the border into Mexico and hang out there for a while before he split for safer climes.

"I don't know, Stu, you're looking strange to me. I hope you aren't thinking about doing something stupid. I want you down on the floor now. Check out those old ladies. Seven old ladies don't just appear out of nowhere. Not one of them is wearing a sweater. I want to know why they're not wearing sweaters. They usually come on a bus or in some church group. Check them out and get back to me."

Stu shrugged. Anything to get out of this stinking room.

Chapter 20

It all seemed to go down in slow motion, to the horror of Hank Owens, who was glued to the overhead monitors in the security room. He watched as Stu Franklin made his way across the casino floor to where one of the old ladies was banging away at a slot machine that promised if you played long enough you had a chance, with ten million other people, to maybe hit the jackpot of $65,778. His gaze swiveled to another monitor that covered the entrance to the casino, where a horde of men, mostly Asian, and led by Harry Wong, who was in charge of the martial-arts exhibition along with another man, were headed.

"Name's Jack Emery, he's the assistant district attorney in Washington, Boss," Richards said. "No one has checked in yet. We sent a limo for Wong and Emery. The others came in two vans. I think there are about thirty-seven of them. They flew in from all over the world."

"Yeah, well, suddenly I'm not liking this," Owens snarled. "First the woman and Winters and whatever crap is going on at the Rabbit Hole, and now this shit with those old ladies who aren't wearing sweaters. I want every man and woman on our payroll on the floor *right now, goddammit*."

"Boss, you sure you want to do that? It's pretty crowded down there for this time of day. With all that action, the customers are going to get spooked," Richards said nervously.

"I don't pay you to think, Richards, I pay you to follow orders. Now, move your ass and get down there yourself. That goes for the rest of you, too. I'll man the monitors."

Owens watched as Stu Franklin approached a row of slots where one of

the old ladies was hitting the SPIN button
with a vengeance. Owens turned up the
volume on Franklin's mike but could hear
only a rustling sound as Franklin leaned
over and said something to the woman.
Owens fiddled with the volume again, then
started to curse.

Isabelle looked up in alarm at the man
standing next to her. Her hand froze in
midair. From across the aisle, Nikki
stopped playing long enough to rummage
in her purse for money, as she watched
the byplay out of the corner of her eye.

"Lady, listen to me carefully, I don't
have time to say this twice. I think I know
who you are, and I don't care. Upstairs,
there's a bunch of guys watching the two
of us. One of them is convinced of who
you are because you all screwed up and
aren't wearing sweaters. I don't have time
to go into detail. Get up, slap my face, and
storm out of here and pray to God your
friends follow you. Someday when this is
all over, take a vacation in the Caymans
and look me up. I'll be on the beach. By
the way, my name is Stu Franklin. Now, do
it and make it look good."

Kathryn was off her stool and ambling around the minute she saw Nikki move toward the exit, where a large group of men were standing as they eyed the casino floor. Her eyes behind her tinted glasses popped when she saw Isabelle wind up like she was going to throw a fast-ball and sock the guy standing near her smack in the nose. "Shit!" Kathryn muttered. She moved then, as fast as the heavy, ugly-ass shoes covering her feet would allow.

Alexis rounded a corner, took in what was happening to Isabelle, and started to beat on Franklin. She then grabbed Isabelle and dragged her toward the exit as she stroked her back and made soothing comments.

Sensing a commotion and seeing the sudden influx of security, Annie and Myra slid off their stools and started jabbering to one another as they tried to head to the entrance. Yoko was left standing in the middle of the aisle when Harry and his group of martial-arts friends started down the aisle.

"Something's going on," Jack said, as

his gaze swept the swarming groups of security personnel.

"No shit!" Harry said. He looked down the aisle and saw the little Japanese lady, who looked like she was going to faint. He squared his shoulders, looked over to his buddies, and started to babble in all eight of his languages. He reached the little lady just as two bruisers who looked like they could move mountains reached for Yoko's arms. In the blink of an eye they were flat on the ground. Harry looked down, and asked, "Are you okay, Mama San?"

The little lady looked up, and replied, "Mama San, my ass, Harry! I need to get out of here; this place is swarming with security. Do something."

Harry almost laughed. He looked at Jack and shrugged.

Jack looked at Harry and shrugged.

They had their marching orders.

One kick-ass distraction coming up. Harry signaled his friends, and the show was on. Men leaped over stools and slot machines, while others flew through the air, to the delight of the customers banging away at the slots. Whistles and bells were ringing all over the place. An entire row of slot machines toppled one by one. A fat little man could be heard screaming that he'd won the jackpot of fifty dollars on the nickel machine.

In thirteen minutes, an unlucky number in Vegas, it was all over. Harry dusted his hands and looked around at the crowd that had gathered. He, Jack, and the others bowed low and smiled.

"Just your ordinary midday entertainment, compliments of the Babylon. Good luck, everyone!" Jack shouted to be heard above the din.

The nickel-machine winner was hopping up and down in his excitement.

"I'm feeling the love for the first time," Harry said, poking Jack on the arm. "You feeling it, buddy?"

"Oh, yeah," Jack drawled. "I hope we're still feeling it when they haul our asses off to jail."

"I'd like to see them try," Harry said, laughing.

"'Mama San'! Shit, Harry, she's gonna make you pay for that one."

Harry laughed again. "Yeah, I know."

One of Harry's guys, Jun Ye Ling, looked at Harry, and asked, "You want to tell us what the hell that was all about?"

"Nah!"

Ling Jun chuckled as he strode past two Vegas cops, who were wielding their nightsticks as they tried to figure out what had happened.

Jack pulled out his cell phone and dialed Lizzie's number. When her voice came over the line, he recounted the events. "They're going to haul us off to jail any minute now, regardless of what Harry says. Call Charles, we're going to need megabail. Just for the record, Lizzie, I don't do well in jail, and Harry . . . well, Harry might reduce the place to rubble. Then there are the other guys . . . Need I say more?" After breaking the connection, Jack said, "She's on it. I think we should just go peacefully. It will give you time to reflect on that Mama San shit you were dumb enough to utter."

"Christ, how I hate you, Jack. But you know what, I'm definitely feeling the love!" He cackled in glee as a straight line of Vegas cops approached.

They all raised their hands and marched peacefully toward the exit.

Lizzie apologized to the table, then lowered her head and whispered what Jack had told her. "So, Mr. Winters, it looks like I have to ask a favor of you. Can your driver take me to the police station so I can bail out the guys?"

"Of course. I'll come with you. Isn't it up to me to press charges?" the old man asked, his eyes alight with excitement.

"Technically, yes, Homer," Cricket said. "But if they book those guys, it's going to be a lot of paperwork. You could call ahead and chop them off at the knees. Or, I should say, you call ahead and tell them it was all a big misunderstanding and to let everybody go. That way the guys won't be filing any lawsuits saying Owens's boys harassed them, and they were just defending themselves. What do you think, Elizabeth?"

Lizzie loved the way her name sounded on his lips. She smiled and nodded. As they walked out of the Rabbit Hole, she risked a quick glance to her left, where a striking blonde, who looked a little hard around the edges, was so intent on not paying attention to them that she stood out like stinkweed in a bouquet of roses.

Cricket picked up on the glance and gave a slight nod. *That's good,* Lizzie thought, *we're on the same page.* Cricket did make her feel . . . funny all over. Maybe she was just coming down with the flu.

Even at noon, the cars were bumper to bumper. Everyone in the limo was on their cell phones, and Ted was on his Black-Berry. Maggie was just going to love all this cloak-and-dagger stuff. Hell, he was loving it himself.

Ted inclined his head to the left, the better to hear the conversation between Homer Winters and Lizzie. He typed faster.

Winters is going to sell the Babylon. He's had enough of Vegas. He's going to look for a buyer. Lizzie says she knows someone who might be interested. Annie? That guy Fish? Maybe partners? Gotta go, babe. You taking good care of Minnie and Mickey?

* * *

Back at The Party Store van, Kathryn shifted gears and pulled out onto Las Vegas Boulevard. "Will someone tell me what the hell happened back there?" She blew her horn, yanked at the steering wheel, and skirted around a MINI Cooper full of lookie-loos.

The women all started to jabber at once, with Annie yapping about seeing a pair of white rhinestone boots in one of the boutiques. "I could see them clear as crystal from where I was sitting. I have to get those. I really do."

"Put a lid on it, Annie," Myra said as she yanked and pulled at the pearls around her neck.

"Who was that guy, Isabelle, and what did he say?" Nikki asked. "The minute I saw the look on your face, I knew something was up. It's a good thing we acted in sync, or we'd be on our way to the police station."

Isabelle took a deep breath. "He warned me to get out and said I should sock him in the snoot. He said his name was Stu Franklin. Maybe he thought the name would mean something to me. I never heard it before. He said he *thought* he knew who I was, and my friends, but the guy upstairs spying on us knew who we were for sure because we weren't wearing sweaters. He said when it was all over I should look him up in the Caymans, he'd be on the beach. He had a microphone on his sleeve—you know, the kind Secret Service guys wear. He had his thumb over it. I did say that, didn't I? He scared the living hell out of me."

"Good thing. You could be a slugger for the Padres the way you hauled off and popped him," Alexis said.

"You did okay yourself when you started beating on him. Boy, did his nose bleed a lot. There was blood all over the place. I guess I don't know my own power," Isabelle said.

"We fooled Harry. He didn't know it was me. He even called me Mama San. Sometimes I'm so good I can't stand myself." Yoko giggled. "Yes, yes, I will make him pay for referring to me as Mama San. But not too much, I think."

"Child, that man saved our . . . bacon. Did I say that right, Kathryn?" Annie asked.

Kathryn nodded, her eyes on the road and the rearview mirror.

"Where *are* we going?" Myra asked.

Kathryn looked over her shoulder. "The only place I can think of for the moment is the condo Rena Gold got for Lizzie and Ted. Someone needs to call them, and sooner rather than later. If we see any other tenants, they'll just think we're a small group of seniors getting together for mahjong or something just as stupid. Tiddlywinks, maybe."

"That was really a little too close for comfort," Nikki said.

"Did any of you see Mr. Fish and his party?" Alexis asked. "They were right there when Harry and his boys arrived. I'm sure it was he, but I didn't want to stay around to make sure. Why did that guy Franklin help us?"

Isabelle felt like the question was directed to her, so she answered. "You know how we all think Lizzie is hot *and* smart, right? Well, Franklin was hot, and I think he's probably pretty smart. He looked sharp to me. I think he was on his way out, and we were just there at the right time to help him out. At the same time, he helped us. He doesn't want to get involved in whatever is happening, but that's just a guess on my part. I can't swear to this, but the way he said he would be in the Caymans, I had the feeling he was going to walk out the door and head for there ASAP. I could be wrong, but that was my thought at that moment. I believe we should think of it as the guy having an epiphany, and we were the beneficiaries, and let it go at that. We don't have a tail, do we?"

"No," Kathryn shot back. "So far, so good."

"I really wanted those boots," Annie grumbled. "It won't be the same if I end up buying them from some catalog. One pair of boots! I'm not leaving here until I get them."

"Annie, dear, I promise you that somehow, some way, you will get your rhinestone cowgirl boots before we leave this fair city," Myra said.

"Oh, Myra, I knew you'd understand," Annie said happily.

The rest of the trip to Rena Gold's condo was made in silence.

* * *

"Well, that was a cluster fuck if I ever saw one," Owens railed at his staff. "I hired you to take care of things. Did you do that? Read my lips, no, you did not. I'm going to dock all of you a day's pay. This shit will be out on the street in seconds. Winters is going to hear about it, and for sure there will be hell to pay. Richards, what's up with the hooker? You on top of that? What's going on at the Rabbit Hole? Where the hell is Stu? His mike went out just when that old dame socked him silly."

"The last time I saw him he was headed for the men's room, his nose was bleeding. Then things went south, and I never saw him again," Oliver said.

"He's not answering his mike or his pager. Send someone to check the parking lot. If his car's gone, we have a problem," Owens snarled.

Quintera, Richards, and Oliver stood rooted to the spot. It sounded to all of them like Hank was saying somehow Stu was responsible for the disaster on the casino floor. All three of them liked Stu.

"He might have gone home to change his clothes if he got blood all over his suit.

You are pretty fussy about us looking like we stepped out of a *GQ* ad, Boss," Richards said in Stu's defense.

"Send a couple of guys to his condo. If they have to, tell them to pick the lock."

Quintera wasn't liking where this all was going. "Maybe the woman broke his nose, and he went to a doctor or the hospital. There was a lot of blood, Boss."

"Then have someone check it out. Do you guys ever make a decision on your own? Do any of you have a clue what's going on?"

"He's one of us, Boss. It don't seem right checking on him like this. And you know what else, Hank, I'm getting a little tired of you constantly telling us how dumb we are. Without us, where do you think you'd be? We've covered your ass for years."

"*Was* one of us. And you were paid to do that. You want out, there's the door, and don't let it hit you in the ass on your way out." Owens smelled revolution in the air. He toned down his anger, and said, "If something happened to Stu, I want to know. If he took himself to the hospital, we'll send flowers. If I have to, I'll buy him a new suit. But if he sold us out and took off, we need to know now. Not later, when our dicks get caught in the wringer."

Richards looked over his shoulder to where he'd left his cell phone on the desk after he heard it ring. He felt like blessing himself at the relief he felt. Anything to get out from under Owens's mean little eyes. He barked a greeting, then listened. He took a deep breath to steel himself against what he had to tell his boss. He closed his cell phone and stuck it in his pocket.

"That was . . . the lady we put in place at the Rabbit Hole. The party sat down and were chatting about nothing, then the woman's cell phone rang and she walked to the door to take the call with her back to our . . . our person. She returned to the table, turned her back again, then whispered something to all of them. They all got up and left. That's all she knows. They had ordered food but paid for it without waiting to eat. She did her best, Boss."

Owens nodded as he stared at one of the monitors that covered a poker table where Little Fish was playing. He pursed his lips as he watched the man he hated with a passion throw down a straight flush and rake in a pile of chips. He was so angry that he was almost cross-eyed.

Quintera's cell rang. He listened. "Stu's car isn't in the lot. Myron should be at his condo in five minutes. Myron said Hattie called the hospital and both clinics. Stu didn't show up. I don't even know if Stu has a personal doctor. I never heard him say he did, but Stu was not one to talk about his personal life. He was a loner, you know that, Boss."

Owens did know that. It was one of the reasons he'd picked Stu to join his inner ring. "What about his ex-wife?"

"She moved back to Texas after the divorce, and before you can ask, I don't know if there's anyone he's seeing on a regular basis. With the hours we put in, I don't see how he could even find anyone who would be willing to put up with his work schedule."

Ten minutes later Oliver's cell rang. He listened and said, "Okay, come on back."

"What?" Owens bellowed.

"Stu's car is in his designated parking

space at his condo. His bloody clothes are in the bathroom. Nothing looks out of place. His refrigerator is full of food. He's got a lot of books, lots and lots of DVDs. Today's paper was on the coffee table, still rolled up. The bed was made, the towels wet like he maybe took a shower. He's got luggage in his closet. Plenty of shoes and sneakers. No computer. The guy has a ton of clothes, so my guy couldn't tell if anything was missing. His golf clubs were by the front door. Toothbrush and shaving gear are still in the bathroom. My guy said Stu is a neat freak."

Owens could feel his stomach muscles knot up. "What about his laptop? Stu had a laptop. I know, because that's how he kept track of his investments."

"Maybe it's in his car, but the car is locked."

"Quintera, call DMV and ask them if they have any other vehicles registered to Stu." Owens knew it was going to be a dead end. Stu had simply walked away. He knew it because if he had been in Franklin's position, he would have done it the same way. He said a mental good-bye to Stu Franklin. There would be no trail to follow, that much he knew. He also knew Stu wouldn't give any of them up. Stu was like those goddamn ninjas that hit the nation's capital—he had simply disappeared into thin air. Bastard!

Chapter 21

Rena's condo, while spacious, was suddenly overcrowded as Lizzie, Ted, and all seven vigilantes moved about. Myra was on the phone with Charles, explaining what was needed to complete the mission. Nikki was talking to Jack, who was growling that she and her Sisters were out of their minds, while Yoko and Harry did a little billing and cooing, the offensive Mama San comment in the holding corral, waiting to be trotted out at another time. Annie was doing her best to track down her rhinestone cowgirl boots. Kathryn was breathless as she spoke to Bert, congratulating him on his appointment as director of the FBI. She did her best to allay his fears where she was concerned by telling him she and the girls knew exactly what they were doing.

Alexis and Isabelle were poring over diagrams on Alexis's laptop from her Red Bag. "As long as we have a *rough outline* of what we're planning, no one will know the difference. We can make it up as we go along. Do you agree?"

Isabelle laughed. Her thoughts were far away, in the Cayman Islands. She wondered if she'd ever get a chance to make the trip. In all probability, no. But a girl could dream, couldn't she?

In the kitchen, Lizzie and Ted were discussing their departure and waiting for Maggie to tell them what time wheels up would be. Ted looked down at the incoming message, and said, "Two hours and thirty minutes. Looks like we're going to miss all the fun."

"Not really. I'll dictate your story to you on the plane. Trust me, it will be the same as if you were there. I can even tell you who's going to win the exhibition. Harry will feed you the terminology when it's time to write up the match."

Ted nodded. "You're looking kind of . . . I don't know, sad, maybe. Is anything wrong, Lizzie?"

Lizzie forced a smile. "What could be wrong? My world is right side up. I just picked up a client who guaranteed my old-age security, and I met some very nice, interesting people along the way. I have no doubt Marble Rose and her mother will make peace with each other at some point in the very near future. I can brag that I actually won forty dollars in a slot machine. I don't think it gets any better than that, do you?"

Ted shrugged just as Lizzie's cell phone rang. She looked down at the caller ID, and a smile to rival the sun split her features. She turned away to take the call. Ted actually stopped tapping his Black-Berry to try to listen.

"When did that happen? Someone just delivered it? Don't you mean if it goes to trial? I think we both know that isn't going to happen. My . . . uh, people don't believe in using taxpayers' money. They prefer to take care of matters on their own. Yes, there is a lot to be said for that. The incoming director of the FBI is in town. You might want to share your newfound treasure with him to . . . avoid any future difficulties. Well, now that you ask, there is something you can do for me . . ."

Ted almost fell off his chair as he tried to hear whatever it was Lizzie wanted the person on the other end of the line to do for her, but he simply couldn't pull it off. He just knew that whatever it was, Maggie was going to go into a snit when he couldn't tell her. He listened again.

"Actually, we'll be wheels up in two hours and fifteen minutes. Yes, well, it was nice meeting you, too. You take care of this end, I'll take care of mine, and I'm sure one of these days we'll meet up again."

Lizzie closed her cell phone, turned around, and looked at Ted, her eyes bright and shiny. Ted thought she was going to cry at any moment. The awesome Lizzie Fox crying. The odds of that happening were about the same as a hurricane hitting the desert.

Ted knew this was a very important moment in Lizzie's life. Sometimes, according to Maggie, people didn't have the good sense to take advantage of such moments.

"Lizzie, it's okay to be tough as nails, and I admire that trait in you. But it's also okay to wear your heart on your sleeve once in a while. I wasn't eavesdropping," he lied, "but I assume that was Cricket you were talking to. Why don't you call him back and invite him to Washington or, better yet, stay over another day? Take some personal time. That guy is yours for the asking. If you want him, that is. I'm a guy, I know these things. There must have been a time in your life when you were . . . you know, into guys and all the romance that goes with it. Let your hair down and go for it. Let it all hang out."

Lizzie's features softened. She leaned over, touched Ted's cheek, then kissed him on the tip of his nose. "I don't know how, Ted," she whispered.

Ted saw the tears, heard the anguish, felt the body tremors. And then the moment was gone, and Ted wasn't sure if he'd imagined it all or not.

"Well, if you think smacking up two million dollars' worth of machinery is going to get you anywhere, you're wrong. That guy is looking for . . . for you, Lizzie. He knows you did it. And he hasn't made a peep in your direction." Ted knew he was losing her right that second. He had to try another tack. "Damn, if that guy isn't the ugliest man I've ever seen. I don't know what you see in him." Lizzie's eyes sparked. That was good, he had her. Maggie was going to be so proud of him.

"You're no prize yourself, Ted," Lizzie snapped.

"I know! I know! You see, now you're getting it! I'm almost as ugly as Cricket. Chicks don't like guys whose hair turns red in the sun. My ears, if I flap them right, allow me to fly. I have too many freckles, I'm skinny, and I don't have a spleen. But Maggie loves me anyway." Then the one word in the whole world that Lizzie detested shot out of his mouth faster than a bullet. "Coward!"

Lizzie's eyes burned so bad she thought she'd been caught in a sand- storm. Her head high, she marched into the bedroom, where she changed her clothes. Skintight leather pants, ankle boots with hooker heels, Harley-Davidson jacket, and a Chanel purse. She picked up her briefcase and marched out to the living room.

The vigilantes stopped what they were doing to stare at Lizzie. They all knew something was different, they just didn't know what it was.

Her voice wasn't brisk and professional, it wasn't lilting and melodious, either. It was dead flat when she said, "I have a few last-minute things to take care of, and with the traffic in this town, it's time for Ted and me to leave. I'll see you all back in D.C." She forced a smile. "I think your plan is awesome, and I wish you luck. See you."

"Something's wrong," Kathryn said, when the door closed behind Lizzie and Ted. "We should have done something. Hugged her, kissed her, *something*. She's always there for us, no questions asked."

Annie walked over to the middle of the circle where the women were sitting on the floor. She flopped down next to Myra. "Lizzie's in love, and she doesn't know what to do about it," she said softly.

Myra nodded. The others looked at each other in stupefied amazement.

"I probably shouldn't tell you this

because Jack told me in confidence, but I don't think he'll mind if I tell you what happened last Christmas with Lizzie." Nikki talked softly, recounting Jack's experience at the cemetery. "And there you have it! There's nothing any of us can do. This is something Lizzie will have to work through."

The silence following Nikki's words was stunning.

"I think we need to finalize our plans, girls," Myra said as she struggled to her feet. "Charles has assured me that while our requests were a bit out of the ordinary, he can and will comply. Actually, he was choking on his own laughter when we hung up. One of the things Lizzie still has to do is get in touch with Homer Winters. He will make his call promptly at seven o'clock. That means we all have to be in position at that time. Now, let's do one more run-through to make sure we don't hit any snags along the way. Positions, girls!"

Lizzie hit every shoe boutique in just about every hotel on the Strip and was told the same thing, there had been a run on white rhinestone cowgirl boots, and they had none in stock in a size 8. Her shoulders sagging, Lizzie climbed back into Homer Winters's limo. "I cannot believe in this whole damn town no one has one pair of those stupid boots. I guess you didn't have any luck, either," she snarled at Ted.

Ted shook his head. Not for all the chips in Vegas would he tell Lizzie he found a pair in a size 7 that he had the store send to Maggie by overnight mail. "We're running late, Lizzie."

"Ask me if I care? The plane isn't going to leave without us since we're the only two passengers. God, I hope there's some food on board."

It was five o'clock, thirty minutes past scheduled takeoff time, and the Gulfstream was burning jet fuel when Lizzie ran up the steps, Ted behind her. The minute they reached the top, the portable stairway was being pushed away.

Ted didn't know why he turned because he couldn't hear anything over the sound of the jet's engines. Lumbering across the tarmac with a horde of airline employees was Cosmo Cricket, who looked like he was shouting at the top of his lungs. As Ted marveled at the speed of the big man he reached for Lizzie's arm and spun her around. "Lizzie, this is where the rubber meets the road. It's your show now."

And then a huge box sailed upward, and Ted caught it. Cricket cupped his hands around his mouth, and yelled, "Boots!"

Lizzie leaned so far out the door, Ted had to hold on to her arm. He knew everyone in Vegas could hear her when she shouted, "I want a plain gold wedding band!"

Cosmo Cricket's fist shot in the air as he was led away by airport security.

The pilot, the copilot, and the steward clapped their hands and whistled.

"Attagirl, Lizzie."

Lizzie looked like she was in a daze as she buckled up. "I did do that, didn't I?"

"Oh, yeah," Ted drawled.

Lizzie closed her eyes, and said, "I've never been married. I wonder what it's like to wake up every morning and have that special person lying next to you. I can't believe I . . . I'm not dreaming, am I, Ted?"

"No, Lizzie, you're not dreaming. I think

you committed big-time, and I think it will
be everything you want it to be. You guys
going to practice law together? I can see it
now, Cricket and Fox. Or, Fox and Cricket.
Who the hell is going to hire you with a firm
named Cricket and Fox?"

Lizzie started to laugh and couldn't
stop.

Ted opened the box he was holding on
his lap and held up a pair of white leather
boots studded with colored rhinestones.
Size 8.

Annie de Silva was going to go over the
moon. His fingers, whose blisters had blisters, tapped the words *Happy ending* on
his BlackBerry.

At six o'clock the vigilantes closed up
the condo and made their way down the
eighteen flights of steps to the back of the
building, which had no windows. There
were three gigantic Dumpsters blocking
the entrance, allowing room for only a single car to pass through. Huge signs in
bright red letters said the Dumpsters were
full and to use the ones on the south side
of the building.

Their vehicle stood, black, shiny, and

ominous, just outside the exit door. Kathryn shivered and observed, "I do believe our ride is here."

The women took a moment to stare at their transportation: a long black hearse driven by Jack Emery, with Harry Wong, his assistant, sitting on the passenger side. Both men wore somber black suits.

No one was in a hurry to climb into the back of the hearse. Jack and Harry had to prod them.

"It creeps me out," Kathryn grumbled.

"What's that smell?" Annie asked.

"Beats me," Jack said cheerfully.

Harry slammed the door shut with such violence that the curtains on the side of the hearse fell to the floor. As one, the women screamed. Harry and Jack laughed.

"How long before we get there?" Isabelle asked in a quaking voice.

"As long as it takes," Harry said. "Lots of traffic today."

The women sat on the floor in the back of the vehicle as they hissed and snarled at one another and blamed Charles for this affront to their dignity.

Annie looked around at their surroundings. "So this is what it's like. Well, when we finally have to take our last ride, we'll know. And I didn't get my boots either. Oh, I just hate this."

Myra reached up and pinched her nose to make her stop talking.

"Just breathe through your mouth," Nikki said, as Annie made gagging sounds.

"You guys better not get sick back there," Jack hooted. "Want some music? There's a DVD player up here." When there were no takers, he observed, "This is really a smooth ride, isn't it, Harry? These babies must have some superb shocks in them."

"SHUT UP, JACK!" Nikki screamed. "Can't you go any faster?"

"Hearses only go twenty miles an hour. That's in the handbook. Harry read it. Fifteen is the recommended speed, so we're five miles over the limit. Just sit back and enjoy the ride, knowing you're going to get out when I bring this goddamn fucking vehicle to a complete stop at the mortuary."

The women clamped their lips shut, until Yoko said, "I feel like something is crawling all over me."

"Me, too," Isabelle said.

Twenty minutes later, Jack said, "Okay, ladies, look *alive* here, no pun intended.

We have arrived! You have to wait while we get out to open the door. That was in the handbook, too. One time, some mortician forgot to lock it, and the casket slid out and landed in the middle of I-95 in Florida. Stopped traffic for days until they could figure whose jurisdiction it was in. That was in the handbook, too. You know, case histories or Mortuary 101, something like that. It never happened again. Families get irate when things like that happen, so morticians have to really be on top of shit like that."

"Kill him right now!" Annie said, landing on the asphalt driveway.

"I would if I had a gun," Myra replied. "Enough already, we don't have much time. We need to get in place."

"What time is it?" Yoko asked.

"Twenty minutes of seven," Kathryn said. "Alexis, where's your Red Bag?"

"Harry took it in."

Jack took a moment to look around at the line of shiny black hearses under the portico. Six in all. He wondered how much it had cost Charles to rent the place for the evening. Probably a bundle. Like Yoko, he was starting to itch. He took one last look around and entered the building. He hated the sound the door made when it locked behind him.

The scent of cloying flowers was so intense, Jack found himself gagging as he followed the women to the front of the building, where somber music was playing in the background. He thought he smelled incense. He passed a chapel loaded with fresh bouquets. He decided right then that he never wanted to live in a place that had such a robust dying business. Twelve lay-out rooms. Translation, according to the handbook, twelve bodies for viewing at any given time. Only six hearses. He shrugged. Two a day would work.

Suddenly, he found himself in a short hallway facing a door that said, in stark black letters, EMPLOYEES ONLY. He opened it and looked inside. Rows and rows of caskets lined the room. Bronze, silver, wood, aluminum, white, big, small. All were on wheels. He turned to run and bumped into Harry, who was bug-eyed. "Chop-chop, Harry, we have to get these back to the . . . what the hell did the handbook call it?"

"THE WORKROOM."

"Yeah, yeah, the workroom. C'mon pedal to the metal, we need to get four of these babies into that workroom."

Harry protested his outrage. "What? You're leaving the decision up to me? No, no! That damn book said the lining had to go with the . . . that thing. You want lavender, you want tufted, you want silk or satin. You want pillows in a different color. Jesus Christ, Jack, it's all I can do to look at these things, much less pick one."

"Okay, okay, let's forget the mix and match and just take the four closest to the door."

"They have price tags on them," Harry said in awe.

"The mortician's handy-dandy handbook did say on page ninety-three that it was expensive to die and to be gentle when mentioning the top-of-the-line prices. Mahogany, as I recall, is the best seller."

"Eat shit, Jack," Harry said as he started pushing one of the caskets out the oversize door. "Oh, damn, they don't turn corners. We're going to need some help here."

Jack froze. "Are you saying you want me to go back to that . . . that *workroom* and tell the women we need help?"

"All right, you're right. I lost my head there for a minute. You help me, then I'll scoot back here and help you. Whee!" he shouted as he took a running leap and pushed a polished-bronze coffin down the hall with so much force it hit the swinging doors and came to a dead stop in the workroom. As one, the women screamed. "One down and three to go!" Harry shouted.

"This is lovely," Annie said as she fingered the shirring on the satin coverlet. "I never really liked lavender. Peach is more subtle."

A glorious, oversize silver coffin appeared. "Two down and two to go," Jack said breathlessly. "What time is it?"

"There's your peach," Myra sniffed. "It's seven ten. Did the actor who is supposed to be impersonating the owner get here yet?"

"I have no clue. As you can see, I've been rather busy."

"We ordered pizza. If you see the delivery-man, tell him to come around back," Kathryn said.

Jack raced back to the workroom, where Harry was waiting for him. "They ordered pizza. Don't say it, Harry. C'mon, c'mon, this sucker is really heavy. How come the lid is closed?"

"Oh, shit! You don't suppose . . ."

"Nah!"

"Check, Jack."

"You check, Harry."

Together they inched up the lid, then slammed it shut. "I guess the owner didn't know what to do with his . . . that person, so he shoved him in here, not knowing our plans. Okay, back him up and take another one. While you're doing that, I have to check to see if our actor arrived and to make arrangements for the pizza."

Harry broke a sweat as he pushed, shoved, angled, and finally parked the spiffy aluminum casket off to the side. He yanked, shoved, and kicked at the wheels of what looked like a solid-oak casket and felt like it. He was waiting at the corner for Jack, who came on the run, then ran back for the last one. Jack was huffing and puffing and looking forward to the pizza when Harry returned to help him maneuver around the corner.

"Done!" both men shouted as they lined up number four next to number three.

"What time is it?" someone asked.

"Seven twenty," Myra said, just as a knock sounded on the workroom door. "I do believe that's our pizza."

Jack opened the door, paid the driver, and accepted four pizzas, while Harry reached for a cardboard tray of soft drinks.

"I think I hear a car. Hurry, Jack, get outside. The minute those guys are in here, lock the door from the outside. Be sure to lock the front door after the actor leaves," Harry said.

Jack was gone a minute later, taking up his position outside the showroom, all but invisible to the naked eye. He listened to four sets of footsteps as they marched down the tile floor to the workroom. When he heard the door clang shut behind the men, he sprinted forward, slid the bar across the door, then ran back to the welcoming foyer, where the somber music was still playing. He paid the actor three hundred dollars and locked the door behind him. He waited behind the frosted glass till he saw the man drive out of the parking lot before he sprinted back down the hall. He was breathing like a racehorse, so he leaned against the wall until his respiration returned to normal. He looked down at his watch. Right on schedule. He slid the bar and opened the door.

A standoff, guns drawn, just like in an old, silly Western movie. Owens whirled, as did the remaining members of the inner ring, at the sound of the door opening. Harry and the vigilantes moved in sync, and before Jack could blink twice, all four men were on the floor. He gathered up the deadly looking weapons and tossed them into one of the sinks.

The women looked at one another and shrugged.

"Let's put Owens on the table, strap him down, and hook up the other three to those contraptions under the caskets. For sure they won't be going anywhere," Nikki said as she whipped out a package of flexicuffs.

The others dragged the members of the inner ring over to the caskets, while Jack and Harry hoisted Hank Owens onto the embalming table. They strapped him down, then everyone washed their hands.

With no seats available, the women slouched against the wall as they ate their pizza and gulped at their drinks. The conversation ranged from Annie's inability to get her white boots with the rhinestones to Harry's certainty that Ling Jun was going to win the competition to Jack saying Vegas sure knew how to make a good pizza.

All four men came around at the same time as they tried to figure out what had happened. Owens roared with rage, while the other three took in their surroundings with fear radiating from their pores.

Kathryn stirred from her spot against the wall and walked over to the embalming table. "Kathryn Lucas," she said by way of introduction. "I'm one of the vigilantes. We brought you here because we want something from you. If you don't give us what we want, we're going to embalm you right here on this table. You will, of course, have to tell us where to send the bodies when we're finished."

Words, some of which the women had never heard before, all of them curses, flew about the room.

"I'm not telling you anything, you'll go to

jail for this. Do you hear me? Don't tell these bitches anything," Owens ordered.

"What do you want to know?" the three tied to the caskets asked.

"It's simple. How, what, when, why, and where's the money you ripped off the Strip?" Nikki asked.

"It was Owens's idea," Quintera revealed. "He said we'd be on easy street and no one would ever know. He said money is power, and we had it. The NGC couldn't touch us. Then that stupid girl came along and screwed things up just by being there. He was the mastermind. Stu got out. He just walked out of the casino today and never came back."

Owens struggled beneath the straps as he bellowed for Quintera to shut his mouth.

A crust of the pizza clutched between her teeth, Annie walked over to the embalming table and flicked at the hoses that drained into a huge outflow port on the floor. She removed the crust of pizza, and asked, "Which one is the intake and which one is the outflow?"

Kathryn pondered the question. "I think

this one drains the blood and that one shoots in the embalming fluid. But, I'm not sure. Do you think it matters, Annie?"

Annie chomped down on the pizza crust. "Probably not. But I'm thinking maybe we should have practiced a little more. What if we make a mistake?"

"Oh, well!" Kathryn said.

"Where's your share of the money, Mr. Owens?" Annie asked.

"I know all about you women. You don't kill people, you just screw up their lives. I'm telling you dickshit."

Alexis and Isabelle walked over to the embalming table and looked around. Something that looked like a pump was sitting on the floor. Neither one knew what it was other than that a plug was in a socket. Alexis turned it on to see if it made noise.

It did. She turned it off. The silence in the room was deafening.

"Where's your share of the money, Owens? This is the last time I'm going to ask you."

"And this is the last time I'm telling you to go to hell."

"Greed is a terrible thing, Mr. Owens," Myra said.

The three men attached to the caskets were jabbering about where their money was. "He has a safe in his office, and that's where he keeps his computer. He sends it all offshore," one of the men said.

Annie walked over to them and stooped so she was eye level with the men. "You know, just because you're hooked up to these particular caskets doesn't mean they're the ones you have to go out in. Take your pick. Silver and peach, bronze and lavender, mahogany with quilted lining. Owens gets the one that's left, and may I say it is the bottom of the line. It wouldn't be my choice at all. Or, anyone's I know, for that matter."

Quintera blacked out. Oliver's eyes rolled back in his head, and Richards started to whimper.

Annie continued, "Your buddy Stu Franklin had his laptop hand-delivered to Peter Udal at the NGC earlier today. Udal, in turn, gave it to their legal counsel, Cosmo Cricket. Now," she said, turning to Richards and Oliver, "if you tell us every-thing we want to know, like the password to Owens's computer and the combination to his safe, we'll let you go, and this will all be just a nightmare you want to forget."

"Are you nuts?" Richards barked. "Do you think for one minute that crazy son of a bitch would tell us *that?* Think again."

"He's probably right," Kathryn said. "You better come up with something fast, or one of you is next on that table." She turned around, and said, "So, it's back to you, Mister Owens. Last chance."

Nikki peered down at a stainless steel tray and picked up what looked like a scalpel. "Does it make a difference where we slice him to insert the tubes?"

"They always do it in the groin area on *CSI,*" Annie chirped.

"Then the groin it is," Nikki said as she sliced away at Owens's five-thousand-dollar suit. "Ah, tighty whities. I would have taken him for a boxer guy. Hey, Yoko, what did the book say about the blood?"

"The book assumed the person was dead, so no blood. As he's alive, it's going to spurt. Even if you get the hose in quickly, it's still going to shoot all over and make a mess. How do they combat that on *CSI,* Annie?"

"I think they only work on dead bodies. Did we decide which is intake and out-flow?" Annie asked. "Or did we say it doesn't matter?"

"I think we're going with *it doesn't matter,*" Kathryn said. "Just slice and dice, and let's get on with it. We can always take a shower later."

Alexis turned on the machine at her feet. Nikki bent over, the scalpel poised. She reached for the band of Owen's underwear and sliced downward, expos-ing his private parts. "Hmmm," she said as she pulled at his left leg. "Right side or left side?"

"Is he a left kind of guy or a right kind of guy?" Kathryn asked.

"Actually, they're hanging in the middle like he can't decide. I can barely see any-thing," Annie chirped. "Go with the right, Nikki."

Nikki backed up a step. "I should be wearing my glasses for this. Did anyone see them?"

"Wear mine, dear," Myra said, fishing in her pocket for her reading glasses.

Nikki slipped them on, and said, "It makes such a difference for up-close work."

She jabbed the tip of the scalpel into Owens's skin, and he yelped so loud the room shook.

"Okay, okay, you crazy bitch. Untie me, and I'll tell you."

"It doesn't work that way. You tell us, *then* we untie you. First, you give us the combination to your safe. We'll call Mr. Winters, who will then have the contents delivered here to us by the same kind gentleman who gave you the story about Stu and admitted you when you first arrived. You know, to satisfy yourself that Stu Franklin was dead, and you were coming to identify the body. Now, what is it?"

Owens rattled off the number. Jack stirred himself to open his cell to call Homer Winters. "Twenty minutes, give or take. Harry will meet the guy up front."

While they waited for their delivery, Annie prowled around the room, checking out all the bottles and jars. The others continued to nibble on the remaining pizza.

"Cover me up," Owens said.

Myra walked over to the embalming table and looked down. "Why should we? You act like there's something to see. There isn't. Now be quiet, or I'll take matters into my own hands. Well, not literally, I'm very careful what kind of garbage I touch. By the way, Mr. Owens, I'm curious about something. Mr. Franklin said you got onto us because of sweaters. Explain that, please."

Owens was so drained he responded. "Old people always wear sweaters when they plan to be in the casinos for a few hours. We keep it cold on purpose so people don't get sluggish. None of you were wearing sweaters. Maybe if one or two of you had had them on, I wouldn't have paid any attention."

Myra looked at the others. She shrugged.

Thirty minutes later, Harry was back with two huge manila envelopes full of cash and Owens's laptop. Nikki popped it open, powered up, and turned to Jack. "I can't transfer any of his stuff until I have a place to send it. Call Mr. Udal and have him give you an account somewhere.

"Let's have your password, Mr. Owens, and don't make me work for it."

"Lucky six."

Nikki typed in the password and sat back as numbers flashed on the screen. Even she was impressed. She heard Jack telling Udal to stay on the line as he repeated the numbers to Nikki, who immediately input them into the computer. She blinked as funds moved at the speed of light until the balance registered zero.

"Done!"

Kathryn walked over to the three men tied to the caskets. "Do you know your account numbers? I wouldn't lie if I were you. Easy, easy, one at a time."

Nikki's fingers went to work. "Funny how these jerks all used the same brokerage, the same banks, the same offshore banks.

"Done!"

"Okay, you got it all. You said you'd cut us loose if we gave it up," Owens said.

"And you believed me? You really are a bunch of jerks. Just lie here and reflect, Mr. Owens. There will be some people here shortly to take care of you." By *people,* Nikki meant Bert Navarro, Duncan Wright, his best field agent, and Elias Cummings, who would be doing the cleanup work.

"Tidy up, girls! Wipe everything down and don't miss anything. Trash in the Dumpster outside. Don't forget the guns in the sink. Jack, did Winters give security the night off?" Nikki asked.

"Yep. The floor is wide-open tonight for anyone interested in trying his or her luck. No rules on this night!" Jack said as he smacked his hands in anticipation of a beginner's gambling luck. Nikki would bring him luck, he was sure of it.

"Girls, it's time to do a little shake, rattle, and roll! Vegas, here we come," Annie said as she led the way out of the mortuary.

Outside in the parking area, all the women said in unison, "I'm not riding in that *thing* again."

"Let's go public and take taxis," Myra said, excitement ringing in her voice.

"Myra, you rock! You really do," Annie said as she walked toward the road that would take them to the boulevard, where they could hail a taxi. "Do you have any idea what kind of statement we could make if we had those boots? All right, all right, Myra, I won't say another word about the boots."

As the first cab slid to the curb, Annie turned. "We did good, girls! I think we earned our money. Now, let's see how much we can *WIN* and get out alive to tell about it."

A tourist who was passing by with his digital camera narrowed his eyes at the sight of the familiar-looking women. He looked over at his wife, who nodded. He snapped and snapped again.

The tourist and his wife went home to Perth Amboy, New Jersey, winners to the tune of $25,000. Compliments of the *Las Vegas Sun*.

Epilogue

Back on the mountain it was still dark out but they were all in the dining room, fully dressed, waiting for Charles to print out the morning editions from the online papers.

Expectations were running high. "There's no way she can't win," Lizzie said. With very little arm twisting, Lizzie had convinced her new employers in Las Vegas and Homer Winters to kick in the money at the eleventh hour to cover Martine's television blitz, which had hit the airwaves with such force, the other side had virtually collapsed from the onslaught.

The women made small talk, nibbling

on blueberry muffins and sipping coffee and juice.

Maggie Spritzer looked around the table and laughed. "C'mon, you know she won!"

Nellie, minus her new husband, smiled as she looked down at her feet. "I never thought I'd be wearing white rhinestone cowgirl boots. Elias says they are definitely me. And, I never thought I'd have Elvis sing 'Love Me Tender' at my wedding."

The others held out their feet to show that they, too, were wearing the coveted boots. Even Myra sported a pair, and said they kept her feet and legs warm.

"Does anyone have any other news? Worthy news?" Kathryn asked.

"What's taking so long?" Nikki asked.

No one answered her.

The front door opened, and a strong gust of wind blew into the dining room. Charles held up a sheaf of printouts and chortled, "We now have a female president. The headline in the *Post* said it was because of a massive influx of money that came in rather suddenly that pushed Connor ahead. Actually, the words the paper used were 'massive onslaught of money at just the right time.'

"Now, ladies, what would you like for breakfast? Just say the words, and it's yours."

"What's that noise?" Kathryn asked. She ran to the door and looked out.

"Charles, it's a helicopter! Who's coming? I didn't know we were expecting company," Nikki said.

"We aren't. All of you stay here, I'll see what this is all about."

"Like he thinks we're going to sit here and wait to find out! I-don't-think-so!" Annie said as she grabbed her jacket, her new boots pounding the oak floor. The others followed suit.

Outside in the blustery wind, the steady *whump-whump* of the helicopter blades was so loud that the women covered their ears.

Kathryn, who bragged that she had the best eyesight of all of them, squealed and yelped, "Look what it says on the helicopter. Air Force One. Oh, myyyy Godddd!"

The women huddled together as they tried to figure out what was going on. A tall, distinguished-looking man stepped to the ground and ran over to where Charles was standing.

"We had a bit of engine trouble and needed to set down. I hope you don't mind. Won't take but a minute to fix. My passenger would like a word with you all. Follow me. Feel free to climb aboard. You have exactly four minutes before I find out what the trouble is. Or isn't," he mumbled under his breath.

The women ran forward and there was the new president-elect of the United States standing with her arms outstretched in the open doorway.

Lizzie was the closest. Martine Connor hugged her. "We developed some mysterious engine problems when we were overhead. We saw your lights and set down. Where did all that money come from? God, Lizzie, how do I thank you?"

"No thanks necessary. We had a deal, Miz President. You renege, and we'll come after you. You know that, right? Doesn't matter if you're the chief exec or not. We have to be clear on that. My ladies are not known for their patience. We need to be clear on that, too."

"Tell me something I don't know. Where I come from, a deal's a deal. Nice boots, Lizzie! Oh, my goodness, I think they found the problem. Come to visit sometime, but be sure to call ahead. I'll be sure to reserve the Lincoln Bedroom."

The newly elected commander in chief reached out her hand to touch each of the vigilantes. She smiled and winked. The women all nearly swooned with joy. The first woman to be elected president of the United States had *touched* them. Actually touched them.

"Sorry, folks, we have to lift off. Thanks for your hospitality, sorry for the intrusion," the distinguished-looking man said. "Back away, please."

When the helicopter was nothing more than a speck on the horizon, the women all started to jabber at once. "What'd she say? Is she going to grant our pardons? What? Tell us right now, Lizzie, or we're pushing you off this mountain."

Lizzie paused for effect. She slowly enunciated each and every word. "She-said . . . '*Nice-boots! Come-for-a-visit-sometime.*'"

The women chased Lizzie all the way

back to the dining room, with Charles in the lead.

"I think I might want some brandy in my coffee this morning," Annie said.

"Sounds good to me," Charles said as he headed for his kitchen.

"Nice going, ladies," he murmured to no one in particular.

FERN MICHAELS is the *USA Today* and *New York Times* bestselling author of *Up Close and Personal, Fool Me Once, Picture Perfect,* and dozens of other novels and novellas. There are over seventy million copies of her books in print. Fern Michaels has built and funded several large day-care centers in her hometown, and is a passionate animal lover who has outfitted police dogs across the country with special bullet-proof vests. She shares her home in South Carolina with her four dogs and a resident ghost named Mary Margaret. Visit her website at www.fernmichaels.com.